The Market ... ...ides
with AnneMarie Brear

ISBN: 978-0-6488003-7-8

First Publication: 2020 AnneMarie Brear.

Cover design by Image: Carpe Librum Book Design

Published novels:

The Market Stall Girl

AnneMarie Brear

Dedication

To my ancestors:
The families of Brear, Gay, Kittrick, Nicholls,
Walker, Ellis and all those before them.

Chapter One

Wrenthorpe, West Yorkshire. June 1913.

Beth Beaumont threw dried rose petals over her older sister, Joanna as she and her new husband, Jimmy Shaw, walked down the path of St Anne's Church.

'Oh, you!' Joanna laughed at her, brushing off the petals that landed on her cream lace bodice.

Beth grinned and threw another handful, showering her new brother-in-law, who she now loved like one of her own brothers. Although sad at losing her sister, who would now be living a few miles away in the village of Stanley, Beth couldn't help being excited as this was the first wedding in her family, and she wanted to enjoy every minute of it.

'Come along.' Their mam, Mary, nudged Beth along the path. 'We've got to get back to the farm before everyone else. There's much to do.'

Beth tossed the smiling couple another handful of petals and then quickly joined her mam in the two-wheeled gig, its wood highly polished and shining.

'Jane!' she called to her best friend since school, who stood out on the road watching the proceedings.

Jane waved and ran over to the cart. 'Doesn't Joanna look smashing?'

'Aye, so she should the amount of money that dress cost us to make.' Mam untied the reins and climbed aboard. 'Are you getting in, Jane Ogden, or what?'

'Hurry up, Jane, or you'll have to walk back with the rest of them.' Beth hitched over in the seat to make room for her friend.

'The three of us can have the tea mashed and the food out before those lot make it down the hill. There's much to do, though Aunty Hilda will have made a start.' Mam twitched the reins onto Snowy's back and the grey gelding flicked his ears and plodded down the road, before turning left into Trough Well Lane, knowing the way home.

Rumbling down the hill on the cart, Beth glanced back over her shoulder and laughed at her brothers Will and Ronnie running behind them. 'The boys are racing us home, Mam.'

'Fools.' Mam chuckled, the frown of worry lifting for a moment.

Beth waved to her brothers and hooked her arms through Mam and Jane's. 'This is such a joyful day.'

Fields on both sides of the dirt lane were farmed by her family. Mostly they farmed rhubarb, but some acres were spared for other crops, or were lying fallow. A rotation system kept the rhubarb growing, two years outside in the ground and then they were harvested and brought inside the dark sheds to be forced grown, while fresh rhubarb was planted outside. However other, smaller crops of vegetables, silver beet, potatoes, turnips and the like were also grown to be sold at their market stall in Wakefield each week.

'Promise me you'll not be in any rush to marry yourself. I've not got the energy to host another wedding for some time,' Mam said as they turned into the farm gates and she pulled Snowy to a stop next to the brick two-storey house, which had been given a fresh coat of white paint especially for the wedding.

'Not likely.' Beth chuckled, scrambling down from the cart.

'No one will have her.' Jane laughed.

In the kitchen, Aunty Hilda, Mam's aged great-aunt, pottered about the cooking range keeping an eye on the fire, which she'd made her primary job. Though over seventy years of age, Aunty Hilda still made the best bread in the area. Each Saturday she would rise early and bake loaves of bread to last the family all week.

'Did it go off all right?' Aunty Hilda asked, bringing another tray of lemon curd tarts out of the oven.

'It was beautiful,' Beth gushed. 'You should have come.'

Aunty Hilda gave her a sharp look. 'And sit in a freezing church listening to Reverend Simmons drone on while my joints stiffen and ache? No, thank you. The man loves to hear the sound of his own voice. Joanna knows I can't stand the cold anymore and that church is like an icebox.'

'Beth get the wedding cake from the larder and take it outside. Make sure you get the cake net for it. I'll not have weeks of work spoilt by flies landing on it.' Mam poured a large tin kettle full of boiling water into two porcelain teapots. 'Here, Jane, take these egg custard tarts out. Cover them with tea towels.'

Beth carefully handled the big square fruit cake, covered in white marzipan, and decorated with fresh pink rosebuds from the garden she'd picked only that morning. The cake was heavy and as her brothers rushed in, she winced at nearly colliding with them. 'Watch out, you daft lumps!'

'Do you want me to take it?' Will, at sixteen was all gangly legs, but working on the farm gave him a burgeoning strength. A handsome lad with the same dark hair and hazel eyes as all the Beaumont children.

'No, I'll take it. Help Jane bring out the rest of the food.'

'No,' Mam said, opening the oven to take out warm potatoes, 'release Snowy into the field.'

Ronnie received a slap on the back of his hands from Mam as he tried to snatch a roast beef sandwich.

Making her way out of the kitchen, Beth walked along the stone path between the kitchen garden beds bursting with vibrant green herbs and the scent of lavender. A grassy area near the orchard was where they'd set up tables with snowy white tablecloths. Shade from the apple, pear and plum trees afforded some respite from the summer sun.

With the cake placed in the centre of the middle table, Beth carefully covered it with the gauze net. Jane and a protesting Ronnie came and went with food, leaving Beth to arrange it all among the tables, while Will turned the horse out into the field behind.

As the tables filled up with delicious plates and bowls of food, Beth took a moment to listen to the murmur of chatter coming down the lane. The bride and groom and all their guests would soon descend on the farm and Beth would be rushed off her feet helping her mam. She quickly took a small slice of honey cake and shoved it in her mouth. It'd been ages since breakfast and likely to be awhile until she ate as she performed hostess duties.

'I saw that.' Will jumped the fence. 'Give us one.'

'You'll wait with the rest.' She handed him a vase of freshly cut flowers. 'Put that on the end table at the back.' Beth surveyed the tables, liking the prettiness of the displays of food and bouquets of flowers with a backdrop of fruit trees.

The sunny days of June had brought out all the flowers, which years ago Mam had planted like a colourful skirt around the house. Mam, when she had a spare moment, liked to relax in the garden and such were her endeavours, they now had so many flowers during the summer months, that they were cut and bundled together to be sold alongside the vegetables on the stall.

Suddenly, Beth realised that she would be manning the stall by herself now that Joanna was a married woman and no longer at home. The concept depressed her for a moment, for she enjoyed the days working on the market with her sister. They would gossip and chat with the other stall holders in all weathers. The stall holders were a type of community and looked out for each other, would mind each other's stall when someone needed a lavatory break or needed to do a quick shop. As of next Tuesday, Beth would be on her own. She wished Joanna wanted to continue on the stall but she'd declared that as a wife she'd need to keep her house in order and look after her husband and Jimmy didn't want her working as he earned a good wage.

Like a human tide, the family and guests poured in through the gates and headed for the tables.

'It all looks wonderful, Beth.' Joanna hugged her.

'You did just as much cooking as I did.' Beth began making cups of tea for the guests, glasses of lemonade for the children.

Dad opened bottles of beer for the men and jackets were removed as the afternoon sun shone from a cloudless blue sky. The back garden flowed with friends and neighbours. Jimmy was popular and had a good group of friends and his large extended Shaw family added to the numbers that the Beaumonts lacked. Her dad, Rob Beaumont was an only child and Mam's siblings had long moved away or died, but having been successful farmers for years, the Beaumonts had a great many friends who all came to share the happiness of the day.

Beth enjoyed seeing the garden bursting with contented people. Weddings were such celebrations. Joanna couldn't stop smiling and Beth's emotions ran high.

Noticing her mam's rosy cheeks, Beth took the tray of clean teacups from her. 'Go and sit down, Mam. You've been at it since dawn.'

'Sit down? With this lot needing feeding and watering?'

'They've been fed and watered.' Beth put the tray on the table. 'They've been here two hours and are having a wonderful time. Go on, I'll see to the tables. Go and sit with Joanna. It'll not be long before her and Jimmy leave.'

'Just a few minutes then, to be social.' Mam was soon in the midst of the other village women, people she'd grown up with and shared the ups and downs of life. Joanna sat next to Aunty Hilda and stories flowed of the past.

On her way back to the kitchen, Beth heard giggles coming from the side of the house, away from the guests. She crept around the kitchen garden and spied her brothers sitting under the elderberry tree sipping bottles of beer.

'William and Ronald Beaumont!' she snapped.

Both boys jumped, spilling their precious beers.

'Jesus, our Beth. You nearly gave me a heart attack.' Will wiped the spilt drink off his good shirt. 'That'll stain now, and I'll be in for it.'

Laughing, Beth sauntered over to them. 'Aye, well, that's your punishment for stealing.'

'You'll not tell, will you, Bethy?' Ronnie, only twelve years old, looked suitably chastened.

'One each. That's it. You take any more and I'll tell Dad,' she warned. 'I'll not have you two spewing your guts up all night, do you hear?'

'Just the one.' Will nodded and gave her a saucy wink.

'I mean it, Will.'

'I'm not a child.'

'Just because you've finished at the grammar school it doesn't mean you're instantly a man.'

'I work as hard as any man on the farm. I'm allowed a beer, for God's sake.' Will took a sip from the beer bottle.

'Mam and Dad wanted you to have a decent education and make something of yourself. Anyone can be a farm labourer.' Beth gazed at him and sighed.

Will shrugged and drank some more. 'It'll be my farm one day. I should understand how it's run.'

'Mam wants more for you.'

'Then she'll have to rely on Ronnie becoming a doctor or something.'

'I don't want to be a doctor! I hate seeing blood,' Ronnie protested, looking ill at the idea. 'I want to drive trains.'

'Will…'

'Leave it, Beth. I get enough of this from Mam.'

It didn't take much for Will to become belligerent these days. As their dad had been, Will, and now Ronnie, was sent to Queen Elizabeth Grammar School in Wakefield to gain an education which would set him up for life, but in reality, he was happiest just working on the farm with Dad and the other men they employed. Mam, coming from a poor mining family had been made up at the idea of her sons attending the grammar school. She saw it as step up in society and begged Will to go on to university and become a doctor or a lawyer. Only Will liked getting his hands dirty and had no head for books. Daily there were arguments as to what Will would do with his future.

She stomped away. She loved her brothers deeply, but they were a pain in the butt most days.

From the larder in the kitchen, she retrieved two plates of egg and cress sandwiches and took them out to the tables just in time for her dad to tap his glass of beer with a spoon.

'Ladies and gentlemen, family and friends, on behalf of my wife and my family, I would like to thank you all for coming here today to help celebrate my daughter Joanna's marriage to Jimmy.'

Everyone clapped and Beth felt the sting of tears build behind her eyes. Joanna and Jimmy stood together, holding hands. Joanna looked so beautiful in her wedding dress. The sight brought a lump to Beth's throat. Her beloved sister was now a married woman. Jimmy would always come first to her now.

'I don't feel as though we are losing a daughter, but gaining a son,' Rob Beaumont continued. 'We are incredibly happy to welcome Jimmy into our family. We know he'll take good care of our lass. We welcome the Shaw family, too. Let our two families forever be united.' He raised his glass. 'To the happy couple.'

Beth wiped tears from her eyes as she raised a glass of lemonade she'd grabbed from the table.

'Isn't it lovely,' Jane said, coming to stand beside her. 'I love weddings.'

'Me, too.' Beth watched her mam kiss her dad's cheek and felt her chest swell with happiness at seeing them smile and joke. It was so rare for her mam to show affection, for she was brought up in a hardworking miner's family where hugs and kisses were as sparse as the food on the table. Yet, Mary Beaumont gave her husband a look of such love that Beth couldn't help but stare. She wished her mam did it more. There were so many times growing up when Beth wanted to rest her head on her mam's shoulder, but it was never encouraged. Instead, Beth would go to her dad or Aunty Hilda and from those two people she received warm embraces and kisses on the forehead.

The Wrenthorpe Colliery Brass Band had been invited to play, many had grown up with her parents, and one member was her mam's cousin, and as they tuned up their instruments, a buzz of excitement flowed between the guests.

'Nothing makes me blubber like a brass band an all.' Jane grinned.

Beth nodded; her throat full as the wonderful sound of the 'William Tell Overture' filled the garden.

Joanna came towards them. 'Will you help me change out of this dress? I can't undo all these buttons.'

Beth followed Joanna upstairs to the bedroom they'd shared all their lives. On Joanna's neatly made bed sat her brown suitcase containing all her remaining clothes, the rest had been sent on ahead to the little house she and Jimmy would be renting in Stanley. Hanging up on the wardrobe door was Joanna's honeymoon outfit, a pretty dress in pale pink.

'I can't wait to go on my honeymoon,' Joanna gushed, slipping off her shoes. 'Two nights in Blackpool. I'm so excited.'

Beth begun unbuttoning the long row of ivory cloth-covered buttons down her back. She'd never known anyone to go on a honeymoon before. Apparently, her Beaumont grandparents had done it. As successful farmers they'd been able to afford such an extravagance. Her mam's side of the family were lucky to get a pie and an ale at the local pub when they got married. 'You lucky thing to be going somewhere as exciting as Blackpool.'

'Well it was a wedding present from Jimmy's grandparents.' Joanna shimmied out of the cream lace dress and Beth took it from her to hang up while Joanna took down the pink dress. 'Jimmy wanted furniture for the house, but we can make do with the bits and bobs we've been given from family and friends. As I said to him, it's not every day you get to go to Blackpool and stay in a hotel, is it?'

'I suppose he's being practical.'

Joanna turned so Beth could do up the zip. 'We can be practical later. I want to go to Blackpool. We'll be the only couple we know who have gone on a proper honeymoon and not just spent a night in some pub in Wakefield. I want to be like our grandparents.'

'And you should go. Mam has always wanted us to be better than others, hasn't she? We are Beaumonts, she always says, and we should act accordingly.' Beth passed her sister the little matching white hat and gloves.

Joanna groaned. 'Lord, how many times has she told us that? You aren't to behave like those common mining kids.'

Beth laughed. 'Yet that was exactly what she was when younger.'

'And what was her answer to that?' Joanna quizzed with a giggle.

'Beaumonts are reputable farmers and as such we must behave as such,' Beth tried to emulate her mam's strong Yorkshire accent.

'Anyone would think we had a thousand-acre estate instead of a rhubarb farm.' Joanna sat on the bed. 'You know, I imagine I first encouraged Jimmy because he was training as an engineer for the gas company and he wasn't a miner from the village.'

'Really?'

'Mam's words always rang in my head not to marry a miner as I could do better. So, I shunned all the village lads.'

'And they called you stuck-up Joanna,' Beth added.

'They did.' Joanna shook her head in bemusement. 'And I've made Mam content by marrying an engineer.'

'But you love Jimmy?'

Joanna smiled. 'Yes, of course. I love him very much. Though it doesn't hurt to keep Mam happy, too, if there is such a thing.'

Beth snorted laughter and gripped Joanna's hand. 'I'm going to miss you.'

'You'll have the bedroom all to yourself!' Joanna chuckled, but tears gathered in her eyes. 'I'll miss you too.'

They hugged each other tightly. Their home life was changing, and Beth knew she wasn't quite ready for it.

Joanna touched Beth's thick cinnamon brown hair, which today was prettily twisted and looped around her head and pinned with rosebuds. 'You're going to have to learn to plait all this hair on your own now.'

Beth frowned. 'I never thought about that. How annoying.' She laughed, glancing in the mirror above the small fireplace. Her thick straight hair gave her nothing but problems. It constantly fell out of combs and pins. Joanna tried to practice different hairstyles on her, but nothing would last long. A thick plait, the end touching her the top of her bottom was the neatest way for her to wear it, without taking scissors to it.

'Promise you'll come and visit me in Stanley. I'm going to be stuck with Jimmy's family on the doorstep the whole time, and, well, they think they are better than they are, especially his Aunt Pat and Uncle Les.' Joanna leaned in close. 'Pat thinks she's posh because she gets all her shopping delivered. By the size of her it wouldn't hurt for her to walk a mile or two and do it herself.'

Laughing, Beth grabbed the suitcase off the bed. 'I'll come and visit as often as I can. Make sure you drop by the stall.'

'I'm going to miss the stall.' Joanna sighed, pulling on her gloves. 'Though not the winter days, freezing my bits off.' She gave the bedroom a last look. 'I'm not a girl any longer…'

'No,' Beth pushed her out of the door, 'you're an old married woman now, ready to nag poor Jimmy for the rest of his life.'

At the bottom of the stairs, Joanna stopped, her expression earnest. 'Make sure you marry a good 'un, our Beth, like my Jimmy. Don't fall for any one flashy or full of himself. You need a man who is kind, above all else.'

'Get away with yourself,' Beth snorted in amusement. 'I'm not marrying for years yet.'

'Probably not. No one will have you or your spectacular temper.'

Beth playfully slapped her sister's shoulder. 'I'm not as bad as I was. I've not been angry for ages.'

'Your due then. Thank heavens I'll not be here to see it!' Joanna laughed.

As the sun slipped down and the lanterns were lit, Joanna and Jimmy were given a huge send off and that started the exodus of the guests departing.

'I'd best be off, Beth,' Jane said, holding a napkin filled with three slices of wedding cake for her grand-parents who she lived with in a little cottage in Al-verthorpe, a village a mile away. 'I'm tired and I'm back to work in the morning.'

'I'll walk with you up the lane a bit.' Beth walked out of the farm's gates with her as the warm summer dusk turned the sky to pink. They waved to other guests leaving, some worse for drink and who sang their way up the lane.

Beth lifted her face up to stare at the streaks of pale lemon and mauve clouds on the horizon as the sun sank lower. 'Thank you for all your help today. You were brilliant.'

'That's what friends are for.'

'Aye, but still, you were a great help.'

Jane plucked a long grass stem from the verge. 'It was a smashing wedding. That's how I hope my wed-ding will be.'

'Oh aye, got someone in mind, have you?'

'Get away.' Jane laughed, blushing.

'So, there is someone! Why didn't you tell me?'

'There isn't, honest.' Her friend looked away.

'Who is he?' Beth prompted. She always knew when Jane was lying for her freckles became more prominent on her face.

Eyes bright, Jane grinned. 'You know that fella, Alfie Taylor, who works outside in the yard at the mill?'

'Do I?' Beth scowled, pondering, then gaped at her. 'Alfie Taylor with the big ears?'

'Aww, don't be nasty.'

'I'm not. It's a true fact, poor lad.'

'Well, any road, he's been coming up to me each day asking if he can walk me home.'

'And have you let him?'

'Once or twice.'

'Jane Ogden!'

'What? There's nowt wrong with us both walking down a few streets, is there? Me gran says I can't be choosy with my red hair and freckles and she's right.'

Beth hugged Jane to her side. 'Nonsense. You're too lovely not to be snapped up by some clever fellow, and your red hair is—'

'Ugly!' Jane spat, having always hated her fire-coloured hair. 'Gran hates it because I got it from me dad and she hated me dad.'

'I hardy remember your parents now,' Beth said sadly. 'It seems forever since you lived in Wren-thorpe with your mam and dad.'

'I was ten when they died. Funny how I don't miss them any more. Gran and Grandad are my parents. They've taken care of me for ten years.'

'You can do no wrong in your grandad's eyes.'

Jane's expression fell. 'I wish he was in better health. Me and Gran are so worried about him. He's not been the same since he fell off that horse and damaged his back. Then losing his job… He's not been the same since. Damn those Melvilles. They didn't have to sack him. He could have worked in some job on the estate.'

'He'll recover and get another job. At least he has you and your gran and you're both working.'

'Yes, but how long will Gran last at the mill? It's getting harder for her each day. I tried to do my work and hers without anyone knowing but it'll only be a matter of time before they realise she's too old to stay on. I don't know what we'll do with only my wage.'

'Don't worry about it until it happens. I'll ask Dad if he knows of anything going about for your grandad.'

'Thanks. At least we're busy at the mill and there's no talk of letting workers go like at some of the other mills. I'd hate to go and find another job.'

'Especially now you've got a fancy man there!' Beth laughed and pushed Jane sideways, trying to lighten the mood.

'Get away with yourself!' Jane scoffed.

'Are you really keen on him?'

'Not as much as I'd like to be on a certain some-one.' Jane nudged her. 'Look who's coming down the lane.'

Beth peered, trying to make out who the distant figure was. Then she saw the little dog dash out of the hedge and realised who it was.

'You can spot Noah Jackson a mile off if he's got his dog with him.' Jane smoothed down her reddish hair, the sun having brightened her freckles.

Beth wanted to tidy herself as well but restrained. Jane already teased her about the Jackson boys and the way they played the fool when she was about. Ever since school, the youngest Jackson boys had been friends with Beth, but not the eldest, Noah.

'My, he is but a handsome devil.' Jane sighed dramatically.

Beth remained quiet, ignoring the way her silly heart responded to the presence of the eldest Jackson brother. She didn't understand why he affected her as he did. She'd known the Jackson family all her life, they lived in the village at the top of the lane. She had gone to school with James and Alfred Jackson, but Noah, being older, had left to go down the pit as soon as he was fourteen. Many said he was wasted digging for coal and his clever brain could have got him into grammar school and maybe even further than that, but his parents needed him earning, as his father, Leo, was often injured down the pit and his mother, Peggy, who worked at the same mill as Jane, tried hard to feed a large brood of strapping boys. A family of seven needed every penny they could earn. Now all five brothers worked with their father down the pit.

Beth watched Noah as he came closer. He wore a white shirt, chestnut brown trousers, his black boots polished. His Sunday best that he wore to church every Sunday. He wore a flat cap, and his hair was the colour of nutmeg, which touched his collar.

The Jackson brothers were known for their good looks, easy smiles, and sunny natures. They had the village girls eating out of their hands. One look, one smile and girls that Beth had grown up with, and even their mothers, were swooning like Victorian old maids.

She understood why, not that she had ever swooned – the idea was ridiculous. Yet, when Noah turned his gaze to her and his smile reached his blue-green eyes, she felt a little short of breath, and mocked herself for such silliness.

'Good evening, ladies.' Noah bent down, picked up a stick and threw it for his little Jack Russell, Patch, who bounded down the lane after it.

'It's a nice evening for a walk,' Jane said.

Beth watched Patch race back to them. 'He's so fast.'

'He's good at catching rabbits.' Noah threw the stick again. 'Did the wedding go well? I know Jimmy from playing cricket against him.'

'It was beautiful,' Jane told him.

'You had a lovely day for it. Barely a cloud in the sky.'

'How's your dad?' Beth asked, knowing through village gossip that Leo Jackson had fallen a few weeks ago and was nearly run over by a coal trolley. He still hadn't returned to his job at the pit.

'He's on the mend, thanks.' Patch jumped up at his leg, wanting him to throw the stick again. 'Stop that. Sit,' he commanded, and the little dog sat at his feet, his eyes adoring.

'Right, I need to be off,' Jane said. 'I'll see you on Saturday, Beth, if I can get half of my shift off.'

'See you then.' Beth waved.

In the moment of silence which stretched between Beth and Noah, and in which Beth felt she really should turn for home, Noah threw the stick for Patch.

'Shame about Emily Davison, isn't it?' he asked, stepping alongside her as she headed back down the lane.

Beth nodded, having read about the suffragette who'd thrown herself in front of the King's horse at the Epsom Derby only a week before. 'It was very tragic.'

'She died fighting for what she believed in,' Noah murmured.

'A brave thing to do. Let us hope the men in parliament start to see sense, and realise women aren't empty-headed fools without intelligent thought.'

He gave a slow smile. 'No one would ever think that of you, Beth Beaumont.'

She lifted her chin in challenge. 'And they'd be right, too.'

'No one would dare mess with you, would they?'

What was he implying? That she was too headstrong, unladylike?

'Anyway, I'm pleased the wedding went well. Your sister has always been nice to me. I wish her well.'

Stopping at the gate, Beth nodded, squashing down the spike of jealousy. Joanna was two years older than her, so at twenty-two she was closer in age to Noah, who she guessed was about twenty-six or so. Did Noah ever fancy her sister? He wasn't married. He'd been courting a girl a few years ago but she called it off and married someone else. At the time, Beth hadn't really wondered about it, but now she was a bit older she thought the other girl must have been mad to reject Noah.

'You look very pretty in that dress, too. See you.' He walked on, whistling to his little dog.

Her stomach clenched at his words. He noticed her dress? Did she look pretty? Her hair was escaping the many pins Joanna had stuck in her thick hair that morning after she'd washed and twisted it up at the

back of her head. She'd also lost a small white rose-
bud from the elegant arrangement Joanna had wound
into her hair.

Beth smoothed down the skirt of her powder-blue
dress with its white lace on the bodice and cuffs. She
adjusted the white silk sash around her waist, happy
she had a tinier waist than many of her friends,
though some had bigger breasts than she did. Was
that important? She hoped not. Still, it delighted her
that Noah Jackson had paid her a compliment. She
fairly skipped back up the drive.

Mam, having changed out of her wedding finery
and into an everyday work dress, was throwing scraps
to the chickens to encourage them into the coop as
Beth walked around to the back of the house. 'What
were you talking to that Jackson boy about?'

'Nothing much. He hoped Joanna had a good wedding day, that's all.'

'Don't be getting mixed up with any of those Jacksons.' Mam shut the door on the coop and secured it.

'I'm not. I was simply being friendly.'

'Good. I'll not have you carrying on with a miner,
even a clever one like that eldest Jackson lad. You
marry a miner and you'll always be poor, I'm telling
you.'

'I'm not carrying on with anyone, Mam.'

'Just think on.' Mam strode past her and into the
scullery.

Beth was reluctant to go inside, even though the
light was fading fast. It was late and tomorrow she'd
be in the fields early, harvesting vegetables ready to
sell on the stall when the market opened on Tuesday.
Her gaze lingered on the pale orange sky, the odd bird

swooping in the distance. Today had been a good day, the sun had shone on their Joanna as she got married, the house had been full of family and friends and Noah Jackson had spoken to her, noticed her. It had been an incredibly good day, indeed!

Chapter Two

Beth placed the tin bucket full of bunches of long-stemmed rosebuds at the front of the stall. The market, even at this early hour on a Tuesday morning, was busy with shoppers and traders. Barrow boys were running up and down the stalls, unpacking produce from the carts and stacking it on the stalls, before going back for more.

Beth and Joanna usually unpacked the vegetables from the farm cart with their dad and Will, but today there would be no Joanna helping. After the excitement of the wedding, Beth felt a little down yesterday and spent the day on her own in the fields harvesting, or in the garden cutting flowers. This morning she'd still felt strange, waking up to see the empty bed opposite. She had to get used to it and be quick about it as this was the beginning of a new period in her life, of manning the stall by herself. Though Jane said she'd help her on Saturday morning, which was their busiest time, and Dad had said he'd pay her.

But the other three days, Beth would be on her own. She'd not buy two cups of hot chocolate in the winter for her and Joanna to wrap cold hands around. They'd not laugh and chat and gossip as they had done for the last five years.

'Your Joanna married then?' Fred, the stallholder next to her, placed a crate of iron tools on his table.

'Yes, thanks, Fred. She had a lovely day.' Beth stacked the lettuces with their crowns facing up, tearing off any broken leaves so the display looked as good as possible.

'That's grand. You'll miss her company then, lass?'

'I will, to begin with, after awhile I think I'll enjoy the peace and quiet.' Beth laughed.

'That'll be a change for you two never shut up.'

'You can talk, Fred Butterworth!' Beth mocked, for the older man, with his round stomach had a booming voice to match and the sweetest nature. She and Joanna thought of him as a kind of uncle after all the years of selling beside him.

Throughout the morning, other stallholders asked Beth how the wedding went and between chatting and serving shoppers, the first day without Joanna passed rather swiftly.

The warm sunshine continued, not abating even as the afternoon drew to a close. Beth packed away the unsold vegetables and flowers into crates and placed them on a handcart. Her family's lock-up was down a side alley off the main outdoor market on Brook Street. In here, Beth stacked the crates and sorted out what vegetables wouldn't be worth selling tomorrow, and which were to be taken home for her mam to use.

'How did you get on, lass?' Rob Beaumont asked, coming into the lock-up.

'Not bad for a Tuesday.' Beth handed him the money wallet which was constantly tied around her waist. 'We need more lettuce and beetroot as I sold out. The warm weather is making people want salads.'

'Will and your mam picked radishes today. You'll have them for Thursday's trade and more onions, too. The tomatoes in the greenhouse will be picked tomorrow.'

She stretched and yawned as her dad pulled the big door closed and locked it.

'Did you miss our Joanna?' he asked.

'Not as much as I imagined I would.' She walked with him to where he'd left Snowy and the cart.

'Don't be telling her that.' He grinned.

'It was a busy day. I didn't have time to miss her. I thought you were letting Will come and pick me up from now on?'

'Aye, I am, but he's gone rabbiting with one of his mates.' He waved to other stallholders packing up. 'Besides, I needed to visit the bank.'

They rumbled away from the market and along the streets of Wakefield, weaving between other carts and carriages. The church bells chimed the hour of five as they left the town and headed north towards Wrenthorpe.

They acknowledged two old men they knew who sat on a bench outside of the Bay Horse Inn and turned left to go under the Potovens Railway Bridge at the same time as a large farm wagon came through. Behind the wagon a man in a gig whipped his horse to pass the wagon, leaving no room for the Beaumont cart.

A jam of sorts formed, created by the impatient man in the gig who whipped his horse and shouted.

'Go back!' Beth's dad yelled. 'Back your horse up. There's not enough room.' He jerked Snowy's reins, edging him to the far side of the road as much as he could.

'You back away, man!' The gig driver hollered, cracking his whip yet again and sending his black horse into a frenzy for the beast couldn't go forward or backwards when the gig's wheels clashed with the Beaumont's cart's wheel.

'You bloody fool!' Dad fumed, pulling Snowy's reins.

Beth held onto the seat's rail, worried the cart would tip and she'd be sent hurling into the patch of nettles lining the railway bank, but more than that she was furious at the reckless behaviour of the gig driver.

The other farm wagon moved on, the driver encouraging his big draught horse to make it up the short incline.

Gripping the rail, Beth leaned over the side of the cart. 'You've room, Dad. A foot or so before the you hit the rut.'

'This damn fool needs to move. Oh, I might have guessed it would be a Melville. Think they own the road, and everything else, they do.' Dad clicked his tongue at Snowy, who threw his head up as the gig driver cracked his whip again.

'Get out of my way!' the gig driver, Louis Melville yelled at Dad, before his horse seemed to jump forward, freeing the colliding wheels.

As the gig came free, Louis Melville turned to sneer at Dad, 'You idiot! I could have been tipped over!'

'I'm the idiot?' Dad yelled. 'All you had to do was wait a few moments until that wagon turned onto the road and then you could have passed me without any issue. You don't own the road, Melville.'

'Don't I? I think you'll find I can own anything I want,' the other man jeered. His eyebrows rose as he looked at Beth fully. 'Watch yourself, Beaumont.'

Dad glared at him. 'What the hell do you mean by that?'

Beth glared back at Melville, angrily, but suddenly her fury shifted, withered, as Melville's top lip curled, and his eyes narrowed on her. She shivered at his intense stare from eyes black as coal and which didn't blink. His sharp thin nose in a narrow face was completed with a scowling mouth.

In a flick of the reins, Snowy broke free of the mayhem and trotted off.

Beth glanced over her shoulder at Melville. She knew of him only by reputation. He was the son of Sir Melville from Melville Manor at Kirkhamgate, a village less than a mile from their farm. Legend has it that her Beaumont great-grandfather saved the current Sir Melville's father's life. In his gratitude, Sir Melville senior signed over five acres of land and the Beaumonts have been farming that land ever since, and subsequent generations even bought more land alongside it to increase their holding. Something the Melville family weren't happy about. It was one thing to give a reward, but totally another thing to add to that and prosper.

'He's a rotten one is that one,' Dad muttered as they trotted down the road. 'Worse than his father, and he was a bad 'un. Thank God Sir Melville had the sense to clear off to Amsterdam and stay there. He's not welcome in these parts and I wish his son would do the same. That whole family is bad news.'

The whole episode had shaken her a little. She hated to see her sweet kind dad angry, something he rarely was, unlike herself, and she hadn't liked the way Louis Melville had looked at her.

'I've not seen him for a long time.'

'Louis Melville finished university and then travelled Europe. He's just returned.'

'How do you know all that?'

'Aunty Hilda is friends with Mr Staines, the Melville's butler. Apparently, Staines's grandfather was once your aunt's beau. She's always kept in touch with the family and even helped Staines get that position at the manor through knowing the former housekeeper there.'

'Is there anything Aunty Hilda hasn't seen or done?' Beth chuckled.

'I doubt it. That's what happens when you live to a ripe old age. You get to know everyone and everything.' Dad gave her a wink.

'I hope I'm like Aunty Hilda when I'm old.' From Sunny Hill, Beth gazed across to their fields below in the shallow valley. Their hired men worked, backs bent spreading the bundles of shoddy, the waste woollen products delivered by the mills to the farm. The shoddy broke down into the soil and provided much needed nitrogen for the rhubarb crops.

'We got a cartload of shoddy delivered, and we'll be getting more tomorrow,' Dad said as he turned into Trough Well Lane. 'I'll have the men busy with that and they'll not be able to help you and your mam with the vegetables, but you'll have Will to help. Reggie will give a hand, too.'

'We'll manage.' Beth turned her thoughts to the hard day's work tomorrow, being in the sheds sorting and cleaning the vegetables and getting them ready to sell on the stall on Thursday. She easily pushed Melville out of her mind and hoped she never saw him again.

~ ~ ~ ~

Noah sat in the tin bath in the scullery, head bent as his brothers waited around outside in the yard until it was their turn to wash the coal dust off their skin. The sun wasn't over the rooftops yet, the day only just beginning.

He'd liked to have soaked for a bit but that was impossible when there were four others waiting to hop in the bath as well. He scrubbed his arms with the cake of soap which was the cheap variety and one that didn't lather too well. His mam refused to spend money on expensive scented soap when she had five sons to feed as well as her husband and herself.

Noah washed away the dust and grit from his eyes, fighting a yawn. They'd just done a week of nightshifts and he had foregone precious sleep to study. He was exhausted, but he needed to keep studying.

'Hurry up, our kid.' Sid thrust his head through the doorway. 'I'm on a promise tonight.'

'Are you heck on a promise,' Alfred snorted, 'and who with?'

'The only promise our Sid will get is his face slapped.' Albie laughed.

'Is it Nessie Lindale? Her with the greasy hair?' James added to the joke. 'You could fry an egg on her head, I tell you.'

'It's not Nessie.' Sid playfully punched James, the youngest brother. 'I ain't telling you lot who it is.'

'It's Jinny Dowes from The Shovel.' Albie grinned. 'She'll have anyone who looks at her twice. I've watched her pulling pints, eyeing up the possibilities as they come in through the door.'

'I bet you're not on her list,' Alfred jabbed James in the ribs. 'Jinny wants a man not a boy.'

'Sod off!' James pushed Alfred.

'Well I'm heading for bed and I don't want to wake up until it's time to go back down the hole again.' Albie sighed tiredly. 'I hate night shifts.'

'Bed is exactly where our Sid wants to be, but not with us.' James winked.

'Aye, well, at least I know how to do other things in bed besides sleeping, young'un!' Sid chuckled.

As his brothers joked and parried punches with each other, Noah got out of the bath and dried himself before donning a clean shirt, underwear, and trousers. He sat on the knee-high brick wall which surrounded the huge copper washing pot and pulled on his socks.

Sid stripped off and climbed into the bath. 'Albie, pour us some hot water!'

Albie collected a bucket of hot water from the copper pot and poured it into the bath.

'Steady on! That's scalding, you'll boil me bollocks off in a second.'

James fell about laughing. 'You'll not miss much!'

With his boots on, Noah shook his head at his mad brothers and went into the kitchen of the small two-up and two-down terraced house he'd been born in.

'Are those lot nearly finished?' His mam, Peggy, stirred a large black pot over the range. She appeared under the weather, her skin grey. 'I've got me shift to get to at the mill.'

Noah's stomach grumbled with hunger and sat at the table. 'Leave that. We can see to ourselves.'

His mam paused, he knew she was torn between making sure her boys got fed and her duty to go out to work, since his dad had hurt himself in the pit and was off work. 'Your dad has eaten. He's gone to The Shovel to meet up with Bill.' She ladled out a portion of porridge into Noah's bowl and pushed a plate of bacon towards him. In the middle of the table was a wooden board holding a bread loaf and a pat of butter and a teapot.

'At this hour?' Noah glanced at the clock; it was only half six in the morning.

'They're off rabbiting. Your dad's taken Patch.'

Spooning porridge into his mouth, Noah didn't re-mark. That is dad was too injured to work but could get up at dawn to go rabbiting with his mate annoyed Noah. His dad, Leo, was often injured lately, leaving his five sons to bring in the money for rent and food. It didn't escape Noah's notice that his dad was hardly around. For the past year, his dad suffered several ac-cidents at the pit, some which Noah found confusing as he and his brothers worked in the same space with their dad. Yet, it was always their dad getting hurt, and the accident usually happened when Noah wasn't looking.

Noah ate to the background noise of his brothers' chatter while his mother readied herself for her shift. 'Have you eaten, Mam?'

'Aye.' She threw her shawl around her shoulders. 'You off to the see that Grimshaw fellow?'

He nodded and poured himself a cup of tea. 'It's our last day of the school term. We'll have four weeks off now. Though Mr Grimshaw has suggested that we work together still. I'll spend a few hours with him a couple of times a week at his house and do the rest here. Today he's set me an exam similar to the main exam I'll sit in September.'

'An exam?' Sid asked, coming into the kitchen, and sitting at the table, his hair dripping wet. 'What for?'

'To prepare me for the teachers' training college entrance exam.'

His mam's blue eyes widened. 'Teachers' college? You?'

Noah buttered a slice of bread. 'It's what I've been working towards this past two years with Mr Grimshaw, you know that.'

'Aye, yes…'

'What, Mam?' Noah swallowed a mouthful of bacon.

'I just thought you'd not go through with it. I considered Mr Grimshaw would realise you're not cut out for that career.'

'Why wouldn't I?' he asked as Albie came to the table. 'Why would I spend all this time studying and not sit the exams in September and November?'

'You left school at twelve. How can you be a teacher?'

31

'Because I've been studying solidly for two years with Mr Grimshaw. You understand this is something I want to do.'

'But you're a miner, son. A son of a miner. A grandson of a miner. To dream of being something other than that is... well... it's getting your hopes up for nothing.'

'You believe I can't become something else?'

'People rarely do.' She sighed. 'I just don't want you to be disappointed.'

'When I don't pass the exams, you mean?' He looked directly at his mother but the question was in the room for anyone to answer.

She coughed for a few moments and then wiped a hand over her tired-looking face. 'I know you're a clever lad, and I understand the need to better yourself but really, when does it actually happen to people like us?'

'It's going to happen to me. I've taught myself to be better educated than I was when in school. I've read books since I was a lad.'

'Aye, always at the bloody library, especially in winter,' Sid snorted. 'Our bedroom is full of books. I can't move for them.'

Noah ignored him. He'd heard that same whine for years.

'How can you afford to go to a teachers' college?' Mam jerkily ladled porridge for Albie, splattering a bit on the worn lino covering the table.

Noah strove for patience. He was certain none of his family listened to him. 'Mr Grimshaw has secured me a grant to help pay for my fees at the college. I'll be a non-resident. He's going to try and find me a

32

position in a school, too, for once I've finished my training.'

'And what school is that?' Mam asked. 'One close by?'

'I don't know. I'll go wherever I can get work.'

'That could be anywhere in the country,' she snapped.

'Or you might get a position in the village school,' Albie said.

'I doubt there's a vacancy. My first choice would be the Queen Elizabeth Grammar School where Mr Grimshaw teaches, but I wouldn't think that would be possible as I'll be a junior teacher and I've not been to university.'

'The posh school in Wakefield?' Albie asked.

'There is only one Queen Elizabeth Grammar.' Noah wondered if his family ever paid any attention to life outside of the pit, the pub and playing football or cricket.

'What about the pit?' Sid scowled, scoffing some bacon.

'If I pass the exams in September and November, I'll be leaving the pit to go to the college.'

His brothers stared at him with black coal-rimmed eyes as though he'd sprouted horns.

'As I said, people like us don't become teachers.' His mam banged the porridge pot back onto the stove and headed for the back door, coughing as she went.

'We can do, Mam, if we try.'

'You're getting above yourself.'

He swallowed a spark of annoyance. 'Is that a crime? Don't you want to see your son do well for himself?'

'How will we manage without your wage, answer me that!' She slammed the door on her way out.

Noah stared down at his bowl. That was the crux of the problem. His mam was worried about money. If he became a teacher and moved away, she'd be down one less wage. Did she assume her sons would be giving up their wages for the rest of their lives?

'I hope you do pass and become a teacher,' Albie spoke quietly. 'One of us should see what it feels like to work above ground for a change.'

'Mam will come around to the idea.' Sid shrugged and ate more porridge. 'She's just in shock that one of her lads is doing something other than digging coal. Dad won't come around to the idea at all, mind. He'll have a lot to say about it and none of it good.'

'I don't care.' Noah drank the last of his tea and stood. 'I'm not digging coal for the rest of my life if there's a chance for something better.'

Noah left the kitchen and collected his jacket from the front room which, years ago, had been turned into a bedroom for him and Sid. His other three brothers shared the biggest bedroom upstairs and his parents had the box room. The house was too small for seven adults, and he longed to be out of it.

All his brothers were at the table as he walked back through to the kitchen.

'Good luck, our kid,' Sid said, pouring out more tea into his cup, the others added their own encouraging wishes.

Noah paused. As much as they fought and bickered, he loved his brothers. He smiled and nodded and left the house.

He missed Patch not being with him. The little dog was usually his constant companion and he was annoyed his dad had taken him. Five years ago, he'd found Patch as a puppy, abandoned in the hedge down a lane, he was starving and wet from recent rain, and his dad declared the scrap wouldn't make it through the night, but Noah had nurtured and cared for the little pup day and night and his reward had been Patch's devoted love ever since.

As he walked along the road, nodding to the odd person he saw, his mind replayed the questions he'd been studying all week. Mr Grimshaw had previously given him mock exams, all readying him for the main one in September. Today's would be the last mock exam and the most important, as it was nearly identical to the one he'd sit in September. He had to pass it. If he didn't, it would mean he needed to study even harder for the next six weeks. Could he do it? Could he pass? Was he cut out to be a teacher? True, he loved books and geography and his main interest was history, but was it enough to work with pupils, to fill their brains with his knowledge? The idea brought him out in a cold sweat.

His footsteps faltered and he stopped. He couldn't do it. He was a miner, and a miner's son. Not an intellectual. He hadn't been to university. His mam was right. People like them didn't become teachers. His dad couldn't even read or write properly, and his mam wasn't much better despite being a mine manager's daughter. What did he think he was doing trying to be more than he was?

'Is everything all right?'

Noah spun around and looked into the concerned hazel eyes of Beth Beaumont.

'Are you ill?' she asked. She held a basket of shopping.

He gazed about realising he'd reached the few shops Wrenthorpe claimed. They were standing in front of the chemist's shop door.

'Noah?'

'Sorry.' He cringed at his own foolishness. 'I'm fine. My mind was elsewhere.'

'Oh, good. I was worried for a moment there.'

'I'm fine,' he repeated. His smile of apology worked, and she relaxed.

'It's another lovely day.' She fell into step beside him.

Surprised she wanted to walk with him, he nodded. 'It is. You are up and about early.'

'Mam wanted some things before I leave to go to the stall. Aunty Hilda has been poorly, and Mam didn't want to leave her.'

'I'm sorry to hear that.' He glanced sideways at her. Beth Beaumont was the prettiest girl in the village and how she hadn't been snapped up yet he didn't know. He'd always been aware of her, watched her growing up, but he had never hung about with her as his youngest brothers did.

Now he had a theory that perhaps Miss Beaumont might be worth pursuing. At twenty-six was he too old for her? She must be twenty for she was in the same class as Alfred and James. Did six years age difference mean much? He wasn't sure. After Lillian, the girl he assumed he'd marry, married someone else two years ago, he'd not taken an interest in the opposite sex. Instead he focused on learning. Night classes when his shifts allowed, or Sunday study when they didn't. Meeting Mr Grimshaw had been the saving of his sanity from the relentless black hole he worked in.

'You've been on the night shift?' she asked.

'Yes. Now I'm on my way into town.'

'Buying something nice?'

'No. I'm sitting a mock exam.'

Beth stopped and stared at him. 'How exciting! What for? Is it to become a mine manager?'

'God no.' He grinned. 'To be a teacher.'

'A teacher?' A look of admiration came over her sweet face. 'That is wonderful, Noah. Truly.'

'Thank you. I've not sat the official one yet, not until September and then again in November for the second part.'

'Even still, it's a credit to you to attempt such a life changing opportunity.'

'Hopefully, if I don't fail.'

'You won't. You're clever. Everyone says so. How many miners do you see who can read and write as well as you do? Or take up extra study?'

'But I'm not properly educated, not like those that come from universities. I left school at twelve and went straight down the pit.'

'Yes, but you've been attending those classes when you're not working, haven't you? The whole village knows how hard you've been studying. You'll be a wonderful teacher because you'll be teaching children that are just like us, village children.' She blushed and looked away from him.

He liked how passionate she was.

'Sorry. I talk too much. Mam says I don't know when to shut up.' Her sunny smile cheered him up no end.

'I don't mind you talking in the slightest. This has been just what I needed. You've helped me get rid of my nerves.' He didn't know this girl well, hardly at all really. She was the daughter of a local farmer and who worked on a stall in the market. What he knew of her came from his brothers who often mentioned the two Beaumont sisters as being right lookers. Joanna had married leaving just Beth unattached, and out of the two of them Noah preferred Beth.

'You've nothing to be nervous about. You'll do amazingly well, I believe it.'

'Thank you.' It greatly surprised him how much her support meant to him. He didn't have a lot of it from his parents, just mainly from Mr Grimshaw and a little from his brothers, not that they cared one way or the other.

'Good luck, Noah Jackson.' She walked across the road and into the butchers who was putting racks of meat into the window display.

He carried on, lighter of spirit. He'd pass this exam and to celebrate he'd ask Beth Beaumont out for a walk or something.

Chapter Three

The Saturday morning crowd spread through the market taking advantage of the fine weather to shop. On days like these Beth was glad to be out in the open area of the market and not in the indoor market which was heaving with sweating bodies, balmy air, and frayed tempers.

'If it's nice like this tomorrow do you want to go for a walk, maybe even a paddle in the beck?' Jane asked Beth as she finished serving a customer. 'I'll walk over after church.'

'That would be grand.' Beth picked up a sack of newly-dug small potatoes and refilled the front of the stall where they had sold out.

'I'll make a stew and dumplings tonight for Grandma and Grandad and they'll eat the rest tomorrow.' Jane spoke as she served the next customer who handed her two turnips and a bunch of celery.

'Mam will let me go out for the afternoon on a Sunday. I'll pack us a picnic, shall I?' Beth stepped back to observe the display and bumped into someone.

'Oh, I am so sorry.' Instinct made her reach out to steady the other person, but she froze as Louis Melville stared at her, eyebrows raised haughtily.

'Is that anyway to treat a customer?'

'Forgive me, I didn't see you.'

'Walking backwards will give you that hindrance.'

'I am sorry.' Beth scooted back behind the stall, embarrassed.

Melville stepped closer to the front of the stall and peered at the vegetables, then at Jane and finally at Beth.

'Is there something you wish to buy?' Beth gripped her hands together. Up close Louis Melville was a severe-looking man, everything about him was thin and narrow. Her mam would say he needed a good feed. His dark eyes were set too close together and deep in his face. She couldn't find one redeeming feature about him.

'Buy? From you? Do I look like a peasant?' He scoffed.

She stopped herself from retorting that he looked like a funeral caretaker being dressed all in black. He carried a gold topped ebony cane even though he must only be thirty years old or so.

His hooded gaze didn't waver from Beth's face. 'Do you know who I am?'

'Yes.' Beth felt Jane stand a little closer to her, looking anxiously at her.

'Good. Then tell your father that the next time he raises his whip to me, he'll be put in jail.'

His threat instantly infuriated Beth. 'How dare you! You were the one who caused all the trouble.'

'Me?'

'Yes, you! If you'd only waited a few moments, we would have safely passed the wagon and you could have gone around him.'

'Your father should have waited for me to pass.'

'Why?' Beth snapped. 'We were on our side of the road. You were foolish and impatient and could have caused damage or injury.'

'How dare you speak to me this way?' His pale face developed two red spots on his cheeks.

'How dare you accuse my dad of being at fault when clearly it was you. Do you suppose the road is for your use only? You're not a king to be bowed down to, you're just a Melville.'

'Beth…' Jane gripped her arm.

She became aware of the gathering standing around watching the argument with open interest, nudging each other, and whispering.

Louis Melville adjusted his cuffs and stretched his neck. 'This will not be forgotten by me.'

Beth lifted her chin, ready to do battle again. 'Nor by me.'

'Do not cross my path again.' He gave her a disparaging once over.

'I don't wish to ever see you again,' Beth flung back at him.

'Leave it,' Jane muttered.

Letting out a breath, Beth watched Melville saunter away, melting into the crowd.

'Nay, lass.' Fred shook his head from where he stood behind his stall next to them. 'What possessed you to get into a ruckus with that man?'

'We nearly had a collision with him the other day and it was his fault.'

'Aye, maybe so, but he and his family aren't nice people. His father, Sir Melville, used to terrorise his tenant farmers and anyone who got in his way. It was a pleasing day when he hopped it to France and no mistake. His son is just like him. Stay away from him.'

Beth nodded and turned away. Now her rage had diminished, her hands shook a little.

'Sit down,' Jane ordered and from a flask poured her a cup of tea. 'Fancy standing up to a Melville.' She tutted. 'Your temper is going to get you in so much trouble one day.'

'Well, who does he think he is, threatening Dad like that?'

'He's the son of a rich man, that's who he is, and they can do as they like. We see him riding in his carriage all the time as he has to pass our cottage to get to his manor. I've seen him on horseback nearly running down children in the street. He's not nice. The last you want is to make an enemy out of him.' Jane went to serve a customer.

Sitting on the stool, Beth sipped her tea. She hoped she'd never see Louis Melville again and with luck he'd soon forget about her, too.

'I've only been gone a few days and here you are sitting on your bum!' Joanna grinned from the other side of the stall.

'Joanna!' Beth put her cup down and raced to embrace her sister.

'That's a nice welcome home. How are you doing?'

'I'm fine. How was Blackpool?'

'Incredible. The sun shone and we were having such an enjoyable time we stayed a few more days. We only come back last night. So, I thought I'd better come and get some food in. Good to see you, Fred.' Joanna smiled to him as he welcomed her back.

Beth took her sister's empty basket from her. 'You've not been home? Mam and Aunty Hilda will want to hear all about it.'

'No, not home yet. I've so much to do to get our little place comfortable. We've got nothing much. The rooms are a bit bare.'

'Well, you did want a honeymoon instead of furniture.'

'I know, but I don't regret it. We've got memories to last us a lifetime.'

'Aye, and Mam would say you can't eat off memories.' Beth laughed. 'What do you want?'

Joanna looked over the produce. 'Carrots, onions, lettuce, potatoes... oh new ones?'

'Dug up only yesterday.'

'Lovely. Do you have any eggs left?'

Jane held up a small basket. 'Only four left.'

'I'll take them. Thanks, Jane.'

'Do you want a cup of tea?' Beth asked, loading the basket.

'No, thanks. I can't stay. I've meat to buy and then I've to go home and cook a meal before Jimmy finishes his shift.'

'You're looking well. Marriage suits you,' Jane said.

Joanna blushed. 'It is good fun, I must say.'

Beth chuckled, glancing at her sister's rosy cheeks. 'No regrets then?'

'No, none at all.'

With the basket full, Beth gave it back to her sister and waved away her money.

'I've got to pay, our Beth,' Joanna protested.

'As if Dad will let you pay.'

'Don't tell our mam then, she'll have something to say about it.' Joanna put her purse away.

'I'll not mention the vegetables, just that you called by.'

'Thanks.' Joanna hugged Beth to her. 'I'll call again next week. And you must come around for tea one evening. You will, won't you?'

'Of course! Try and stop me.'

'Come on Friday. Bye then. Bye, Jane.'

'Bye, Joanna.' Jane packed away an empty crate. 'You didn't mention Melville.'

'No. He's not worth the worry. I doubt we'll cross paths again. Now what shall I put in this picnic for us to have by the beck tomorrow?'

~ ~ ~ ~

Basking in the sunshine, Beth lay on the grassy bank by the trickling beck. The sweltering summer had dwindled the water flow substantially. It was too low to swim in, as they had done in previous summers, but she and Jane had taken off their shoes and stockings and lifting their skirts high, they'd paddled and splashed each other until they couldn't feel their toes any longer.

The picnic spread between them, they chatted and gossiped, enjoying the day off work and a day together. In the midday heat, fat bees buzzed between the pink and white flowers of the clover, a green-eyed dragonfly hovered over the trickling water and in the trees came the call of a wood pigeon.

'Did you hear about Janice Hubbard?' Jane asked, biting into a jam tart.

'No.' Beth lay staring up at the sky, trying to make pictures out of the fluffy clouds.

'Aye, she's got herself in trouble with Jem the butcher's apprentice in Alverthorpe. Imagine. They're getting married next weekend.'

'Where did you hear that?'

'Janice used to work on the next machine to Peggy Jackson, but she stopped coming a few weeks back. What we understood to be her putting on weight was actually a baby, which she can't hide any longer.'

'She and Jem?' Beth swiped at a pestering fly near her face.

'Aye. Can you imagine doing it with Jem from the butchers?'

Beth chuckled and squinted at Jane's screwed up face. 'Well, she'll never go short of meat now, will she?'

They both laughed.

'It's a hefty price to pay though for meat on your table each day. Every night having Jem's huge hands pawing at you.'

'She must like it, or she'd not be in the family way right now.'

'I stood behind him once at the Post Office. He stank.' Jane shivered.

'Aren't you lucky you've got the lovely Alfie instead?'

'No, I ain't. We're just friends.'

'I bet he wants more than that and I think you do, too.'

'Maybe.'

Beth raised her head. 'Really?'

'Aye, why not? We're twenty years old, Beth, not sixteen. It's time we were wed.'

Lying back down, Beth closed her eyes. She didn't want things to change again. She was still getting used to Joanna having got married and living away from the farm. 'Not yet, Jane. There's no rush.'

'I'm not rushing. I'm just not closing myself off to it. Why are you against it?'

'I'm not. I never said I was, but I don't want to be tied to a man and a house and always having to put my husband first and not simply do whatever I want.'

'Maybe because you've never been in love?'

'Maybe. Yet think of how many women have very little happiness just because they believed they were in love and are now stuck with a man who rules their every move? How can that be love and how can it be just?'

'You sound like a suffragette.'

'And what's wrong with that if I do? They are fighting for us, for us to have rights.'

'I'm surprised you've not joined them.'

'I would if I could, but I promised Mam I wouldn't. She says I'd let my temper get the better of me and end up in jail and embarrass the family.'

Jane snorted a laugh. 'She's right, too. Look at you with that nasty Melville fella yesterday.'

Beth sighed and closed her eyes. 'Don't mention his name. Horrid man.'

'If you had your pick of a man who would you have?' Jane teased. 'Would you have someone like Melville who is nasty but also rich and able to give you everything? Or someone handsome and poor like Noah Jackson?'

46

Beth sat up. 'I'd rather be a spinster for the rest of my life than be with someone like Melville even with all his family's money.'

'And Noah Jackson and forever being poor?'

Heat flushed her cheeks. 'Noah is lovely, and he'll not be poor all his life. He's training to be a teacher if he passes his exams.'

Jane's eyes widened. 'How do you know that?'

'He told me the other day. I met him at the shops early in the morning. He was on his way to sit a mock exam.'

'What's a mock exam, for goodness sake?'

'Apparently something like a practice exam? Not sure.'

'You spoke to the handsome Noah…' Jane said dreamily. 'Cor, he's a looker and no mistake. He's different to all the other village fellas, even to his own brothers. He acts differently, as though he thinks before he speaks. I don't know what it is, but he stands out. People see him.'

Beth stared at her friend. 'Goodness, Jane, that's deep and meaningful.'

Jane chuckled and blushed. 'Gran says I'm a romantic. I've been ploughing my way through one of Jane Austen's novels, *Sense and Sensibility*. You know my reading isn't great, not like yours, but I'm getting through it. Noah reminds me of Colonel Brandon.'

'I won't argue with you about that, however he's not as rich nor is he a colonel.' Beth laughed and laid back down and closed her eyes. Her thoughts centred on Noah. He had a way about him, dignified was the only way to describe him. He was a rare specimen, being a working-class miner, yet studying to better himself. He walked with his head held high, his shoulders straight and a look in his eyes that spoke of a thinker, someone who took notice of everything. She'd like to be his friend.

With the sun burning her face, she slipped her straw hat over her eyes, breathing in the aroma of straw and grass. Her body relaxed, softened, as she listened to the trickling water.

'I do love summer,' Jane murmured. 'When in the mill, I dream of days like these.'

'Be careful of daydreaming, you'll lose a finger or two in your machine.'

'Don't remind me. Young Florrie got her hair caught in a machine last week. Nearly scalped her it did. If it wasn't for the quick thinking of Nellie Cartwright in quickly turning off the machine, I dread to imagine what might have happened.'

'I wish you didn't have to work there.' Beth felt the sun heat her clothes and skin.

'I'd like to work in a shop.'

'Then apply to some in town,' Beth said from under her hat, feeling drowsy.

'I might do. Boy, it's hot. I'm off to paddle.'

Beth closed her eyes, listening to Jane splash in the water. Perhaps she should, too. Or at least get out of the sun and sit in the shade for a bit.

She heard a rustle, a pant. Then a wet nose jerked the hat off her face and a tongue licked her cheek. She jumped up in surprise. Patch barked and rummaged through the picnic food.

'Patch! Patch!' Noah came running over the bank. 'I'm so sorry. I thought he was hunting for rabbits.

Stop that, Patch!' He pulled the dog away by his collar. Too late, Patch had scored himself a jam tart.

Laughing, Beth packed away some of the food and secured the lid on the basket.

'Bad boy.' Noah pushed Patch off the blanket. 'I'm sorry, Beth. We've disturbed your picnic.'

'It's fine. We can afford to lose the odd jam tart. We won't starve. I packed too much anyway.'

Jane stood in the water; her skirts held bunched just below her knees. A look of amusement on her face.

Beth looked up at Noah, shading her eyes from the sun. He wore brown trousers and a white shirt with the sleeves rolled up and a flat cap on his head. He looked masculine and his smile made her stomach flip. 'Care for something to eat or drink?'

'Thank you. A drink, maybe?'

'Sit down.' A little nervous, Beth opened the picnic basket lid and Patch stuck his head in it once more.

'Patch! I swear to God, dog.' Noah rose to his knees to drag the panting dog away.

'Here, Patch.' Jane waded to the edge of the bank and picked up a stick, which she threw along the beck.

Patch raced after it, splashing through the water, scaring birds as he made a lunge for the floating stick.

Pouring Noah a drink of lemonade, Beth handed him the cup and then poured another for herself.

Together they watched Jane and Patch play.

'Did you pass your exam?' she asked, extremely aware that Noah was sitting just on the other side of the blanket. That twice in a week she'd seen and spoken to him. It excited her that he seemed to like her company. Who would have dreamed it?

Noah glanced away from the dog to her. 'I did. Just. Mr Grimshaw says my spelling and grammar needs improvement before September, but he was happy with everything else.'

'You must be relieved?'

'I am, though I shall spend the next eight weeks studying hard to improve my weaknesses. I want to pass the proper exam easily, not just scrape by. So, I need to double my efforts.'

He was truly dedicated. She felt lazy by comparison.

'What made you want to be a teacher?'

Noah sipped his drink. 'I like learning, finding out new things. As a kid I was forever wanting to know about things. I asked so many questions to my parents, but they didn't have the answers, which frustrated me. So, I joined the library and started reading. It gave me a sense of accomplishment to learn something new and to keep learning. Then about two years ago, I met Mr Grimshaw by accident when I sat next to him on the horse bus in town. We got chatting and he told me that he was a teacher. I thought it would be grand to help children learn, for gaining more knowledge gave me a sense of fulfilment and it might them, too.'

'It's a noble profession.'

'I agree. Mr Grimshaw gave me his card and we soon became good friends as well as pupil and teacher.'

'He must be a nice man indeed to help you so much.'

'I can never repay him. That man has spent so much time on me, shaping me to be someone who could one day teach children, to fill their heads with knowledge that may one day change their lives.' Noah's blue-green eyes glowed with affection.

'You're going to be a brilliant teacher.'

Noah smiled self-consciously. 'I have to pass the exams first.'

'Then what happens?'

'I go the teachers' training college in Leeds for thirty weeks. Mr Grimshaw has secured me a grant to go as a non-resident.'

'Leeds?'

'Yes.' He looked sheepish. 'I've not told anyone about that yet. My family will go mad when they learn I'll be going to Leeds every day. I should reside there, really.'

'Then why don't you?'

Noah shrugged. 'Many reasons. My mam hasn't been well lately. I like to keep an eye on her, and I can't do that if I'm living in Leeds. My dad and brothers take advantage of her. Also, if I stay living at home, I can perhaps pick up some part-time work, pulling pints at night or something and earn a bit to give to my mam.'

'Travelling to Leeds and back every day and then working at night sounds exhausting.'

'I can do it for seven months and then I'll be trained and hopefully will get a position at a school close by.'

Beth poured him some more lemonade. 'I hope it works out for you, Noah, I really do.'

On the path behind them at the top of the bank came the sound of hoof beats. Once more a dog came bounding over the bank, only this time, the brown dog snarled and growled at them.

Frightened, Beth shot to her feet and Noah moved around closer to her. Patch came racing out of the water, barking.

'No, Patch!' Noah ran to grab him as the brown dog attacked Patch.

A horse rider appeared at the top of the bank.

'Your dog! Call him off!' Beth shouted, then realised with a sickening thud that it was Melville, who often rode the lanes on his bay stallion.

Melville peered down at them, a self-satisfied smirk on his face.

'Call your dog off!' Noah yelled, struggling to keep the big brown dog from biting the much smaller Patch.

The fighting dogs grew more frenzied. Noah bent to pick up Patch and Melville's dog took the advantage and lunged into them, biting Patch's leg, making him yelp. It then turned to Noah and scraped his forearm with its sharp teeth. Noah shouted and kicked at the dog.

Beth picked up the picnic basket and hurled it at the dog, screaming at it.

Jane squealed as Melville rode his horse down the bank, as though to charge them all. Chaos reigned. Cracking his riding crop over his dog's head, Melville managed to get the dog under control.

Panting, blood oozing down his arm, Noah cradled a whimpering Patch.

Beth stood beside them, raging. 'You're a stupid fool, Melville. Your animal could have killed Patch or one of us. He should be shot.'

Wheeling his horse about, Melville glowered at them. 'That dog was as much to blame.' He pointed at Patch. 'He wanted to take on Zeus. It is to blame. If I had a gun with me, it would be dead by now.'

Noah stiffened. 'Your damn dog came for us. Patch was protecting me.'

'Need a silly little mutt to protect you, do you? What kind of man are you?'

'One that will kick your arse if you're brave enough to get off that horse.'

'You're not worth my time. What is your name? I'll bring charges against you for being a public nuisance.'

'You'll bring charges against me?' Noah thrust Patch into Beth's arms. 'Like hell you will.'

'No, Noah.' She grabbed him. 'If you touch him, he'll have the police on you before you get home. He's that type.'

'Listen to the girl,' Melville crowed. 'It seems she has more sense than you even if she is nothing but a common farming wench.' He pointedly looked at her bare feet. 'What a disgrace.'

'How dare you! Get away from us.' Beth took a step towards him. 'Constable Murdoch is friends with my dad. Shall I go and tell him what has happened today?'

Melville leaned down from the saddle, eyes piercing. 'Are you threatening me, you little bitch?'

Beth squared up to him. 'I'm not scared of you. You're nothing but a spoilt bully!'

'Beth!' Jane came running to her side and pulled her away. 'Stop it!'

Laughing, Melville sat back in the saddle. 'You've got some spark, haven't you, stall girl?'

'Leave us alone.'

Melville rode back up the bank, his panting dog trailing behind. At the top Melville wheeled his horse about to face them. He pointed his crop at Noah. 'Don't cross paths with me again, or you'll be sorry for it.' Digging his heels into the horse's flanks, he set off down the lane.

'Oh, my Lord.' Jane, hands over her mouth, surveyed the destroyed picnic, the blood seeping from Patch's leg and running down Noah's arm.

'I've got to take Patch home.' Noah started up the bank.

'Wait. Come to my house. It's closer.' Dejected, Beth picked up the scattered remnants of the food and with Jane's help packed it into the basket, which now had a loose lid after Beth had thrown it.

Having put on their stockings and shoes, the group made their way along the lane towards Beaumont Farm without talking.

Her mam was bringing in the washing as they rounded the back of the house.

Aunty Hilda sat on a chair in the garden, shelling peas. 'What's all this then?'

'Noah and Patch have been attacked by a vicious dog,' Beth gushed.

Aunty Hilda put the bowl of peas on the floor and carefully rose. 'Come away in. You'll need ointment put on that arm and we can bandage the dog.'

'Thank you.' Noah followed the old woman into the scullery.

'Beth?' Mam walked towards them carrying the washing basket on her hip. 'What's happened?'

Beth repeated what had taken place down by the beck.

Mam tutted. 'Are you hurt?'

'No, but Noah is and his dog.'

'Noah Jackson?'

'Yes.'

Mam tutted again and went inside, and the girls followed her.

In the kitchen Noah sat at the table with Patch on his knee.

'Take the dog, Beth,' Mam instructed.

Gently she took Patch from Noah, aware of her hands touching Noah's leg and her stomach twisted as she caught Noah's gaze.

'Let me look.' Mam peered at Noah's arm, while Aunty Hilda filled a bowl with salted water and took a clean cloth from the drawer. 'You'll not need stitches.'

Mam took the bowl from Aunty Hilda and dabbed away the blood. The saltwater made Noah flinch. 'Is that your blood on your dog?'

'No, he was bitten too.'

'I'll look after him.' Aunty Hilda took Patch into the scullery to check his wound and Jane went with her to help.

'Thank you for this, Mrs Beaumont,' Noah said, watching her clean up his arm.

'You shouldn't be messing about with a vicious dog.' Mam dried his arm. 'Beth hold this bandage on the cut while I bound the arm.'

'His dog attacked us.' Noah gazed at Beth and she blushed, but held the pressure.

'Wasn't it just you and Jane on the picnic?' Mam asked, not looking up as she wound the bandage.

'It was,' Beth defended. 'Until Patch found us and licked my face while I was dozing in the sun, cheeky boy.' She smiled at Noah.

Mam's hands paused only for a minute as she glanced between the two of them. 'Don't be getting any coal dust in this cut. Keep it covered. Watch for infection.'

'Yes, Mrs Beaumont.'

'Clean it again with salted water in an hour or so. If it starts to swell or get hot and red, go to Doctor Beatty straight away.' Mam cleaned away the bowl of water and the dirty cloth.

'Thank you. I will.'

Jane brought Patch back in with a bandage wrapped around his leg. 'He's fine. Two puncture wounds. Aunty Hilda has washed them well.' She kissed the top of Patch's head. 'He was so brave.'

'Thank you.' Noah took Patch from her. 'We'd best be getting home.'

'Don't carry that dog all the way home. He can walk. He's got three other good legs, but you've only got one good arm,' Mam instructed.

'Yes, Mrs Beaumont.' Immediately Noah placed Patch on the floor.

'I'll walk with you to the gate.' Beth dashed out of the door before her mam could call her back.

'Thank you, all of you.' Noah nodded his head and walked outside.

Patch hopped towards Beth. 'Good boy.' She bent and gave him a pat.

Walking down the drive to the gate, she didn't know what to say to Noah, but also regretted he was leaving.

'You were great today, Beth.' Noah stopped at the gate, watching Patch sniff in the tall grass on the other side of the lane.

'It's a shame Melville spoiled our picnic. I wanted to ask you more about teaching.'

'Oh?' He seemed surprised by that.

'Yes. I don't know anyone who has become a teacher.'

He laughed. 'I'm not one yet.'

'But you will be.'

'I hope so.'

'Will you move away when you do qualify?'

'No, I don't suppose I will. If I can find a position in Wakefield, I'll be satisfied.'

'Me too,' Beth burst out and instantly wanted to die. Why had she said that out loud?

He stared into her eyes. 'Would you like to go for a walk with me next Sunday after church?'

'Yes. I'd like that.'

His smile made her heart thud erratically. 'Good. I'll call by about one o'clock if the weather is fine? Though I'll see you in church anyway and we can decide then.'

She nodded, too excited to speak.

'Beth!' Mam stood at the front door. 'Come in now.'

'I'd best go.' Beth couldn't stop smiling.

'See you on Sunday.'

'Beth!' Mam called again.

'Bye.' Beth ran back to the house, feeling as light as a bubble. Noah Jackson wanted to go for a walk with her! She could barely believe it. He liked her. She thought her smile would split her face she was so happy. However, her smiled died at her mam's scowl.

Chapter Four

'Here, Beth.'

Beth turned from serving a customer and smiled in relief at Flo from the haberdashery. 'Flo, you're a star.'

'Don't I know it.' Flo, an old school friend of Beth's, worked as an assistant at the haberdashery stall at the indoor market and made dresses as a side income. She handed over the parcel to Beth. 'I couldn't match the same lemon material of the dress for the satin sash so it's white instead, which matches the white lace at the throat and sleeves.'

'Thank you so much.'

'Two dresses in one summer, you must be flushed with money?'

'I've saved,' Beth explained. 'Besides, Mam paid for the bridesmaid dress for Joanna's wedding. This dress is my wages for last month and my dad always gives me extra money.'

'You're lucky. I wish my dad would.' Flo touched the parcel. 'Thankfully, I got it done this week. Normally, it takes much longer, but since you're a friend I put you before some of me other clients and finished it late last night. Are you going somewhere special?'

'No. I just wanted something pretty before the winter comes. Thanks again.'

When Flo left, Beth tucked the parcel under the stall and served another customer who wanted a dozen eggs and a bunch of carrots. Saturday's were the busiest day and she wished Jane had been able to help her, but Jane had to work at the mill.

Beth thanked the customer and instinctively turned to the next one who wanted the last bunch of flowers picked from the garden just that morning and a bunch of mixed herbs as well as two turnips, a small brown paper bag of strawberries and a handful of radishes.

With that customer dealt with, Beth took a sip of water from the bottle she kept under the stall. All week she'd been excited about Sunday. Working hard in the fields or on the stall didn't matter. All she fantasised about was going for a walk with Noah. She still couldn't believe it. Out of all the girls in the area, Noah Jackson had picked her. Yes, it was only a walk, and she mustn't get ahead of herself, but still, Noah had asked her.

With a beaming smile, Beth looked to her next customer, a wealthy woman dressed in amber-coloured silk and with long feathers in her hat. 'Yes, madam. How can I help you?'

The woman's gaze skimmed over the stall and rested on Beth. Her thin pointed nose rose in the air slightly. After a moment she walked on.

Beth stared after her. The woman reminded her of someone, but she didn't recall ever seeing her before.

'She wasn't too taken with your vegetables.' Fred laughed from behind his stall.

'No, it didn't seem so.'

'Melvilles are weird folk.'

'She was a Melville?'

'Aye. Sir Melvilles daughter. Can't remember her name. She's spent many years in Switzerland at some finishing school and then went on a Grand Tour around Europe with some elderly aunt as the posh folk do.'

A spark of jealousy flickered in Beth. How must it be to live without a care in the world, to travel on a whim?

'I don't suppose I've ever seen her in the market before,' Fred murmured as he fixed the handle on a hammer.

'No, nor have I.' Beth frowned. Why would the Melville woman do so now?

She dismissed the woman from her mind and served another customer, a regular who chatted to her for awhile about the size of strawberries and whether they were better than raspberries.

When Will and Ronnie came to help her pack away at noon, Beth suppressed her giddiness that to-morrow was Sunday and she'd see Noah. She hurried the boys to secure the lock-up and pack the cart. She was eager to get home and have a bath and wash her hair, also she wanted to try on her new dress.

As they entered the village, they passed a gig and Beth stiffened at its occupants, Louis Melville, and his sister who she'd seen at the market earlier today. Both of them stared at her, but Louis suddenly grinned and whispered something into his sister's ear and she laughed as well.

Were they talking about her? Beth swallowed; the hair rising on the back of her neck. Was Louis telling his sister about the confrontation at the picnic? He must have said something to his sister for why else would she come to the stall and study Beth as if she was an exhibit? By the look on her face she hadn't approved of what she saw. She thought Beth to be inferior, her expression made that clear.

Beth seethed. How dare the Melvilles look down on her. Her family owned land just as the Melvilles did. Albeit not as much, nor did they have the vast amount of money the Melvilles obviously had, but still, she wasn't a beggar in the street, and she deserved to be treated with some respect.

'Do get Snowy moving, our Will,' Beth urged as they made their way home.

'She's been working in the field all day. She's tired.' Will gave Beth a sharp look. 'What's your hurry anyway?'

'I want to get home, that's all.' She took the reins from him.

'Hey! What are you doing?' He snatched them back.

'Let me drive.'

'I'll not.' Will glared at her, affronted. 'I'm in charge of the cart, Dad said.'

'I'm older.'

'I'm a boy.'

She squared up at him in the seat. 'And that makes you better than me?'

'Now, our Beth, steady on.' Will concentrated on the road and flicked Snowy's reins a little to urge her on as they turned into Trough Well Lane.

'Don't ever imagine you are better than me William Beaumont just because you're a male, understand?' she fumed.

'Calm down, will you?' He frowned at her.

'Give me the reins.'

'No.'

'Stop it you two,' Ronnie called from the back of the cart.

'What's wrong with you?' Will muttered as they turned into the gates.

'Nothing.' Beth grabbed her parcel and basket, jumping down from the cart before Snowy had barely stopped. She ran inside and straight upstairs to her room. Seeing the Melvilles had taken the shine off her day.

~ ~ ~ ~

'I said you're not going.' Mam stirred the batter for the Yorkshire puddings, her face set.

'Why can't I?' Beth stood on the other side of the table, still dressed in her new lemon and white lace dress that she'd worn to church. Mam had just told her to take it off and do some weeding in the kitchen garden.

'You've things to do.'

'I'll do them when I get back, I promise you.'

Dad came into the kitchen, yesterday's newspaper under his arm. 'What's all this?'

'She wants to go walking with Noah Jackson. I've said no. She's got work to do.'

Rob Beaumont's eyebrows drew together. 'It's Sunday and she works all week. Let her go.'

'She went gallivanting off last Sunday and look where that got her, in a scrap with a Melville.'

'That wasn't my fault,' Beth argued.

'You were still involved though, weren't you? And with that Jackson fellow.'

'Melville's dog attacked us!'

'You're not going.' Mam turned her back on them and thudded the bowl onto the shelf above the range.

Dad jerked his head towards the door, indicating that Beth should go.

She grabbed her straw hat and left the kitchen.

'You've let her go!' Mam's raised voice made Beth pause outside the door.

'Aye, I did. She deserves an afternoon to herself. She works hard.'

'She's going walking with a Jackson.'

'Aye, and is that a crime now?'

'Rob!'

'Mary, lass, Noah Jackson is a good fellow. He's a man going places, learning to be a teacher. He's not his dad.'

'He's still a Jackson and they are all as bad as each other. They think they can do as they like, and their good looks will get them out of everything.'

'Mary, love.'

'Don't Mary love me, Robert Beaumont. You'll be the one comforting our lass when that Jackson lad throws her over for someone else.'

Beth heard a door slam and hurried down the path to the drive and ran to the gate where Noah waited for her.

His smile wiped away the scene with her mam and she grinned back at him, butterflies circling in her stomach.

'Where do you want to go?' he asked.

'Anywhere away from here.' She looked back at the house and saw Mam at the bedroom window which faced the lane.

'There's a brass band playing in the park.'

Beth turned away and gave him a huge smile. 'Sounds perfect.'

As they walked up the lane towards the village, Beth asked after Patch.

'He's fine. It took three days for him to walk on that leg, but he's doing it now. My family have been making a fuss over him, so he's happy as a pig in muck right now.'

'That's good, and your arm?'

He flexed the injured arm. 'All good, too. It hurt for a few days, swinging a pick underground didn't help, but I kept it as clean as I could, which is difficult being a miner. My mam is forever at me to change the bandages. It's starting to heal now. It'll be a tattoo scar, no doubt.'

'A tattoo scar?'

'Yes, when a miner gets a cut on his skin, the coal dust gets in, no matter how hard we try to keep it clean. The coal dust shows up black when the skin heals. All miners have their work tattoos.' He showed her his wrist and the fine line of blue-black scars.

'I never knew that.'

'You aren't from a mining family.'

'No. My mam's family were. She was the first in her family to marry a farmer and not a miner.'

'Lucky her. She got out of it. No one ever gets a decent life from working in a coal mine. It's nothing but hard dangerous work for basic pay which barely keeps a roof over your head.'

Although she didn't hear bitterness in his voice, there was a resigned tone. Beth wondered what her mam thought about having escaped that life. She'd never asked her. Although the Beaumonts worked hard, they earned good money and were much better off than the miners. Mam had left her mining village in Outwood and its damp terraced houses and poor underfed inhabitants and found herself mistress of a large farmhouse with plenty of food and space and fresh air. The Beaumonts had not only worked the land for years but owned it and not rented. Something rare unless you were gentry.

Her mam had done well for herself. Beth rarely saw that side of her mam's family. Her mam's parents were dead, and her mam's sister had moved to Leeds. Only her brother remained in the terrace house in Outwood, but he had argued with Mam years ago and they'd not spoken since.

'Thank you for agreeing to take a walk with me.' Noah smiled. 'I expected you to have a beau by now.'

'No, I've been asked before by some of the lads in the village, but I wasn't interested.'

'What made you say yes to me then?'

Beth shrugged. 'I liked the look of you,' she said cheekily. 'And you're clever, so I've been told. Some of the lads I went to school with are as dumb as rocks.'

Noah laughed. 'Not for the first time in my life I'm glad I made the decision to educate myself.'

Beth relaxed and lifted her face to the sun. She liked Noah Jackson.

They heard the band before they saw it. Couples strolled the path around the park and parents sat on

66

blankets in the sunshine. Children were running around the grassy parkland, chasing balls and each other.

'May I buy you a drink?' Noah asked.

'Yes, thank you.'

A little wooden cabin selling bottles of drink and pots of tea was at the edge of the park and they strolled over to it.

A football came whirling past Beth's head.

'Sorry!'

Noah turned and swore. 'Albie!'

Beth recognised James and Alfred Jackson paying football with the other two Jackson brothers that she didn't know as well, with them being older than her.

'Hiya, Beth!' Alfred called, running over to her Noah.

'Go away, Alfred,' Noah muttered.

Within seconds all the Jackson brothers were crowded around Beth.

'So, this is why he didn't want to play football with us.' Sid pushed Noah's shoulder.

'Who could blame him?' Albie said kindly. 'You are very pretty, Miss Beaumont.'

'The prettiest girl in the village,' James added, giving Beth a playful nudge.

'Thank you.' Beth blushed.

'It's just Beth Beaumont,' Alfred joked. 'Why are you all being so soft? I used to sit behind her in class and pulled her pigtails.'

'Yes, you did!' Beth accused, chuckling.

'What do you see in our Noah, Miss Beaumont?' Sid asked boldly. 'He's no better than any of us.'

Beth grinned. 'Really? I highly doubt that for I know that James can't spell for toffee and Alfred talks with his mouthful. Remember, I spent years with them at school. I'm aware of all their bad habits.'

The brothers teased each other, agreeing with Beth.

'We're having a drink now. Go away, you lot.' Noah steered Beth by the elbow towards the tea cabin and away from his brothers, who now were whistling and hollering like loons, kicking the ball high.

'I'm sorry about that,' Noah said, waiting in line.

'It's fine. I've known James and Alfred for so long. They are no different since we were kids.'

He passed her a small bottle of ginger ale. 'One day they'll grow up.'

'I doubt it, they are males.'

Noah raised his eyebrows in amusement. 'Shall we walk to the other side? We can hear the band better.'

'Yes, all right.' She walked beside him, waving to those she knew. They stood in the shade of a large pin oak and listened to the band play.

It was difficult to talk when the band played so loudly, but Beth was content to listen and watch the other people enjoying their Sunday afternoon. That she stood with Noah made her swell with pride. Some of the villagers noticed the two of them together and heads were bent close and they whispered. Beth didn't care. He had chosen her.

Noah took their bottles back to the cabin when they'd finished and suggested a stroll around the perimeter of the park.

'Summer is my favourite season,' Beth said, skirting a child playing with a hoop.

'Mine is spring. I like to see the new flowers, the blossom, the baby animals in the fields. In spring you know you have months of pleasant weather ahead. Not that I see a lot of it working underground.'

'No. But soon you will see it every day, from a schoolroom window.'

'We can agree that winter is the worst month?' He stuck his hands in his trouser pockets. 'I hate getting up in the dark and coming home in the dark.' He shivered. 'I'll never get used to it.'

'Imagine living in a country that is always warm.'

'Like the south of Italy or on a Greek Island?' He raised his face to the sun. 'To travel…'

'Wouldn't it be wonderful?' She couldn't imagine visiting such distant places.

'Mr Grimshaw has been to France and Germany. He has told me about his trips. I am envious. He paints such thoughts in my mind of diverse cultures, strange food and languages.'

'I'd like to see the pyramids.' Beth sighed dreamily. 'I've seen them in books.'

'Do you go to the library often?'

'Yes, as much as I can.'

'Perhaps we can go together and have a look at the large atlas they have in there. Have you seen it?'

'The one on the stand in the corner by the window?' She glowed at the idea of spending more time with Noah.

'Yes.'

'I have seen it but not dared to turn the pages.'

'Mr Grimshaw and I did once, a few months ago. It's beautifully illustrated.'

'Illustrated? What is that?'

'Drawn art or stencilled print work, that sort of thing. Drawings are on nearly every page of the atlas about that particular country and all in colour.'

'I didn't know the drawings were called that. In colour, too. Fascinating.' She felt rather stupid all of a sudden.

Her schooling had been adequate, but she'd left school at fourteen, knowing how to read and write, to work on the farm and the stall with Joanna. Her parents didn't push for her to learn more. They were farmers. Girls got married and had babies in her family, they didn't become doctors or teachers, though her mam was vocal about her and Joanna marrying well, preferable another farmer with land.

Noah kicked a runaway ball back to some youths. 'What do you like to do in your spare time, apart from having picnics?'

Beth brushed away a fly. 'I like walking, reading, spending time in the garden, that kind of thing. Mam would wish me to be better at my needlework, but I find it rather boring.'

'What do you read?'

'I do enjoy stories. The Bronte sisters and Charles Dickens. You?'

'I'm the same, though my time is now spent on studying geography and history, mathematics and so on. I don't have the time to simply relax with a good story.'

She realised that his knowledge far outweighed hers. Would he find her wanting? Could she hold a stimulating conversation with him, or would he soon grow bored? It was only her love of reading books that had widened her knowledge somewhat. Suddenly it wasn't enough. Noah was a miner, but he was better educated than she was, through his own efforts. He'd taught himself, pushed himself to learn, to educate himself to make his life better. She felt ashamed she hadn't the drive to do the same, but then could she? Did she want to be a teacher or a nurse or a governess? The answer was no.

Was she happy to work behind a stall or toil in the field until the day she married? It was the only thing expected of her. Was it enough? She'd never really considered it before because she was happy. She loved her family's farm and enjoyed working on the stall. If she left the stall to do something else, what would her parents say?

'What are you doing on Tuesday?' Noah asked as they found themselves back at the tea cabin. 'I finish at four o'clock all week.'

'I'm on the stall on Tuesday. There isn't a market on Mondays and Wednesdays.'

'Did you want to go to the library with me on Wednesday?'

'I'd like that.' She thought for a moment. Wednesdays were field days, sorting vegetables and cutting flowers ready for the stall the following day. However, if she woke early and did all her jobs without taking a break, then she'd be free in the afternoon. 'I can meet you in town about four-thirty?' she asked hopefully, desperately wanting to spend more time with him. 'Does that give you enough time after work?'

'It does. I'll try and get above ground a bit sooner than normal and wash quickly.' He grinned. 'I'll meet you outside of the library.'

Chapter Five

Impatient to be gone, Beth worked like a demon on Wednesday. She was up with her dad at dawn and out in the fields as the sky was changing from navy to coral.

'What's your hurry, lass?' her dad asked, as she wheeled the barrow out of the shed. She'd already collected the eggs, fed the hens, and let them out. She'd walked the mile to Henderson's Dairy and bought a bucket of fresh milk and carried it home, a task usually allocated to Will, but he was full of cold and so she'd done it for him.

'I want to go into town later.' She collected a gardening fork and a spade. 'If I get everything done, Mam won't find reason to stop me.'

'Why do you need to go into town?'

Beth paused. Should she tell her dad? He was usually easy-going and had allowed her to meet Noah on Sunday, but still her mam had a thing about the Jacksons, whatever that was, and perhaps she shouldn't mention Noah again just yet. 'I'm going to the library.' It wasn't a lie.

'Your mam wouldn't stop you going to the library. She likes you reading.'

'Not if I haven't got all my jobs done, she doesn't.' Beth pushed the wheelbarrow towards the large vegetable garden in the field closest to the house.

'I'm going into town myself about three, if you fancy a lift?' he called to her.

'Thanks, Dad.'

She began forking the weeds out between the rows of lettuce which were covered with protective netting to keep the rabbits from eating them. She worked steadily for an hour until her mam brought out a cup of tea for her.

'Your dad says you want to go into town?'

'Aye. To the library.'

'Can you pick me up some red wool from Mrs Flannery's shop on Westgate, it's not far from the library. I've already paid her, so it's just a pickup. I want to finish making that scarf for Will for winter.'

'Aye, of course I'll get the wool.' She sipped her tea. 'Is he feeling better?'

'Yes, he's playing it on and Aunty Hilda fusses over him. He's only got the sniffles and acts as though he's at death's door.'

'He'd never last on the stall in winter.'

Mam went to turn away but stopped. 'I'll get your dad to give you some money for the tram back as it'll be late.'

'Thanks, Mam.'

'After you've done in here, there's marigold seeds to sort and bag in the potting shed. Oh, and yesterday I potted up half a dozen pansies for you to sell tomorrow. Will can load the cart this evening when your dad returns.'

Beth nodded, finished her tea, and handed the cup back to her mam.

Mam peered at her. 'Are you all right?'

'Aye, fine. Why?'

'You didn't mention much about your walk with that Jackson lad when you returned home on Sunday. I didn't want to bring it up in case you had a falling out.'

'I think it would be difficult to have a falling out with Noah. He's so kind and considerate. We had a nice walk around the park and listened to the band for a while. Noah bought me a drink and then we walked some more before coming home.'

'I noticed he didn't walk you to the gate.'

Beth knew her mam would have been watching the lane for sight of them. 'No, we parted at the top of the lane, there was no point in him walking down the lane, only to turn around and walk back up it again.'

'What's a couple of hundred yards to him? He's fit and healthy, isn't he?'

'Yes, but he lives along the other way.'

'I'm aware of where he lives, but he still should have walked you to the gate. That is the proper way to behave. But then he is a Jackson so it's to be expected.'

Her words riled Beth. 'What have you got against the Jacksons, Mam?'

'Nowt. I care nothing about any of them.'

'Then why haven't you got a kind word for them?'

'Because I know that kind of folk. Lazy, liars and not worth feeding.'

'That's unkind. Noah and his brothers are good, hardworking men.'

Mam snorted. 'Not like their father then.'

'I don't know much about him, nothing at all, really.'

'Best keep it that way. Nothing good comes from a Jackson.' Mam stormed away and Beth watched her go.

Continuing her digging, Beth pondered on her mam's behaviour. Never had she seen her so catty against a family as she was against the Jacksons. Had she fallen out with Mrs Jackson at some point in the past? She knew Peggy Jackson worked at the mill with Jane, but Jane only mentioned her briefly and always said she was a hard worker who liked a laugh and was fiercely protective over her lads.

It was all such a mystery.

~ ~ ~ ~

Noah buttoned up his waistcoat and tucked his tie in as Sid came into the room.

'Look at you, all spiffy. Where are you off to?' he said, throwing himself onto his bed. 'Aren't we were going to the football try-outs this afternoon? It's on from four till six o'clock.'

'Nope. I'm off to the library.'

'God, could your life be more boring, man? Come to the try-outs with us. I reckon we all might make the team this season.'

'I've a better option than spending the afternoon with you rowdy lot.' Noah laughed.

'There's only three more try-outs left, and you've not been to any so far. Alfred definitely has a spot, I reckon. Tell me, what is better than playing football with your brothers and then going for a pint?'

'Spending the day with Beth Beaumont.' Noah grinned.

That made Sid sit up and give him his full attention. 'Miss Beaumont again, hey? Is this getting serious then?'

'It might be. We'll see.' Noah shrugged, not wanting to give too much away just yet. He wasn't sure himself what to think. He should be concentrating on his teaching career, not pondering about a pretty lass. But Beth had managed to get under his skin, and he was enamoured by her. He liked her sweet smile, that flash of her eyes when something caught her interest. The way she had jumped straight in to help him when Melville's dog attacked him and Patch, had not left his mind. She had spirit and courage and a lovely laugh.

He liked the shape of her body, the supple strength she had, the straightness of her back, the lift of her chin. Her dark hair and hazel eyes made him lose his thoughts and he longed to kiss her and feel what it would be like to hold her against him.

A pillow smacked him up the side of his head. 'What the hell!' He glared at Sid.

'I've asked you a question three times!' Sid sighed. 'Stop pondering that Beaumont lass and listen to me.'

'What?' Noah smoothed down his hair he'd carefully combed.

'Do you reckon Dad'll be going back to work tomorrow? He hinted as such just now.'

'Aye, probably, but for how long, who knows? Not one for working is our father, is he?' He checked his boots were clean and polished.

'Not since Alfred and James left school and joined us. He spends more time injured than underground.'

'I agree. It's been annoying me that he spends more time at the pub than working. The six of us should be raking the money in now, and Mam could stop working at the mill, which would help her chest. We could move out of this dump and get something nicer, but no, in the last few years Dad has been working less and less.' Taking his best jacket from the peg behind the door, Noah shrugged it on.

'Well let's hope this time he stays underground for longer than a few weeks before he hurts himself again.' Sid frowned.

'Let's hope so. Oh, and don't allow James to get legless before the game. He can't hold his drink.'

Sid laid back on the bed with the newspaper. 'I ain't his nursemaid.'

Noah walked into the kitchen to find his mam peeling potatoes.

She glanced at him. 'Where are you off to?'

'The library.'

'You live at that place.'

'I need to study.' He didn't want to mention Beth to her just yet.

Her hands stilled but she didn't look at him. 'You know I'm proud of you, don't you?'

'Are you? I'd never realise it.' Noah checked his appearance in the small mirror above the fireplace. He straightened his tie. Patch sat waiting for his attention and he gave the dog a quick ear fondle.

'I just worry, that's all. Teachers don't get paid a lot of money.'

'Nor do pit men.'

Her head dropped a little more. 'I just worry, that's all. If you move away and your dad hurts himself again then it's less money coming in to feed us all and pay the rent.'

'Is money all you care about?' Noah tried not to be annoyed with his mam but lately her constant going on about money was driving him mad.

'Feeding us all isn't easy. I've had to manage for years on your dad's wage which barely covered the rent!'

'That shouldn't be a problem now though, should it? Not with us all working. You get most of our wages.'

'Mr Grimshaw will encourage you to leave here if you can't get a place in a school in this area.'

'Mam, I never said I was moving away. I have to pass the exams first, anyway. Let us cross each bridge as we come to it.'

She nodded and sighed despondently.

'Mam, there will be a time when all us lads will get married and move out of here. You'll not have our money then to buy food and pay the rent. We'll have our own families to support.'

'That's what I'm afraid of. Your dad and me ending up in the poor house.'

He stared at her disbelief. 'The poor house? Where has that idea come from? We'd never see you go to somewhere like that or let you go short, you know that.'

She glanced up at him with a haunted expression. 'Ignore me.'

Noah sensed something was wrong. He understood his mam well, and although she'd deny it, he knew he was her favourite and she'd never keep something from him. 'Mam I love you. You'll always be looked after by me, whether I'm married or not, working close by or further away.'

'Aye, I know.'

'Then what's wrong? You've been acting strangely for weeks. You're always sniping and being short-tempered with us all. That's not you. I've not seen you smile in months.'

'It's nothing, son. Get off to the library.'

'I'm not going anywhere until you tell me what's upsetting you.'

'Noah, please…'

He stood close to her and placed his hand on her shoulder. 'Tell me.'

She sighed deeply, unhappily. 'I might as well tell you as you'll find out soon enough if we get evicted.'

'Evicted?' His mouth dropped open in shock.

'Your dad has debts, lad.'

Noah's stomach dipped. 'Debts?'

'Aye.' She continued to peel the potatoes. 'He's been losing money on the greyhounds, the horses, the football…' She shrugged one shoulder. 'Anything and everything it seems.'

Anger burned through Noah quicker than a wild-fire. 'Then he'd better get himself back to work, hadn't he?'

'He's going in the morning.' She dunked her hands into the dirty water and began peeling another potato.

Noah grabbed her hand. 'Where is your wedding ring?'

'Er…'

'Don't lie to me, Mam.'

She wouldn't look at him. 'Pawned.'

'Mam!'

'Your dad promised he'll get it back.' Her tone was resigned.

'Sid!' Noah barked, furious. When his brother raced into the kitchen, Noah held up their mam's hand. 'Dad's pawned her ring to pay for his gambling debts.'

'No!' Sid looked horrified. 'Oh, Mam.'

'It's all right,' she pleaded. 'Don't make a fuss.'

'No, it's not all right.' Noah stormed to the door. 'We don't pawn things in this house.'

His mam abruptly laughed mirthlessly. 'Lad, I've been pawning stuff since I married your dad. You were just too little to know about it.'

'What else has been pawned.'

'Enough now, Noah.' Mam waved him away. 'I don't want to talk about it.'

'Where's Dad?'

'At the pub,' Sid answered.

'What money is he using to buy pints with?'

Mam continued to peel the potatoes.

Noah took down the jug on the mantelpiece where he knew his mam put all their wages each week. The jug was empty. A cold rage circled his head. He tipped the jug upside down to show Sid.

'We have six wages coming in,' said Sid, sitting at the table and allowing Patch to jump up onto his lap. 'How the hell are we not managing on six wages?'

Noah's blood turned to ice as his mam's face paled. 'Because Dad's using Mam's wage to gamble and he's not working himself, is he? Dad is spending our hard-earned money, leaving none for rent and bills. That's why Mam's ring was pawned and God knows what else.'

Sid stared at Noah. 'That can't be right...'

'Mam? Am I telling the truth?' Noah asked, trying to keep his anger in check.

'He said he'll get the money back.'

'Are we to be evicted?' Noah prodded.

'Not if we can catch up on the arrears in the next few weeks.'

Noah opened the door as Albie, Alfred and James came through the scullery.

'We're off to the try-outs. Are you coming, Sid?' James said.

Albie stared at them in turn. 'What's happened?'

'You tell them, Sid. I'm going to be late.' Noah turned to his mam and he rammed his flat cap on his head. 'We'll talk about this later.'

He marched out of the back yard and down the cut between their house and the neighbour's and onto Potovens Lane. His anger fed his foul mood and his fast pace as he headed out of the village and towards Newton Bar where he'd catch the tram into town.

He needed to lose his anger before he saw Beth, or it'd ruin their afternoon, but it was hard to shake off the fear of eviction and all because of his dad's self-ishness. His relationship with his dad had never been great. Leo Jackson was one for giving slaps first and asking questions later. He was hard man who gave lit-tle affection to his sons and not much more to their mam. All their lives they'd been frightened of him, of his shouts and sullen silences. True he could laugh and joke with them but only when he deemed it the time to be jovial. Leo Jackson spent as little time as possible in the family home. Always had somewhere to go, people to see and petty deals to drum up which might nab him a few pennies. Pennies which went down his throat in pints of ale.

Noah never understood why his pretty mam had married such a man.

His father's selfish behaviour only convinced him more to become a teacher and better his position in life. His mam's words about moving away also rang in his head. Before he'd had no intention of moving away but now, he was beginning to think it might be a solution. Perhaps, once qualified, he could apply for a position in a private school with better pay. Or become a tutor to a wealthy family. Was that even possible? He'd ask Mr Grimshaw.

One thing was for sure, he'd not be living in a cramped, damp pit house, that's for certain. He'd not subject his future family to such soul-destroying conditions.

Once on the tram and heading into Wakefield, he cooled his temper and thought of the pleasant afternoon with Beth.

She was waiting for him out the front of the library on Drury Street and his stomach flipped at the sight of her. Her welcoming smile delighted him like nothing else. This lovely girl filled his head day and night and the quickness of it surprised him. Was she the one he needed in his life? Was it too soon to know the answer or to even think of such a question?

'I was early,' she said as he walked closer to her. 'I had to collect some wool for my mam.' Beth held up a string bag showing red balls of wool inside.

'Shall we go inside?' He took her elbow and escorted her into the building. He found it refreshing that she didn't simper and giggle as most girls did.

They found the old atlas on its stand by the window and thankfully no one was studying it. Like all libraries, the atmosphere was soft, silent, as though the books held their breath suspended, waiting for someone to choose them.

Noah felt such a sense of peace in the library. It was his favourite place to be when the frosty winter weather prevented him from walking the fields. Amongst the tomes he would hide from the world which demanded that he dig coal deep underground and instead he was transported to anywhere he chose.

'We should make a plan,' Beth whispered, her eyes bright with excitement.

'A plan?' Noah turned a page carefully, valuing the ancient book.

'Yes. A voyage to other countries and plan a route.' She frowned. 'Or does that sound silly?'

'It sounds interesting.' He grinned. 'You start.'

'I'd like to see the pyramids.'

'Right. So how do we get to Egypt? Leave London and go by boat the entire way, or shall we cross the Channel and go overland?' He turned the pages until he came to the United Kingdom and put his finger on London.

'Overland. We cross the Channel and go to France.'

'France.' He turned more pages until he found France.

'Oh look, the Eiffel Tower.' Beth leaned closer to study the picture of the famous tower.

'We should stop in Amsterdam and see the sights?' Noah prompted, enjoying the game.

'Yes, and then…' Beth ran her finger down the length of France. 'Either we go over the Alps to Italy or down to Spain?'

Noah's chest tightened as he stared at her profile as she bent over the book. The sunlight streamed through the large window, highlighting her cheek-bones, her lips. She wore her dark hair up under a straw hat, but tendrils had come loose and lay wispy over her delicate ears. He ached to touch her, to run his fingers over her sun-kissed skin, to—

'We could leave from Marseilles?'

He cleared his throat and concentrated on the large map in front of him. 'Italy?'

'Yes. Let's cross the Alps into Italy. Shall we go to Rome?'

He nodded, pretending to be serious when all he wanted to do was take her in his arms. 'One day I want to travel to Rome,' he murmured, wondering if ever such a thing would come true.

'And you shall. I know it.' She beamed up at him, and at that moment, Noah felt a pull on his heart, and he knew he was lost. Beth Beaumont. There would be no other woman for him.

Her gaze locked with his and an unspoken message was shared. They'd found what they didn't realise had been missing.

They spent the next half an hour planning their imaginary trip across Europe, studying the town and cities, delighting in the illustrated pictures of famous landmarks of each country.

'Shall we go for a cup of tea?' Beth said as they closed the large tome as the librarian told them they'd be closing soon.

'I'd like that very much.'

Walking back through the library, they whispered where they should go when an older man carrying books came up to them.

'Mr Jackson. The book you ordered has come in. It's behind the desk. Do you want it today?'

'Yes, thank you, Mr Hancock.'

They followed the library clerk to the main desk and Noah received the book he'd ordered on world geography, which was wrapped in brown paper and tied with string.

Once out of the library, they headed down Westgate to a tea room.

'Here, put your book in my bag.' Beth opened the string bag for him to pop the book into. 'There's no point in you carrying it when I've a bag.'

'It'll make it heavier for you.'

She laughed at him. 'I carry heavy crates of vegetables every day. I can carry a book and some wool.'

'Ah, true. But I can carry the bag.'

'No, you won't.' She stopped before the tea room door. 'And I'm buying this time, too.'

Noah jerked to a halt. 'You certainly are not. What a suggestion!'

'You bought me a drink at the park.'

'And I'll buy you every drink while ever you're in my company, Miss Beaumont.'

She raised an eyebrow at him. 'I am capable of buying us both a cup of tea and a piece of cake.'

He frowned. 'Are you a secret suffragette?'

Beth put her hands on her hips and glared at him. 'What if I was?'

Her anger amused him. 'Go inside and find a table while I order.'

'Mr Jackson, I—'

'Miss Beaumont, as beautiful as you are, you're not buying me a cup of tea.' He walked towards the counter but not before seeing her blush when he called her beautiful.

Over tea and cake, they discussed the pros and cons of the suffragettes, and Beth told him she'd like to be one, but her parents forbade it. Then they discussed their families and work.

'What time are you expected back home?' Noah asked as they left the tea room after he had paid. The sun was slowly descending, but still high enough to give good light. The church bells around the town rang in the hour of six o'clock.

'As long as I'm home before dark, Mam won't mind.'

'We could watch the football try-outs or the cricket practice.'

'Why aren't you playing this year? You always play cricket in the summer.'

'I gave it up this year to study.'

'Good on you for such commitment.'

'Sometimes I question myself about it, when my eyes are stinging with tiredness and my brothers are begging me to do some activity with them and I keep turning them down.'

'It'll not be forever.' She stopped and a smile lit up her face. 'I know. Let's go to the park and hire bicycles for an hour.'

'Really? At this hour? The hire stall will be closed.'

'No, I saw an advertisement in the newspaper that they didn't close until seven in the summer. That gives us some time.'

'Let's go then.'

She clapped and then gripped his arm. 'Wonderful. I love riding bicycles. I ride Will's all the time.'

'Why don't you have your own?'

'Mam reckons it's not very ladylike.' She shrugged, disappointedly.

'Well, your mam isn't around, is she?'

She clapped again. 'I knew you wouldn't be too serious and like to have fun.'

Having caught the tram, they were soon at Thorne's Park and hired two bicycles for half an hour. Freewheeling down a hill, dodging people walking by and horses and carts, Beth laughed and raced Noah along the paths. They stayed in the grounds of the large park, keeping away from the horse traffic and trams. Noah peddled beside Beth, watching the happiness radiate out of her, and had never felt more alive in his life.

Chapter Six

'Maybe we can have a double wedding?' Jane asked.

Beth laughed as they walked along Lindale Hill Lane. They'd spent the day at Jane's grandparents' cottage, painting the kitchen and generally tiding the place up. The job was too much for Jane to do alone, and her grandad had hurt his back, which meant he found physical work painful, and so Beth had offered to brandish a paintbrush.

After finishing the kitchen and clearing away, they decided on an afternoon walk to clear their heads of paint fumes. Besides, as the September weather was unpredictable, they knew they'd not have many more opportunities to take walks before the chilly weather descended.

'Well, we could,' Jane defended.

'Are you serious with Alfie Taylor now?'

'We've been walking out for five months, give or take.' Jane blushed.

'And you're talking of marriage?'

'Aren't you with Noah?'

'Not at all.' Beth pulled at a tall blade of grass lining the dirt lane.

'Don't you want to marry him?'

Beth gave her a lofty look. 'We're friends. Nothing has been declared.'

'It's been months since you started walking out with him and you didn't answer my question.'

'Two. Two months we've been walking out if you can call it that.' Beth's heart fluttered as it always did at the mention of Noah.

Since that day in July when they visited the library and rode the bicycles in Thorne Park, they'd spent every Sunday together – seven Sundays learning about each other. She had adored every moment of it. However, it was becoming increasingly difficult for Beth to hide her feelings for Noah and she wasn't entirely sure how he felt about her.

Not once had he touched her in any way other than to take her elbow to help her up into a tram, or some other kind gesture. A few times, he had put his hand out but withdrawn it quickly, and once or twice she noticed the way his gaze lingered on her lips and her toes had curled in anticipation of him kissing her, but he hadn't.

She ached for him to hold her. Was that very wanton of her? She didn't care. If he kissed her, she'd kiss him right back and enjoy every second.

But she knew he was growing anxious about his exams. The first exam was to be next week and he was spending every moment studying for it and she encouraged him too, which was why this Sunday she was painting Jane's kitchen and not with Noah, so he could spend the day reading his books in readiness for Wednesday's exam.

'You're lucky snagging such a good looking and clever man, Beth. You're the envy of every girl in the district.'

Beth swelled with pride. 'He is handsome and clever.'

'And kind?'

'Yes, he is. I've found nothing bad about him yet. Though Mam hasn't a pleasant word to say about him or any of the Jackson family.'

'But why?'

'I've no idea and it's tiring keeping my mouth shut when she goes on and on about untrustworthy Jacksons and that I'll have my heart broken if I keep seeing Noah.'

'It doesn't make any sense why she would be so against him.'

'I need to find out.'

'Especially if Noah asks you to marry him.'

The thought made Beth tingle with excitement. 'If I ever did marry Noah, and I'm not saying that it's something I'm always thinking about…' Beth paused, for she did daydream about it more than she should, 'then I would want a June wedding, like our Joanna's. I'd like a sunny day, with flowers and bunting and girls in pretty dresses, lots of food and drink and my mam and dad hosting the party in the garden.'

'Your Joanna's day was special,' Jane agreed, gazing out over the fields ready for harvesting. 'It went off perfectly.'

'As a wedding should, don't you agree?'

'Mine won't be like that.' Jane sighed. 'I'll be lucky to have a few sandwiches in the garden of the pub.'

Beth chuckled at her friend's forlorn face. 'Nonsense. As if I'd let that happen?'

Jane relaxed. 'I'd be able to have a cake?'

'I'd make it myself.'

'God, no. You're a terrible cook.'

'Hey, cheeky!' They fell together laughing and didn't notice the horse and rider until it was nearly upon them.

They turned at the pounding hooves and Jane screamed as the horse reared. Beth pulled Jane to one side in fear of being struck down by the threshing hooves. Frightened, they stared up at the rider.

Louis Melville.

Beth's stomach somersaulted.

'Get out of my way,' Melville sneered, his horse snorting, foam frothing out of his mouth, sides heaving.

'We didn't see you.' Beth took another step back into the weeds lining the lane.

'You should be looking. Riders cannot slow a galloping horse immediately without doing damage and my horse is worth more than you two are.'

'A horse isn't more important than two human lives.' Beth faced him. 'You would have seen us for a hundred yards or more. You had plenty of time to slow down. You wanted to run us down.'

Melville leaned down from the saddle.' If I wanted to run you down, then I would have done so. Now get out of my way.'

Beth smelled some sort of alcohol on his breath and recoiled. 'You're the devil, Louis Melville.'

'Really? The devil, am I?' He grinned evilly. 'Maybe I am as you say!' He brought his riding crop down across Beth's shoulders.

The shock of the action and the sting of the whip made Beth gasp. A burning fire ran across her left shoulder. Rage burst out of her. She grabbed the horse's reins and yanked them. Melville's horse jerked its head up, skittering sideways, dragging Beth forward.

'Let go, you bloody fool!' Melville brought the crop down again, hitting Beth's shoulder and chest.

She cried out at the pain.

Jane screamed.

Beth, still holding the reins, pulled again, trying to unseat Melville. She wanted his riding crop and to use it on him.

'Beth! Stop!' Jane screamed.

Melville kicked his horse, trying to bring it under control. Enraged, Melville whipped Beth again. The sting arched her back. She let go and ran. She stumbled and fell to her knees, Jane's screaming in her ears. A shadow fell across from her. She tensed waiting for the horse's hooves to rip into her body.

The ground pounded beneath her hands and knees as the horse circled her.

'Stop! Stop!' Jane's yelling filled the air.

Then all she heard was the thundering hooves as Melville galloped away.

Jane ran to Beth's side and helped her up, crying heartbrokenly.

Beth winced at the pain of the lashes. Anger and humiliation kept her tears at bay. Hatred of the man fuelled her strength as they turned and headed for Beth's farm.

'You're not to tell anyone,' Beth whispered, leaning on Jane as they walked. Her shoulders felt on fire.

'What? Why not? He should answer for this, for what he did to you!'

'No. Dad will want to kill him and I'm not having that. It'll be Dad in a police cell, not Melville. He's too rich to be brought to justice and I can't have my family's name dragged through the mud. Mam would never forgive me.'

'It's not right, Beth.' Jane wiped her face.

'I don't care what is right or not,' Beth snapped. 'I shouldn't have grabbed his horse's reins. I shouldn't have spoken to him at all and let him go past. This is my fault. My temper did this.'

'Melville did this!' Jane hissed, dusting off Beth's skirt. 'He could have killed you.'

'Don't be stupid. I got whipped, that's all.'

'That's all?' Jane's eyes widened. 'Why are you protecting that monster.'

'I'm not. I'm protecting my dad.' The notion of her dad finding out brought the tears to her eyes. Her dad would lose his mind over something like this and the gun he used to go hunting would be used on Melville, she had no doubt about that.

'I think you're wrong,' Jane murmured.

'Promise me you'll not speak a word of this to anyone?'

'But…'

'Promise me, Jane. If you value our friendship, you'll keep quiet.'

Jane nodded.

They didn't speak again until they entered the farm and Ronnie came running past with a few of his mates. 'Our Joanna is here,' he said, scooting past them, kicking a football to his friend.

Beth straightened and tidied her hair. 'Do I look all right?'

Jane patted Beth's collar down. 'Aye.'

Adjusting the straw hat better on her head, Beth squared her shoulders.

'I'm not coming in.' Jane took a step back. 'Your mam can read me like a book and will know something's happened.'

Beth took a steadying breath. Jane was terrible at lying, many a time in their childhood they'd been caught out doing something wrong just by Mam peering at Jane, who instantly caved.

'I'll see you on Saturday evening at the harvest dance?' Beth squeezed Jane's hand in thanks.

'Aye, see you on Saturday. I'm bringing Alfie. Obviously, he's not from the village, but he knows enough people.'

'Good.'

Although shaken, Beth kept her head high as she entered the kitchen where her family had gathered and forced a smile at her sister. 'This is a delightful surprise.'

Joanna hugged Beth and Beth tried not to wince as she pressed the area where Melville had whipped her.

'I've news,' Joanna said, sitting back at the table.

'Oh?' Beth sat also, her legs were shaky now that she was home and safe.

'You're going to be an aunty.' Joanna beamed.

'A baby!' Tears spurted from Beth's eyes and she gripped her sister's hands.

'Isn't it wonderful?' Mam mashed more tea into the pot.

'I'm to be a granddad,' Dad boasted proudly.

'It makes me feel even more ancient,' joked Aunty Hilda.

The family erupted into happy chatter and after a few minutes, Beth excused herself and slowly climbed the stairs to her bedroom.

With the door shut and locked, she eased off her blouse and cried at the red streaks across her shoulders. Her corset had taken most of the blows of the whip across her back, but she felt beaten and sore, and incredibly angry.

Melville would pay for what he had done.

~ ~ ~ ~

Beth tapped her foot in time with the band as she watched couples dancing. Children ran about the yard beside St Anne's Church as the harvest festival dance brought in the villagers. After closing the stall at midday, Beth had helped her mam and Aunty Hilda to ferry the baskets of food up to the church. Inside the church a table groaned under the weight of the produce donated from local farmers. Tomorrow after Sunday service, the food would be given to the poor as tradition, but none of that was on Beth's mind as James Jackson grabbed her hand. He swung her out into the centre of the yard to dance and she laughed as he twirled her about.

'I've not danced with you in years.' James grinned. 'But now you're Noah's girl I can take advantage.'

'Where is Noah?'

'He'll be along shortly. Had his head in his books again. Do us a favour will you and make him smile. The man needs to relax.'

'I can do that.' She squealed as James lifted her off the ground and spun them around.

Once the dance was finished, James disappeared, and Beth went in search of Jane. The setting sun glowed over the yard, sprinkling gold. Lanterns were lit and a bonfire sent sparks up into the evening twilight.

'There you are,' Jane said, coming out of the church with Alfie close behind. 'I've been looking for you. I've been speaking to your mam and Joanna.'

'I was dancing with James Jackson.'

'Speaking of which…' Jane nudged Alfie in the side. 'How about a dance?'

Alfie, tall and thin, looked pained. 'Do I have to?'

'I've finally got a fella and he doesn't want to dance!' Jane gave him a raised eyebrow.

Alfie was saved by an old school friend of Beth and Jane's, Dulcie Greenbow, who came up to them, a hand on her large pregnant stomach.

'It's grand to see you both,' Dulcie said. 'I've not missed a harvest dance in my life and just because I've moved to Thornes doesn't mean I can't come back and enjoy it with my family.'

'My sister, Joanna said the same thing.'

'Aye, I saw your Joanna. Me mam said she'd married a few months ago.' Dulcie eyed up Alfie. 'And who's this stranger then?'

Jane bristled for everyone knew Dulcie was a maneater. She'd married two years ago when her escapades of hanging about with lads tripped her up and she became pregnant. 'This is my Alfie.' Jane linked her arm through Alfie's. 'How many babies have you got now then, Dulcie?'

Dulcie tapped her stomach. 'This is my second one. I'm not a rabbit, Jane Ogden.'

Beth hid a grin. 'Is your husband here, too, Dulcie?'

'God no. Seth's at the pub with his mates. I'm staying the night with Mam and Dad. I'm in no hurry to return home to washing and cleaning.' Dulcie gave Beth a superior stare. 'You not got a fella yet, Beth? You don't want to wait around forever, you know, or you'll be left on the shelf.'

'You make it sound like a death sentence.' Beth chuckled.

'Well, who wants to be an old maid?'

Jane crossed her arms over her chest. 'Just because we weren't having babies at eighteen, Dulcie, doesn't mean we're old maids. We're only twenty.'

Dulcie shrugged a shoulder. 'I'm just saying, that's all. There's not many of us girls who went to school together aren't married by now. In fact, I suppose it's just you two left?'

Jane bristled. 'We'll get married when we're ready.'

'You might but Beth doesn't even have a bloke, does she?'

'Aye, she does.' Noah suddenly stood behind Beth and wrapped his arm around her waist.

Dulcie's eyes nearly popped out of her head.

Beth smiled up at Noah. 'I'm glad you could make it.'

'I've not missed one yet. Besides, I need to dance with my girl.' He took her hand and pulled her away from the others, but not before she heard Jane tell

Dulcie that Beth was courting Noah Jackson and didn't they make a handsome pair?

Beth shivered in Noah's arms, enjoying the intimacy of being close to him.

'Are you cold?' he asked, gazing down into her eyes.

'No…' She stared back, wishing he'd kiss her.

Noah groaned softly. 'When you look at me like that, Beth all I want to do is kiss you.' He leaned closer to whisper in her ear. 'You're all a think about and I want to kiss you until I can't breathe.'

'Shall we find a dark corner and practise doing just that?' she whispered back, her heart beating fast like a drummer in a march.

Noah took her hand and guided her away from the crowds, the bonfire, and the music. Behind the church they found a large bush and beyond that a waist-high stone wall. Noah jumped it and then helped Beth over, which was difficult in her tight lemon dress, but she didn't care if it ripped. For the first time in two months, they were not being sensible, not being courteous and well-mannered towards each other.

Giggling, she fell into Noah's arms and he was kissing her. Their mouths melded; arms tight around each other. Beth raised a hand and threaded her fingers through Noah's hair just above his collar. He groaned against her mouth.

It gave her a sense of power to make him react so physically to her touch. He rained kisses down her neck, and she stared up into the deep mauve-coloured sky as the first stars twinkled.

'I've wanted to kiss you like that since the summer.'

'Then don't stop.' She brought his head down for another kiss, feeling the tenseness in his shoulders. She leaned back. 'What is it?'

'You don't know what you're doing to me, Beth. You're innocent…'

She cupped his cheek with her hand. 'I've lived on a farm all my life. I do know what happens.'

'Aye but we…'

She silenced him with another kiss, pulling him closer and she could feel by the bulge in his trousers just how much he wanted her, and she smiled inwardly.

When some lads ran by, hollering and messing about, Noah pulled away. 'We should get back.'

'We should.' Beth tucked her arm through his as they walked along the path around to the front of the church.

'Beth!' Joanna came out of the little gate. 'I've been looking for you.' She smiled at Noah. 'You'd best get back to the party. Mam's not in the best of moods that she couldn't find you.'

Beth sighed and the three of them headed into the throng of people. Noah stopped to talk to some friends, while Joanna steered Beth to where Jane and Alfie stood talking to a family who used to live next door to her before she moved to Alverthorpe.

'Oh, so you're back?' From nowhere Beth's mam was by her side. 'You do realise that people saw you leaving with Noah?'

'So?'

'Don't so me, girl,' Mam whispered harshly. 'That's not how you were brought up. No daughter of mine leaves a party with a man, especially not a Jackson.'

'Mam we are courting.'

'Are you just?' Her eyebrows rose nearly to her hairline. 'We'll see about that.'

~ ~ ~ ~

Noah chipped away at the coal seam. Shirtless, the stifling heat in the pocket of blackness where he worked sent trickles of sweat down his body, to be soaked up by the waistband of his trousers.

Weak electric light flickered, highlighting the wall of coal in front of him, and gave him glimpses of his brothers working alongside. The mine owners had recently installed the new electric lighting, something not all pits had. Such a new invention to have underground helped to make the pit less dangerous, or so they were told. Noah didn't believe everything the owners told them. A candle underground was a good indicator of gas, and many miners still preferred to have candles lit right alongside the new-fangled electric lighting.

His brothers didn't speak, instead they worked hard at swinging picks to break up the coal seam or wielded the shovels to fill the tubs. Then two of them would push the cart back up to the bottom of the shaft and have it identified and labelled with tokens belonging to the Jacksons.

At the dark, hot, and airless coalface, Noah hunkered down and rhythmically chipped away at the coal. Around him came the noise of his family working, but also the creaks and groans of the earth moving, shifting. Old miners said the mine spoke to you if you listened carefully. The old timers knew when a fall was to happen, or a flood. The mine was always a female and like any female, a man had to watch and listen to not feel her wrath. Those that took the creaks and groans for granted often didn't make it out alive.

'Pay day, today,' Sid said, hunkering down beside Noah.

'Aye.'

'I'm not paying me union fees today.'

Noah paused, thinking he'd not heard him correctly. 'What?'

'I ain't paying the union today.'

'Why?'

Sid signalled for Noah to follow him further away from the others. 'I need every penny,' he practically shouted in Noah's ear so he could hear him over James and Albie's shovelling of coal into the tubs.

'What for?' Even in this dim light, Noah knew Sid could lip-read him; it was a talent all miners acquired working in such a noisy environment.

Covered in coal dust, the whites of Sid's eyes showed his worry. 'Never mind.' He scuttled back to the face and rapidly chipped away at the coal.

Frowning, Noah walked back to his own position and continued working. Why wasn't Sid paying his dues? It would cause nothing but hassle. Union dues had to be paid. It wasn't an option.

Was Sid paying off their dad's debts? Noah thumped at the wall, annoyed at his father who knelt only yards away from him. So far, his dad had worked every day since rejoining the team, but was he still gambling? Mam refused to speak of it, and after recouping her wedding ring from the pawnbrokers, she'd asked Noah to not bring the subject up again.

He wasn't a praying man, and didn't believe in God, but that was something he kept to himself so as not to upset his mam, and for her he attended church every Sunday and sat through sermons that made no sense to his logical mind, but now he prayed to any deity that might be taking heed that his dad wasn't gambling.

A nudge from James told him their shift was done. He'd been lost in his thoughts and hadn't realised. Shrugging on his old shirt, his stomach clenched. Tomorrow he'd receive his exam results, and he'd know if he'd failed or passed.

With his family, he walked through the dark tunnel. Their lamps shrouded them in an eerie glow as they walked, tired and unspeaking, the mile to the cage train, which would then take them another mile to the bottom of the shaft. There they'd climb into a tiny cage and be cranked vertically up to the pit top to be spewed out into the daylight.

Noah thought of Beth and his exam results. It had been three weeks since that anxious day he'd sat with one other man in Mr Grimshaw's school room at the prestigious Queen Elizabeth Grammar School and completed the exam. Mr Grimshaw said he'd know the results by the end of the month. Tomorrow would be the thirtieth of September.

In an orderly queue they waited to be paid from a window in the pit office by one of the clerks and standing next to the window was the union man,

Morrison, to collect their dues and mark it off against their names in his book.

Noah watched Sid, standing in front of him, collect his wage and then step around the union man.

'Hey, Jackson, dues if you please.' Morrison frowned at Sid. 'Does it look like I'm standing here for the good of my health, man?'

'I can't. Not this time. I'll make it up to you next week.'

Morrison stiffened, taking it personally. 'You're not paying your dues?'

Noah collected his wages, aware that everyone in the queue was watching the scene. To not pay your union due could have serious consequences.

He pulled Sid to one side. 'What are you playing at?'

'I need the money.'

'What the hell for?'

Sid scuffed his boots, sending a shower of coal dust from his clothes.

'Sid, for God's sake, what is it?' Noah wanted to shake him.

'It's Meg.'

Confused, Noah scratched his head. 'Meg?'

'Meg Boycott. I've been walking out with her.'

'And?' Noah didn't know this Meg, or that Sid had a serious girl.

'She's having a baby.'

Noah stared dumbfounded. 'A baby? Are you sure?'

'She's late with her monthly show.'

Noah scrambled for the right words. 'She might be late for some other reason...'

'That's what I said,' Sid whispered, 'but she said her breasts are tender and she feels sick on waking each morning.'

Noah groaned. 'Bloody hell.'

'Aye, tell me about it.' Sid hung his head.

'What do you want to do?'

'I'll have to marry her.'

'Do you like her enough to do that?'

'Aye. She's bonny and a laugh. We'll rub along well enough. Besides, she's having me kid.'

'And you're sure it's yours?'

Sid took a step back, his eyes wide in his black face. 'Aye. She's a good girl. Not free and loose or anything.'

'She was with you,' Noah pointed out.

'She says she loves me, and she wanted me to be her first.'

'And now you'll be the last.'

'I don't need this from you, Noah. I'm worried enough.'

'Right, well…' Noah rubbed a coal-covered hand over his coal-covered face. 'Just go pay your dues.'

'But I need the money to get wed.' Sid's expression was more of a man going to the gallows.

'I'll help you. Just don't piss off Morrison.'

'Really? Look, don't tell anyone just yet. I'll have to speak to her father, and everyone knows he's a grumpy old git. I need some time to get used to this and I need to buy a ring and… and…' Sid's shoulders slumped. 'I don't know what I need.'

'A pint more than anything.' Noah grinned. 'Come on. We'll sort this out over an ale. It'll be fine.' He threw an arm around Sid's shoulders and walked him back to the office.

Chapter Seven

Serving her last customer for the day, Beth kept looking down the length of the market for sight of Noah, who said he'd come and see her after he'd been with Mr Grimshaw.

She was nervous the news was bad. Noah would be extremely disappointed, and she'd hate to see him despondent.

'Not a bad day, lass,' said Fred, packing away his own goods.

'Yes, not bad at all.' She packed away the carrots into the crate and topped them with the turnips.

A cool wind scattered dropped rubbish and bits of paper around the market area as Beth stacked the crates on the cart. It had rained this morning and dark clouds threatened more rain for tonight. Late summer weather had been replaced by autumn. She wasn't looking forward to winter and standing behind the stall in the bitter cold for months on end.

She glanced up as a cart rumbled past. Brook Street was crammed with heavy traffic as stallholders packed away. Will was late and that didn't improve her mood.

After stacking the last of the crates on the hand-cart, she said goodnight and waved to the other stall-holders and pushed the cart to the lock-up. The wind whistled around her ankles, billowing her skirts as she unlocked the large door, wondering where Will was, or Noah. Having patience wasn't something she was good at.

'Ah ha!'

Beth spun around at the voice. She stared at Louis Melville. 'What do you want?' she asked abruptly.

'Nothing.' He gazed around but kept his distance from her as other stallholders put away their goods in the lock-ups next to hers.

'Good, then go away.'

'You're a plucky little thing, aren't you?'

She ignored him and pushed the cart into the lock-up, cursing her brother's lateness.

Suddenly Melville was right behind her and she froze.

'I just wanted to be friendly. Our last encounter was… regrettable.'

Beth slowly turned and glared at him in revulsion. 'You whipped me like a dog and expect me to be friendly with you? You're lucky I didn't call the police!'

'That was a misunderstanding, and one that fills me with shame. I'd had too much to drink and my senses weren't in their correct order. I can only apologise.' He bowed like a gallant knight. 'I will make it up to you.'

'I don't care.' She kept hold of her temper. 'Please leave. My brother is due any moment.'

'You have courage, Miss Beaumont. Spirit. I like that. What other young woman would lunge at a horse to unseat its rider? I was suitably impressed by your daring. I can honestly say I've never been more enthralled by a young woman.'

Beth stared at him. What on earth was he meaning?

Melville leaned against the wall. 'In fact, I spoke about you to my friends. They say I should find out more about you. A few of them even wanted to meet you. They don't trust me when I extol your beauty and character. Some of my friends even believe your selfless act to protect yourself and your friend was commendable. None of us could imagine that any young woman would dangerously lunge for a horse as you did.'

'You deserved it.'

'Perhaps I did. However, I would wish for you to forget the incident and then we can start again as friends.'

Had he gone mad?

Beth took a deep breath. 'Why would we be friends, Mr Melville? We do not mix in the same society.'

'That will change. I shall invite you to Melville Manor for dinner. Would you like that?'

'I don't think so.'

'Come now, surely you wouldn't want to miss an opportunity to dine at the manor?'

'I would, actually.' She found it hard to comprehend they were having this conversation.

He took a step back and twirled his cane. 'I will make it worth your while to be my friend.'

She scowled, not understanding. 'What do you mean?'

'As I said, I like you. Admire you even. You are different, which is so refreshing to me. I feel we might become good friends.'

'You do?'

'Of course. A pretty girl like you, well…' He again stared around at the lock-up at the empty crates in the corner, the handcart. 'You'll never be much more than a market stall girl, will you? However, I can offer you the chance to escape all this.' He waved his hand, his tone superior. 'Surely you must dream of having more? I can give you that.' He nodded eagerly as though the idea had only just come to him. 'Yes, I can give you so much, Miss Beaumont. Nice clothes, jewels… I can make your dreams come true.'

'My dreams are none of your concern.' She folded her arms and tilted her head. He was making fun of her. 'Please leave.'

He laughed. 'My you have spunk. I adore it. You've shown courage each time we've met. You're like an untamed horse.' He stepped closer to her. 'And I wish to be the one to tame you,' he whispered.

Beth shivered in revulsion.

'What the hell is going on?' Noah demanded from the doorway.

Beth jumped and dodged around Melville to Noah, thankful for his presence. She gripped his arm.

'Melville?' Noah's fists clenched at his side.

'I'm simply enquiring about the Beaumont stock.' Melville walked out of the lock-up and then turned back to them. 'I have an offer I was asking Miss Beaumont to consider about supplying my home with their produce.' His eyes narrowed on Beth, daring her to refute the lie. 'I'll leave you to ponder the suggestion, Miss Beaumont.'

'My answer is no.' Beth spoke as he moved away.

Melville's smile was as cold as the wind blowing down the street. 'Have some time to consider it. There is no hurry.'

Beth watched him saunter away, swinging his cane. She longed for the wind to blow his top hat off his ugly head.

'Why on earth was he here? Surely he should talk to your dad about supplies?'

'Forget him.' Beth felt the anger in Noah's stiff body. She still held onto his arm and rubbed it with a forced smile. She gazed into his eyes and impulsively leaned forward and kissed him.

Noah stilled for a second and then crushed her into his arms and kissed her back.

Beth curled her fingers into his jacket, glorying in the wonder of his lips on hers, his strong body under her hands.

Eventually, they pulled apart and smiled into each other's eyes.

'I've been wanting to do that all day.'

'Me too,' she breathed. 'Let's do it again.'

He chuckled and lowered his head to kiss her again, pulling her tight against the length of him. She loved the feeling of his body against hers. Now it made sense, the talk of love, the need to be with someone. She never wanted to let Noah go.

'Hey, you two, give it up,' Will yelled from the cart outside, pulling Snowy to a stop.

Reluctantly, Beth stepped away from Noah and faced her brother. 'Where have you been? You're half an hour late!'

Will climbed down off the seat and began unloading the farm's crates into the lock-up. 'One of the cart's wheels came loose. Dad and I had to fix it and it took longer than we expected. Then I got caught up in the traffic on Saville Street.'

Beth and Noah helped him until the cart was empty.

Locking the door, Beth smiled at Noah. 'You'll come with us?'

'No. I'm going to Mr Grimshaw's house for dinner. I just wanted to come and see you first. I was worried I might have missed you.'

'Oh!' Beth clapped her hands over her mouth. 'Your results!'

His smile wide, his expression filled with joy. 'I passed.'

'You did!' She threw herself at him and he swung her around, drawing looks from the last of the stallholders still closing up.

'Thank you for believing in me.' He squeezed her hands.

'I always knew you could do it. Roll on the next one in November.'

'Yes, I've completed the first step.' He helped her up onto the cart. 'I'll see you on Sunday?'

She nodded down to him. 'You will. Perhaps you'd like to come for Sunday dinner?'

'I'd like that.'

'I'll talk to Mam and let you know at church. Enjoy your evening with Mr Grimshaw.'

He waved her off and they smiled at each other until the cart turned the corner and he was no longer in view.

'You really like him, don't you?' Will asked.

'I do.'

'Mam won't like it. She barely tolerates you walking out with him. She'll not want a Jackson sat at our table.'

'Well, it's time she got over her dislike of the Jackson family. Noah has done nothing to her.'

Will shrugged as though the whims of their mam was a mystery to him.

Beth stared straight ahead and tried to form the words in her head to broach the subject with her mam.

Of Melville's ridiculous proposition she was dumbfounded. The man was obviously sick in the mind. Yet a part of her was intrigued by this change in him. He'd gone from a monster to someone who gave apologies and compliments. She didn't understand it. Part of her was still so angry at his humiliating treatment of her and yet another, mature part of her wanted to forget all about it and think only of the future with Noah. Only, Melville seemed keen on becoming her friend. Did she want that? In truth it was better to be his friend than his enemy, but something niggled in the back of her mind that Melville was wanting more than he was saying and it worried her.

~ ~ ~ ~

'I said no.' Mam stood sprinkling flour over the table and then started rolling the pastry dough.

Beth seethed as she washed the plates from breakfast. 'Can you tell me why Noah can't come on Sunday?'

'I don't want a Jackson in my house.'

'Noah is a good person, kind and decent.' Beth glanced at Aunty Hilda, who sat in the corner cutting up apples for the pie Mam was making.

'He'll be the first Jackson to be so.' Mam blew hair out of her eyes as she flipped the pastry over and rolled it again.

'I don't understand any of this.' Beth wanted to throw a plate at the wall.

'The Jacksons are no good. I told you that months ago.' Mam buttered the pie dish. 'You said you had no interest in Noah Jackson and then the next minute you're walking out with him.'

'I didn't expect any of this. We just happened to get talking and then suddenly we found we really liked one another.'

'Has he asked you to marry him?'

'No. It's only been a few months.'

'If he does ask, say no, for your own sake.'

'What? Why?' Beth, hands soapy, stared at her mother.

'If he's anything like his father, and I'm sure he and his brothers are, then you'll be saving yourself heartbreak.'

Heartbreak?

Finally, something made sense to Beth. 'Did you and Leo Jackson once have an understanding? Did Leo Jackson break your heart, Mam?'

Mam's hands stilled. 'As if I'd let a Jackson break my heart. Don't talk nonsense. Go out and help your dad. They're harvesting the last of the fruit trees.'

Beth dried her hands on the towel, her mind whirling. 'Mam—'

'Go, lass,' Aunty Hilda shooed her away, a knowing look in her eyes.

With a last glance at Mam's bowed head, Beth donned her coat and left the house. Had her mam and Leo been courting years ago? It seemed incredible that no one had mentioned it before. She'd always assumed Dad had been her mam's first love.

In the fields behind the garden, her dad, Will and Reggie, their one constant employee, were up ladders picking the crop of apples, plums, and pears.

'I'm here to help.' She resisted the urge to shake Will's ladder to make him squeal.

'Good, lass.' Dad climbed down the ladder and emptied his bag into a wooden wheelbarrow. 'Come with me and you can help sort them.' He pushed the barrow into the nearby shed and tipped out its contents onto a low sorting table.

The morning sun held no heat and the shed, with its double doors open for light was cold and draughty.

Beth wrapped a hessian apron around her waist and began sorting the apples by size into separate barrels. Any that were damaged by weather, birds or insects were put into a separate barrel to be made into cider.

'You'll have a nice selection to sell at the market tomorrow,' Dad said, sorting out a few apples.

'Dad…'

'Mmm.'

'Why does Mam hate the Jacksons? Is it because she once had some friendship with Leo Jackson?'

Dad kept his head down, sorting. 'That's your mam's business. You need to ask her.'

'I did and she won't speak of it. I'm not stupid, nor am I a child. I asked if Noah might come for Sunday dinner, and she said no, and that she won't have any Jackson under her roof.'

'And you're keen on the eldest Jackson, aren't you? You've been spending a lot of time with him.'

'Yes, I am keen on him.'

'Does he feel the same?'

'I believe so, yes.'

Dad sighed and threw a damaged apple into the cider barrel. 'Your mam was and still is a pretty lass. Like you, really. Such lovely hair and those eyes. You also got her temper.' Dad smiled. 'Every man in the village and beyond wanted to walk out with Mary, me included. I thought she was the best girl in the world. For some reason though, Leo Jackson won her heart when we were young, still at school.'

'I never knew that.'

'Leo was a bit of a lad. Liked his drinking, sport, and the girls, but he was proud as punch to have the prettiest of them, Mary, on his arm. Everyone expected them to marry. I was green with envy.'

'Why didn't they?'

'When we were about eighteen, Leo was taken by a new pretty lass, her name was Peggy and she'd moved to Wakefield from Wales as her father had secured a manager's job at one of the local pits. Leo met her at some miners' picnic and well he was smitten by all accounts. He played off Mary and Peggy at the same time. Rumours spread and your mam was hurt. Next thing we knew, Leo and Peggy were married and weeks later Peggy's round stomach was rather noticeable. Her son was born only six months after they married.'

'She was with child when they married, and that child was Noah?'

'Aye. Leo believed he was being clever having two women after him. He broke your mam's heart, and he never apologised, never explained. She hated him after that.'

'But Mam married you so she must have put him in the past?' Beth found it difficult to imagine her mam being in love with Leo Jackson. Noah's dad, on the few times she'd seen him, wasn't as handsome as her dad. Leo Jackson always appeared untidy as though he'd not washed the coal dust off himself properly. Mr Jackson was always one of the men sitting outside of the Malt Shovel pub.

Dad inspected an apple and placed it in the barrel for the stall. 'Mary and I married a year later. It wasn't easy though. My mother, your grandma, didn't want me to marry Mary. She felt Mary wasn't good enough to marry into the Beaumont family, coming from poor mining stock. My mother and Mary never got on. After Leo's betrayal and my mother's dislike, my sweet Mary became hard and laughed less. Mary was always trying to prove her worth to my parents. She worked hard on the farm and in the house but having two strong women under the same roof was like a constant war.'

'How sad.' She had very little memory of her grandma Beaumont, a woman who was a vicar's daughter and well educated and with exacting standards. Was her mam still trying to live up to her mother-in-law's ideals? Is that why she never rested and relaxed but was always doing something; cleaning, cooking, helping dad with the farm's paperwork, visiting friends, helping the poor in the area. Beth had never seen her mam doing nothing. Even at night, her mam would be sewing, darning, or knitting, polishing the few pieces of Beaumont silver, or stuffing more feathers into pillows and so many other jobs. Not once had Beth seen her mam read a book by the fire or sit with a cup of tea and stare at nothing.

Dad threw another apple into the barrel. 'I'm telling you this, so you can understand why your mam reacts the way she does to the name Jackson.' He took off his hat and scratched his head. 'I wish you had picked another young fellow to be sweet on, lass.'

'Noah is a good man, Dad. He's a hard worker and is trying to better himself. I'd like him to come on Sunday.'

'Aye, I know. I've nothing against the fellow, honestly, but Mary…'

'She can't blame Noah for being born.'

'But she does, lass. He was the reason Leo and Peggy married.'

'That's not fair.'

'Nothing is when love is involved.' Dad gave her a fleeting smile and walked out of the shed.

~ ~ ~ ~

Standing behind the stall the following day, Beth huddled into her coat as rain lashed the marketplace. The low grey clouds kept customers away and the takings were dismal and so was her mood.

Mam's refusal to have Noah come for dinner remained a sore point. Beth had tried once more to talk to her mam about it but had been met with a stony silence and a shake of the head from Aunty Hilda, who obviously knew the history of Mam and Leo Jackson.

'You look miserable.' Joanna grinned, coming around behind the stall and giving her a hug.

'What are you doing out in this weather?' Beth stood and gave Joanna the stool to sit on.

'I had shopping to do, nothing in for tea, and Jimmy's parents and aunt and uncle are coming around later as it's his dad's birthday.'

'Are you baking a cake?'

Joanna snorted. 'Not likely. I've bought one from Linton's Bakery. That way there are no complaints.'

'What else have you bought?' Beth peeked into her sister's basket.

'Pork pies, some tarts, bread and the cake. I'll make some sandwiches. I can't afford to do much else.' Joanna leaned back and wiggled her feet. 'These boots are killing me. My ankles are swollen from all this walking.'

'Take the tram home.'

'Aye, I will. So, how are things with you?'

'Fine.' Beth pulled her coat tight as rain blew in on an angle under the stall's awning.

'Are you sure?'

Leaning against the back of the stall, Beth sighed. 'I really like Noah Jackson.'

'That's nice.'

'But Mam hates all the Jacksons.'

'Oh, yes.'

'Dad told me it is because Leo Jackson and our mam were courting and going to marry until Leo met Peggy and got her with child.'

'No!' Joanna sounded as surprised as Beth had been.

'You didn't know either?'

'Not at all. Poor Mam. She had her heart broken.'

'Yes. But it also means she'll never accept Noah.'

'I'm certain she will, in time. None of it is his fault, is it? Just take it slowly.'

'I want Mam to like Noah the same as she does with your Jimmy.'

'As I said, it'll take time.' Joanna tilted her head to one side. 'You and this Noah are serious then?'

'I think so.'

'Have you kissed him yet?

'Joanna!' Beth hissed, glancing over at Fred who was reading his newspaper.

'Well? Have you?'

'Yes. Hundreds of times.' Beth grinned, remembering the feel of Noah's lips on hers. 'It's wonderful.'

'Make sure that's all you do!' Joanna laughed. 'Seriously, I'm so happy for you.'

Beth shivered as the rain fell. The awning flapped in the wind. 'What to do about Mam though?'

'Leave it for awhile. There's no rush is there?'

'No.'

Joanna stood. 'I'd best be getting back.' She kissed Beth's cheek. 'I'll come to the farm next week. I might be able to talk to Mam about Noah.'

'Thank you. Oh, and I've started to knit a little jacket for the baby. It's terrible. You'll have to unpick most of it when it's finished but at least I've tried, and it stops Mam from getting on at me for not doing my share.'

'What are you like?' Joanna shook her head in amusement as she left.

By the end of the day, Beth was more than happy to pack up and head for the tram. In the cooler months when the weather was bad, and the customer numbers low, Will didn't come to collect her or bring extra vegetables for the next day. She had enough stock to last and catching the tram saved someone from leaving their work on the farm to collect her.

The tram terminated at Newton, leaving her a couple of miles to walk home, which in the rainy conditions she was not looking forward to.

With her basket hooked over her arm, Beth alighted the tram, a wet breeze teasing her hat from its pins.

Head down, she strode down Wrenthorpe Road and under the railway bridge, her thoughts on Noah and her mam. Wagons and carts passed, and she wished Will, or someone had thought to come and pick her up, but perhaps they were busy with storing the last of the harvesting.

A horse snorted making her jump. The carriage stopped beside her, but she paid no attention to it.

'Miss Beaumont.'

Beth glanced over her shoulder at Edwina Melville leaning out of the window. 'Will you not ride with me and save yourself from this terrible weather?'

'No, thank you.' Beth kept walking, surprised that Miss Melville would consider stopping and offering her a lift. She didn't know the woman at all, only that she was Louis's sister.

'Miss Beaumont, please. It is awfully frightful out there.'

'I haven't much further to go. Good day.'

The carriage caught up to her and Miss Melville opened the carriage door. 'Please, I insist.'

Beth huffed. 'Why?'

'Because… because it's the correct thing to do. A young woman shouldn't be out in this weather.'

Suddenly Louis Melville stuck his head out, he'd been hidden in the shadows of the carriage. 'Miss Beaumont, do get in. My sister is correct.'

She glared at him. 'Would you offer a ride to anyone else? I don't think so.'

'We'd like to be your friend,' Miss Melville uttered, glancing at Louis as though for confirmation she was saying the correct thing. 'The Beaumont fields have been neighbours to our fields for decades. In fact, our two families have history, do the not, Louis?'

'Indeed, we do.' Louis nodded. 'We, my sister and I, feel we should become better acquainted. I would be honoured if you became my sister's friend. She doesn't have many in this area as she spends all her time in London.'

'I'm certain there are more suitable women for her to befriend.' Beth walked faster.

He leaned out of the door in his sister's place. 'Really, Miss Beaumont. Can you not be civil?'

'To you?' Beth snapped.

Melville climbed out of the carriage and came to her as the rain fell once more. 'Have you contemplated my proposition?'

'Not at all.' Beth quickened her steps.

'Miss Beaumont.' He walked beside her. 'Do consider all I can offer you. It is a change to your future and your family's future.'

'I don't need anything from you, nor does my family.'

'Really?' He mocked. 'You'd never have to walk in the rain again if you allowed me to look after you. I would treat you as a princess.'

'What do you think my mam and dad would say to your proposition?'

He reddened. 'Would a marriage proposal from a Melville be so abhorrent to them? I could give you everything.'

Beth jerked to a stop, eyes wide in disbelief. 'Marriage? You aren't serious.'

'Yes, of course. What did you assume I offered?'

'To be your… your…'

'Mistress?' Melville chuckled. 'It did cross my mind, but I knew a well brought up girl like yourself would never accept that. No. I propose marriage, my dear, as much as it surprises me. It seems it is you that I want more than any other woman I have met. It's quite the laugh, don't you agree?'

'You don't even know me,' she whispered in shock.

He squinted through the rain at her. 'That can be rectified. I'm aware of your background and I know there isn't a prettier young lady in all of the district than you.' His eyes narrowed. 'I want you to be my wife, and I always get what I want, Miss Beaumont.'

Beth blinked. Was he threatening her as well as proposing? This had to be a dream. It was ridiculous. She laughed.

Melville stepped back, confused. 'You find my offer insulting?'

'I find it unbelievable.'

'I can have my pick of women, Miss Beaumont, women who are much higher in status than a simple farmer's daughter.'

'Then perhaps you should ask them and leave this farmer's daughter alone?'

He grinned. 'How easy that would make my life. However, I don't desire them. I want you.' The rain dripped from the brim of his top hat. 'Do you not want to live in luxury? To further your father's prospects? With Melville support and contacts, he could supply more markets, buy more land, employ more people. Your brothers would prosper, too. I've spoken to my sister about it and she is of the opinion that we'd make a good match. What's more, she is willing to help present you into our society. Isn't that admirable of her?'

'I don't know what to say...'

He took a step back. 'Do think about it.'

'Louis, enough,' Edwina's whine was clearly heard from within the carriage. 'I want to go home. The girl clearly isn't interested. Find someone else to play with.'

'Be quiet, Edwina.' He gave his attention to Beth. 'I'll leave you to digest my intentions which are honourable and true, and remember, as my wife you will have everything you ever longed for and more.' He touched the rim of his hat with his cane and re-entered the carriage.

Standing in the rain, Beth watched the carriage lurch past and let out a shivery breath. Melville wasn't serious, surely? He was toying with her, playing a game. As if he was serious? She should laugh for really it was such a joke. Louis Melville from Melville Manor couldn't possibly want to marry her. He'd have the pick of the ladies in the area, many daughters of wealthy gentlemen would happily become his wife no doubt. He didn't need or want a farmer's daughter, really. He had to be joking, playing some sort of ridiculous game. He and his sister must be laughing now, making fun of her.

She hated him and he could shove his offer where the sun doesn't shine.

Thoroughly wet, the rain dripping off her velvet hat, she headed for the village and home. Melville's shocking and unexpected offer would be her secret just in case he was making fun of her. It was all so unbelievable.

Chapter Eight

Beth filled a customer's basket with potatoes and carrots. 'Anything else, Mrs Fisher?'

'I'll have five onions, please, oh and throw in a turnip. My George likes a turnip every now and then. You'd best give me a good bunch of those peas, an' all.' Mrs Fisher's beady gaze studied the vegetables on the stall.

'Is Mr Fisher's back better?'

'Aye, he's up and about but not at work yet. He'll help our son deliver coal, instead of digging for it. Easier on his poor old bones, so he tells me.' Mrs Fisher, dressed all in black, crossed her arms with a sniff as though her husband's ailments were a cross she must bear.

'There we are, all done.' Beth totalled up the amount on a notepad and showed it to Mrs Fisher, who promptly paid her.

'How's your sister? She's not on the stall any more?'

'No, not since she married. She's having a baby now, too.'

'Oh, bless her.' Mrs Fisher took the basket from Beth. 'Tell her I wish her well, won't you?'

'Will do, Mrs Fisher. See you next week.'

Behind Mrs Fisher, Beth spotted Noah coming to the stall. She smiled, devouring him with her eyes.

She'd not seen him for nearly a week, not since last Sunday when they had gone for a walk, and she'd told him her mam didn't want visitors for dinner. It had been a little white lie, but she hadn't been able to confess that her mam hated all Jacksons.

Noah came around behind the stall and took her hand, not able to kiss her in front of the whole market. 'I've missed you.'

'I've missed you, too.' She ached to kiss him. He still had coal-rimmed eyes, which no matter how much coalminers washed their eyes, they still had the telltale signs of being down the pit.

'I'm off to spend the evening with Mr Grimshaw. He has some new books he wants to show me. He says they will help me with my next exam.'

'That's kind of him.' Beth broke away to serve another customer.

'Are we meeting up on Sunday?'

'Yes, unless you want to study?'

'No, I need a break. I've been at the books every night this week.' Noah pushed his hands into his pockets. 'Is Jane helping you on the stall tomorrow? I know sometimes she works the odd Saturday with you.'

'No, she's got a full day's shift at the mill.'

'Shame. I was wondering if maybe she could man the stall while I take you out for a bite to eat somewhere.'

She finished serving and smiled at him. 'I would like that. I finish up here at noon. We can go afterwards?'

'Yes, excellent. It'll be harder to meet once the cold weather comes. My house is bursting with my brothers, so I can't ask you to come there.'

'I don't mind, honestly. I'll go anywhere as long as I see you.'

He took her hands. 'I'll work something out when winter hits properly.' Suddenly his expression brightened. 'There's a comedy show on at the theatre in Northgate tomorrow night. I saw the sign as I was passing on the tram just now. Shall I go and get us tickets?'

'Oh, yes, that would be wonderful.'

'Your mam and dad will allow you to go?'

Her happiness evaporated like water in sand. Her mam was becoming more irritated by Beth's every mention of Noah. 'I'm sure they will. I'm not a child. I'm twenty and a trip to the theatre is hardly shocking.'

'We can have something to eat at midday and then we can go home and get ready for the evening. Sound good?'

She nodded eagerly, then noticed her mam standing on the other side of the stall. 'Mam? What are you doing here?' It was rare for her mam to come to the stall. If she needed anything Beth usually got it for her and brought it home.

Mary Beaumont stared at Noah and then down at their joined hands and her lips thinned.

'Mam, this is Noah Jackson.' Beth kept his hands in hers. 'Noah, this is my mam, Mary Beaumont.' She introduced them properly even though they both knew of the other.

'Please to meet you, Mrs Beaumont.'

A muscle worked in Mam's jaw, as though she was chewing something.

Beth waited for her to say something. Her body gave off signals that she was unhappy with what she saw.

'Mr Jackson, I believe congratulations are in order for passing your first exam?'

'Thank you. I passed and must sit the second exam in a few weeks.'

'From miner to teacher. How interesting. You must be keen to start your new career?'

'I am, madam.'

'A career that will no doubt take you away from this area?'

'No, I shouldn't expect so. At least, not if I can find a position in a school close by.'

Mam's gaze lingered on Noah for a moment more and then she blinked and turned to Beth. 'I've come to help you pack up early. Aunty Hilda doesn't want a fuss for her birthday, but I'm putting on a tea for her. Joanna is already at the farm.'

'You never said this morning.'

'I hadn't decided, and you know Aunty Hilda doesn't like admitting she's getting older and birthdays remind her of that.' Mam glanced at Noah. 'Sorry to cut short your visit, Mr Jackson, but we must get on.'

'Of course.' He stepped aside as she started to fill the crates that were stacked against the wall with produce. 'Mrs Beaumont, I wish to take Beth to a theatre show tomorrow evening. Do I have your permission?'

Mam's hands stilled slightly, and she took a long moment to answer. 'You are to bring her straight home, Mr Jackson, once the show has ended.'

'I will, certainly.' He smiled at Beth.

Letting out a breath, Beth continued packing up, giving Noah a secret smile.

'See you tomorrow,' he whispered and then headed down the market.

'Thank you, Mam.'

'Don't thank me,' she snapped. 'He'll break your heart. You've been warned. So, don't come crying to me when it happens, and you're left with nothing.' Mam stacked a crate on the handcart, her face stony.

~ ~ ~ ~

Beth held her sides as she laughed at the comedy duo on stage. Beside her, Noah chuckled, and she loved seeing him so happy. The act had the audience roaring with laughter, the comic timing and witty banter proved to be a big hit.

Despite the coldness from Mam for going out this evening with Noah, Beth was enjoying herself. She felt for the first time a grown woman. It was as though she had shed her youth and become some other person, a more mature aspect of herself.

Getting ready for tonight she had washed her hair and Jane had arranged it on top of her head with combs and pins. She'd worn her blue dress and added a splash of perfume, a gift from Joanna last Christmas. Tonight, was her first proper night out with a man, not just a walk along the lanes or a bicycle ride around the park. No, this was courting, in the grown-up way, and she couldn't help but fizz with excitement.

How proud she'd been walking into the theatre on Noah's arm. They'd acknowledged a few people they knew. Beth had smiled at customers who frequented her stall. The buzz of anticipation filled the theatre's foyer as people gathered expecting a fun evening ahead.

Taking their seats, Beth had chatted away to Noah, talking about the afternoon they'd spent walking the streets in town and having a light meal at a little café in Mary Street. Afterwards they'd travelled back to Wrenthorpe and parted ways to get ready for tonight. She was so relieved that they never had any awkward silences.

Even in the dimly lit packed theatre, Beth was aware of Noah sitting close beside her. His thigh touching hers, his hand often reaching out to grasp her hand. She knew it had to be enough, but she wanted more.

When the act finished and the stage was being prepared for the next one, Noah took Beth's hand in his and gently squeezed it. 'Are you having a nice time?'

'The best.' She leaned her shoulder against his. 'Thank you for suggesting we come to see this. I've not laughed so hard in ages.'

'Nor me.'

The curtain rose for the next act and they faced the stage, but something made Beth glance up to the more expensive seating boxes on the left and her stomach clenched. Louis Melville sat staring at her. He gave a little wave. His sister and two other men made up his party.

Beth focused on the stage. Why did he of all people have to be here? She wished she'd never looked up.

The rest of the show passed her by. She smiled when others laughed, not able to find any enjoyment in the funny antics on stage.

'Are you all right?' Noah asked as they left the theatre and flowed into the street with the crowd.

'Yes. I'm fine.'

'You didn't find the end of the show very entertaining?'

'I did, yes.' She slipped her arm through his as they walked down the road to the tram stop. 'I'm only tired, that's all. Sorry.'

'You don't have to be sorry at all. You've been at work this morning, standing on your feet behind a busy stall and then we walked all around town this afternoon. It's now gone ten o'clock, of course you'd be tired.'

'It's Sunday tomorrow, I won't have to be up for six o'clock. I'll have a lie in.'

'Want to go for a walk after church?'

'I'd like that.' She smiled up at him and he leaned down and gave her a brief kiss.

The tram held only them and two other people, drunk young men a little worse for wear who were singing loudly. Beth ignored them and chatted to Noah for most of the journey to Newton, trying to put Melville out of her mind.

On the walk from Newton to Wrenthorpe, Noah kept his arm around her waist, stopping every now and then to kiss her. Once in the village, they stopped in the shadows along the street and kissed properly.

Being in his arms felt like heaven. Their rising passion was hard to control however, and panting, Noah pulled away.

'Beth…' He leaned his forehead against hers. 'We should get married.'

She gasped, staring at him in the darkness lit only by a streetlamp twenty yards away. 'Married?'

'Yes. You don't want to?'

'I do! Oh, Noah!' She threw herself into his arms as he laughed and crushed her to him. 'When?'

'I'd marry you tomorrow, my darling, but your parents might have something to say about that. What about next spring?'

'Sounds wonderful.'

'By then, hopefully, I'll be a teacher and although I'll be at the teacher's college, I'll be searching for positions, too. I can save over the winter for a house for us. I don't want to rush this, Beth, and start our marriage with no money. We can achieve better than that if we are clever about it.'

'I agree. I'll save every penny, too.'

He looked into her eyes. 'I love you, Beth Beaumont.'

'And I love you, Noah Jackson.'

They pulled apart as a carriage rumbled down the street. Hand in hand they walked, happiness uniting them in a warm cocoon. The carriage slowed and in the dim light from the streetlamp, Louis Melville's pale face appeared from within the carriage. His gaze never left her face as they drove past.

She shivered.

'You're cold?' Noah asked, taking off his jacket and placing it around her shoulders.

'You'll walk me all the way home, won't you?'

'Absolutely. As if I'd leave you alone in the dark.'

She relaxed and squeezed his hand. A part of her wanted to confide in Noah, to tell him all what Melville had offered her, but another part of her kept her quiet. No good would come of her mentioning Melville's offer to anyone. It meant nothing to her, and the man probably wasn't serious. Soon, no doubt, Melville would grow bored of her and she could forget all this nonsense.

Chapter Nine

'You're joking, aren't you?' Peggy Jackson stopped scrubbing the clothes in the copper boiler.

Noah leant against the doorjamb of the little scullery which jutted out from the kitchen and where the family took a bath and his mother washed the clothes. The sun was not fully up, and he'd just told his mother he wanted to marry Beth. 'Why would I joke?'

'Because you're not in any position to take on a wife.'

'How am I not? I'm earning.'

'But you'll be earning less once you're a teacher. There's no extra shifts and overtime for teachers, you know, not like down the pit.' Bent over the tub, she plunged the shirt back into the water.

'If I'm struggling on a teacher's wage, I'll take on extra work by tutoring in the evenings.'

His mam shrugged. 'You'll need to keep that Beaumont girl in style. She's come from a comfortable farm. She's not going to want to live in a place like this and how can you afford more?'

'I'll work something out. We aren't thinking of marrying until the spring. I'll save my money.'

'And see your family go short?'

'Mam, there's seven wages coming in. I'll pay my board but I'm not paying more to compensate Dad's gambling. He's got to stop. I've told you this.'

She tutted and kept scrubbing. 'What's her family got to say about it?'

'I've not spoken to them about it. It's just something Beth and I discussed the other night and again yesterday after church.'

'You'd better bring her to see us then, hadn't you? I should meet the girl. If you are serious?'

'I am. It's what we both want, and I thought you might like to know my plans.'

'What plans are these then?' His dad came up behind Noah.

Peggy straightened. 'He's getting married.'

'Married? I didn't even know he was courting.'

'That's because you take no interest in anything other than yourself,' she snapped. Then a devilish look came into her eyes. 'He's walking out with Beth Beaumont, Mary's girl.'

'Mary Beaumont's girl?' His dad seemed impressed.

Noah sensed something was in the air. 'So?' he asked his dad.

'Good luck to you, boy. Is she in the family way?'

'No, she bloody isn't.' Noah pushed past him. 'And I'm no longer a boy.'

In the kitchen, Noah grabbed his flat cap and coat, ready to walk to the pit, but his parents' talk stopped him. He stepped to the door to hear better.

'It's a funny old world isn't it, Peg?'

'How so?' Mam answered.

'Well, I nearly married Mary and now my son is going to marry her daughter. If I had married Mary and not you, none of this would be happening.'

'If you hadn't got me pregnant you might have married her in the end anyway.'

'No, you had taken my fancy. I made the right choice.'

'Did you? Sometimes it doesn't feel like it, Leo.'

'What does that mean?'

There was a long silence. 'Nothing. Let's hope Noah is happier than we are. At least he has chosen his girl without pressure, unlike us. He'll do better than we did.'

'We've done all right.'

'You think? Scraping by day by day? You're hardly in work now, yet you spend every penny that comes into the house leaving me to make one shilling do the work of two.'

'Don't start nagging, woman.'

'At least the boys are hard workers, and hopefully they'll follow Noah's example and improve themselves, unlike you did.'

'I've tried my best.'

'No, you didn't, Leo. You see to yourself and leave me to deal with everything else. You've always done it and I'm tired of it.'

'You're a miserable cow, Peggy. You're never satisfied, are you?' His dad stormed into the kitchen and Noah quickly pulled on his coat. His mind whirling with the images of his dad and Mary Beaumont courting. Did Beth know?

'Where are the others?' his dad grumbled, finishing his cup of tea.

'I'll hurry them up.' Noah went to his bedroom where Sid was lacing up his boots. 'Get a move on, Dad's in a mood.'

He called up the stairs for his brothers and they came stampeding down, complaining and yawning.

In the kitchen, Mam gave them bacon butties to eat on their way to the pit and a snap tin each, which held their midday meal and a flask of tea on top.

Like hundreds of others, the Jackson men joined the crowd of workers walking to their jobs in the brisk autumn morning.

Sid came alongside of Noah. 'I've spoken to Meg's father. He shook my hand and welcomed me into the family. I'll tell everyone else tonight after work.'

'When are you getting married?'

'I'll see the vicar on Sunday and have him read the banns.'

'I'll be doing that myself next spring.' Noah grinned.

'Get away!' Sid punched him in the arm. 'Who's the lucky lady? The Beaumont girl?'

'What's going on?' Albie jogged up to join them, followed quickly by Alfred and James.

'What's happening?' Alfred asked.

'Our kid here is getting married,' Noah put in quickly, punching Sid back.

'Get away!' James laughed. 'No one would have him!'

Sid grinned. 'I'm not the only one, either. Noah's getting married next spring.'

'No!' The brothers all looked amazed.

'To Beth?' Alfred asked.

'Aye to Beth.' Noah swelled with pride being able to say it.

'And you, Sid? Is it Meg?' James asked. 'Or is it some other poor lass, who's blind and feeble?'

'No, it's Meg, you cheeky blighter!' Sid grabbed James and hauled him off his feet. 'My Meg isn't blind or feeble. She's a lovely lass.'

'You lot! Stop messing about,' their dad shouted from behind where he walked with some of his drinking buddies. 'It's too early for your nonsense. Anyone would think you're still bloody kids.'

They settled down and once more the only sound was the hobnailed boots ringing on the cobbles as the sun slowly made its way over the village rooftops.

~ ~ ~ ~

'Terrible news.' Dad shook his head while reading the morning paper.

Beth looked up from her breakfast of eggs and sausages, building up the courage to mention Noah's proposal.

'What is it?' Mam poured out more tea into her cup.

'Yesterday, in Wales, a mine collapse at Senghenydd. Hundreds trapped, one dead, but they expect more as the rescue continues.' Dad bit into his toast.

'Tragic.' Mam buttered her own toast. 'It's a dangerous job. Those poor families. I lost an uncle in a mine collapse and my granddad lost all the fingers on one hand when it got trapped between two trolleys.'

Beth shuddered, hating the thought of the frequent mine accidents that happened all over the country, and in their own district.

'Aunty Hilda is still in bed?' Beth asked.

'Yes. Her arthritis plays up once the weather turns colder. She's getting worse each winter.'

'The boys?'

'Will's harnessing Snowy to the cart and Ronnie is outside feeding the chickens. Why?' Mam ignored her toast, waiting for Beth's response.

'There's something I want to discuss with you both.' Beth licked her dry lips and took a sip of tea.

Dad folded the newspaper and cut a piece of sausage. 'What's that then, my lass?'

'Noah and me.'

'I knew it had something to do with that Jackson fellow.' Mam threw her toast onto her plate.

Dad indicated for Beth to continue.

'Well, Noah and me... We are...' Beth felt she couldn't breathe. 'You see...'

'Out with it, lass.' Dad frowned. 'Has something happened?'

'Yes, but in a good way.'

'What?' Mam's lips thinned.

'Noah and I want to get married, next year, in the spring,' she gushed in one breath. Under the table she twisted her hands together in anguish.

'That's champion news, isn't it, Mary?' Dad beamed. 'Both my two girls to be married. Imagine!' He left this chair and came around to kiss her cheek. 'I'm pleased for you, lass, I am. He's a good lad. Decent.'

'He wants to come and see you, Dad, of course, but I wanted to give you some notice first.'

'Champion. He can come and see me whenever he wants.'

'It is a bit sudden, isn't it?' Mam murmured as though each word was difficult to pronounce.

'We've been walking out together since the summer,' Beth defended.

'You told me at Joanna's wedding you didn't want to marry for some time yet.'

'That was before I met Noah.'

Mam stirred her tea, her expression blank. 'Are you sure this is what you want?'

'Yes, it is.' Beth nodded too much, and her voice was too high, but she couldn't help it. She wanted them both to be happy for her.

'He'll be a teacher soon. Didn't you say a while back?' Dad asked, resuming his chair.

'Yes, he sits his next exam soon.'

'Marriage is forever,' Mam said tersely. 'Something you need to seriously consider. Him as your husband, every day for the rest of your life.'

Beth swallowed.

'They've made a sensible decision, Mary,' Dad cut in, 'they're not marrying until the spring, which is months away. Beth can change her mind in that time if she wishes to or, if not, then she'll know for certain Noah Jackson is who she wants.'

Mam jerked up from the table. 'On your head be it.' She marched from the room and outside.

Dad sighed. 'She'll get used to the idea, lass.'

'Noah isn't his father.'

'No.' He added more tea to his teacup. 'Just give your mam some time. She never expected that one day Leo Jackson would be tied to her in some way. Now they will be. It'll take her some adjusting. Be patient with her.'

Beth nodded.

Her thoughts about her mam and Leo Jackson kept her company as she set up the stall an hour later. Fred was chatting next to her about his whippet, Dolly, who came with him sometimes to his stall in the summer but in the colder months she stayed at home.

'I've bought Dolly a new coat. Well, I say bought, Mrs Worth next door made it for her out of an old flannel dressing gown. Dolly feels the cold. She's as snug as a bug in a rug now though.'

Beth nodded, half listening to him as she loaded the front of the stall with carrots and radishes, onions, and potatoes.

For some reason, she wished Will had stayed with her this morning after dropping her off, but he was needed at home to manure the forcing sheds in preparation for the new crop of rhubarb. Soon they' be lifting the outside crop of rhubarb and the back-breaking work needed all hands. It was the one time her dad employed more men to join Reggie as labourers. The task of lifting acres of rhubarb demanded strength and Dad was happy to pay young men to work for a few weeks until the crop was in the forcing sheds.

Once finished setting up the stall, Beth had a few customers. Fred was now talking to Mrs Rogers, the stallholder on his other side and so Beth poured herself a cup of tea out of the flask. The early morning frost still remained glimmering on the rooftops, but the sun was climbing higher though it held no heat in it.

She served another customer, chatting about the briskness of the morning and the arrest and escape of Sylvia Pankhurst which had been reported in the newspapers a few days ago. Secretly, Beth cheered at the daringness of Sylvia Pankhurst and all the suffragettes. If only she could be as brave and make a stand with them.

When the customer left, Beth's stomach churned as Louis Melville stepped up to the stall.

'Good morning, Miss Beaumont.'

'What do you want?'

'What a charming greeting.' Melville smiled with thin lips.

'I'm busy. I don't have time for your games.'

'I play no game, Miss Beaumont.' He selected an apple and bit into it.

Beth fumed. She folded her arms and glared at him.

'Have you thought more about my proposal?'

'None at all. It's not worthy of my time.'

He threw the apple onto the ground where it rolled into the gutter. 'Are you saying I am not worthy of you?'

'I'm saying I do not wish to marry you.'

'Perhaps that is because we are not well acquainted with each other yet. We should remedy the situation. Shall we say… dinner tomorrow night at Melville Manor about eight o'clock?'

'You can say all you like, Mr Melville, but I shan't be coming to your dinner. I don't want to get to know you. Forgive me for being so blunt, but there is no point in continuing this discussion any further. Thank you for your proposal but I decline.'

Melville's cheeks reddened. 'You are being hasty. Shall I speak to your father, perhaps?'

'No!' Beth barked, then noticed others had turned to look at her. She stepped closer to the edge of the stall the vegetables between them as a barrier. 'I don't wish to marry you. Speaking to my father will be of no use to you.'

'Come, come. Marriage into the Melville family will be of great benefit to you and your family. You must consider that at least.' His smile didn't reach his eyes, which narrowed on her like a hunter spotting his prey. 'My sister would be an asset to you as well. She has many friends and spends a good deal of time in London. Would you enjoy seeing London? We would be a jolly party the three of us.'

'No, thank you.' The thought of spending any time in his or his sister's company left her cold.

'Obviously, I've not given you enough time. I'll leave you to think about it some more and will come back and see you on Saturday.'

'Don't bother.' She forestalled him. 'There really isn't any point.'

Why wasn't he taking her seriously?

'Now, Miss Beaumont, you are being too hasty. If it is courting, you wish for then I can do that. Perhaps not in the way that your people conduct such things but, in my society, we do a similar activity. Would you care to accompany me to the park on Sunday? We can take a stroll. My sister will be happy to be your chaperone.'

Beth gave a mocking laugh. 'Chaperone? I don't need a chaperone, thank you very much. I know how to conduct myself.' She shook her head. 'Why am I even discussing this? No, Mr Melville. I will not go to the park or to the moon with you. I have no wish to do anything with you. Please leave me alone.'

Melville stepped aside as a large woman scowled at him as she wanted to be served.

Beth gave her attention to the woman, but Melville stayed beside the stall until Beth had finished serving.

He gave her a tight smile, or what passed for a smile in his rigid expression. He looked so out of place in the market, wearing a top hat and a suit that would probably cost more than an average person's monthly wage. At once she felt sorry for him.

'Mr Melville. I thank you for your kind offer and I am honoured, truly, but I can't marry you.'

'May I ask why?'

'Because we are two hugely different people from different backgrounds.'

'That can be rectified. With time and learning you will be able to grace any ballroom in the county. My sister and I will help you. I've told you how much I admire you and, in time, I'm certain you will come to feel the same about me. I will do my utmost to make you happy.'

She sighed for he seemed genuine and earnest. He was a man she didn't understand. One moment he could be evil and then the next he offered her the world. 'Mr Melville… I am to marry someone else.'

'That man you were with at the theatre?'

'Yes.'

'A simple common man,' he scoffed. 'You can do so much better than that, Miss Beaumont. You are wasted marrying into the working class.'

'There is nothing common about him.'

'What can he give you that I can't?' he snapped.

She was growing tired of this conversation. Standing still was making her cold. Turning, she restocked the produce she'd sold. 'You have your answer. Good day, Mr Melville.'

'In all good conscience I cannot leave you to such a fate, Miss Beaumont. You deserve better than a simple man who will drag you into poverty and get a child on you every year.'

'My life and my choices aren't any of your business, Mr Melville.' She gave a taut smile to a customer who asked for a pound of potatoes.

When she looked up, Melville was glaring at her. He turned sharply on his heel and strode down the market.

She let out a breath and finished serving.

'What did that toff, Melville, want, Beth? He was standing about your stall a long time.'

'He wanted nothing, Fred. He obviously had time to waste.'

'Well, they do, don't they? Posh folk have nothing worthwhile to do really.' His laugh boomed out over the stalls. 'He took a shine to you and no mistake. But I don't like the look of him, lass. Be careful with that one.'

'I don't intend to ever speak to him again, Fred.' She poured out another cup of tea, her first one having gone cold.

Chapter Ten

Beth waited by the gate, rain threatened, and she hoped it would hold off until Noah had arrived. In the distance she saw Patch running in and out of the hedge bordering the lane. Gathering up her skirts, she ran up to meet Noah as he walked down towards the farm.

'I do enjoy how you greet me, Beth.' Noah joked as she flew into his arms and he twirled her around, making Patch bark.

'It feels like forever since I've seen you.' She kissed him hard on the mouth and he laughed.

'It's been four days.' He kissed her tenderly, holding her tightly to him.

'Four days too long.' Tucking her arm through his, they walked back to the farm. 'What's this?' She took the bottle from him.

'I brought a bottle of Madeira. We could have a toast once I've spoken to your dad.'

'Excellent.'

'I didn't want to turn up empty-handed.'

'Sid said this morning in church that you were busy studying and that's why you weren't there.'

'Yes, sorry. But I needed to finish my notes on the maths that Mr Grimshaw set me to practise. Church, I'm afraid, wasn't high on my list, much to my mam's disgust when she found out I was coming here. She said I could have gone to church and then studied and not come here.'

'My mam said something similar.'

'My career and you come before Reverend Simmons's boring sermons.' Noah shrugged, glancing at the rhubarb fields half-lifted.

'You'll go to hell,' she joked.

'What a way to go though!' He tickled her waist.

She squealed and dodged away from him. 'Mam's put a tea on.'

'Lovely, I've not had anything since breakfast.'

Beth paused when they reached the gate. 'Don't be... offended if Mam is a little uptight. It's nothing to do with you, it's just her way.'

He nodded and took her hand. 'It'll be fine, don't worry.'

Inside, Noah shook hands with her dad and gave the Madeira to Mam, before nodding to Aunty Hilda, Will and Ronnie.

'Sit down, lad,' Aunty Hilda said, bringing out a blackberry and apple pie from the oven.

'Thank you. Sorry I have Patch with me. He doesn't leave me alone on my days off.' Noah took off his coat and Mam hung it behind the door in the scullery.

'He'll be fine in the scullery,' Mam said.

'May I have a word, Mr Beaumont?' Noah asked.

'Course you can, lad. Come into the front room.' Dad led him out of the kitchen.

Nervous, even though she knew her dad would give his permission, Beth paced the kitchen.

'For goodness' sake, girl, sit down,' Mam commanded, going from table to oven. 'You're under my feet. Here, mash the tea.'

'Sorry.' Beth set to work, wondering how long it took for her dad and Noah to talk.

'He's a handsome lad, that's for sure.' Aunty Hilda chuckled, sitting at the table. 'Better looking than his dad, and Leo was a right good looker.'

Beth grinned. 'There is no one in the whole district more handsome than my Noah.'

Mam grunted, taking out forks from the drawer.

'He's good at football and cricket,' Will mentioned, helping himself to a ham sandwich only to get his hand slapped by Mam.

'Wait.'

It seemed forever that Noah and Dad were gone. Beth kept glancing at the mantel clock. What on earth could they be talking about for ten minutes?

'I'm hungry,' Ronnie whined. 'I want to go and see my mates before it rains.'

'You'll wait until your dad returns,' Mam said, pouring out glasses of Madeira.

'Let him go, Mam,' Beth begged.

'He'll wait.' Mam's stern look was one that they knew well and knew to abide by.

A door closed and Beth held her breath as Dad and Noah came back into the kitchen, all smiles.

'Looks like we're gaining another son, Mary.' Dad beamed, patting Noah on the back.

Beth jumped up and ran to her dad and kissed his cheek. 'Thanks, Dad.'

'You're welcome, my lass. He's a good bloke. Got a good head on his shoulders. I'm pleased for you both.'

'Welcome to the family, Noah.' Mam's tone wasn't cold, but it wasn't warm either. She had a brittleness about her that made Beth wary and also a little angry. Couldn't her mam be happy for her today?

'A spring wedding then?' Aunty Hilda asked, her pale blue eyes smiling happily from her wrinkled face.

'Yes, March?' Noah looked to Beth as he took a seat next to her at the table.

'March, yes.' Beth thought her heart would explode with happiness.

'And you'll be a teacher by then?' Mam inquired.

'Aye, hopefully. I just need to pass my next exam in two weeks.'

Mam passed around a plate of ham sandwiches. 'You'll probably move away then to a bigger town where there are more schools, or perhaps into the countryside where teachers might be needed?'

'I'm not sure yet. Personally, I'd like to stay in Wakefield if I could. Maybe even get a position at the school here in Wrenthorpe. It depends on demand.'

Mam's hand faltered slightly as she poured out the tea. 'Wrenthorpe? Surely, you'd want to stretch your horizons for somewhere better? A prestigious school would be a boost to your career.'

'We will have to see. I need to pass the next exam first.'

'I'm sure you will.' Mam left the table to top up the teapot.

The meal progressed with toasts of Madeira and plates full of sandwiches and salads, pie, cakes, and many cups of tea. The rain fell outside, but in the Beaumont kitchen a happy atmosphere pervaded the room, though Beth was aware that Mam never spoke to Noah again.

After clearing away the table, Will brought out a pack of cards for them to play. Dad begged to be excused, needing to be out in the sheds, Aunty Hilda fell asleep in her chair by the fire and Mam disappeared upstairs, leaving Will, Beth, Noah and Ronnie to play away the afternoon hours until the rain stopped and Noah could walk home.

Donning her coat, Beth gave Patch a good scratch as Noah said goodbye to everyone, including Dad who came out of one of the sheds to see him off.

'That went well, didn't it?' Noah said as they strolled around the puddles hand in hand.

'Yes.' Beth watched Patch as he sniffed the grass verge. 'Hopefully, next time Joanna will be there, and Jimmy, too.'

'How about next Sunday you come to mine? Mam said she wants to meet you.'

'That would be lovely.' It was difficult to comprehend how much her life had changed in such a brief time. Courting a man and marriage had seemed so far off only a few months ago. This time last year she'd been happy working on the stall with Joanna, going shopping with her or Jane, climbing into the hayloft with Ronnie to throw straw down onto Will's head, sneaking Will's bicycle out without Mam knowing and riding down the lanes, exhilarating in the freedom of pedal power and being able to ride to Jane's house in a matter of minutes.

Her life had been non-eventful, blessed even, for none of her immediate family had died or were ill, they lived a good life on the farm with plenty to eat, good clothes and a nice house and her days had rolled one after the other without inflicting sudden blows to the everyday routine she enjoyed and took for granted.

Now it felt as though she'd been living in a bubble, not actually experiencing anything. Meeting Noah, falling in love, had heightened her senses. Things became sharper in focus, highlighted to make her see and feel clearer than ever before. No longer was she a child, but a young woman, ready to embark on a new phase of her life, which was both scary and exciting in the same breath.

'I hope your mam likes me one day.' Noah broke into her thoughts.

'She will. Mam is a strange one. She's not very emotional but that doesn't mean she doesn't feel. She just keeps it all close to her chest.' Beth paused, looking towards the top of the lane, which rose up the hill. 'Is that your dad?'

Frowning, Noah nodded. 'Yes.'

Leo waved and hurried down to them. 'I'm glad I caught you before I got to the farm.'

'What's up?' Noah asked, slapping his leg for Patch to come.

'Your mam has had a bit of a turn.'

'How bad?'

Leo Jackson eyed Beth as he spoke. 'She's out of breath, you know how she gets. I was on my way to fetch Doctor Beatty, but you've younger legs than me. Can you go and fetch the doctor? I'll return home.'

'Where are my brothers?'

'They've gone out rabbiting with Sid's ferrets, except Albie, he's at home with your mam.' Leo held out his hand. 'You must be Miss Beaumont?'

'Yes, I am. Nice to meet you properly, Mr Jackson.' She shook his hand.

'You're pretty as a picture.' His hand lingered in hers a moment longer. 'You're just like your mam,' he whispered, a faraway look in his eyes.

'I'll go and fetch Doctor Beatty,' Noah said. 'He won't like to be disturbed on a Sunday afternoon.'

'No, he won't but tough.' Leo Jackson whistled for Patch and strode away.

Noah pulled Beth into a tight embrace. 'I'll try and come around and see you after my shift tomorrow. I'm still on the early shift for a few more days.' He kissed her gently.

Beth held him tightly, kissing him back. 'I hope your mam gets better soon.'

'It's her chest. Years of breathing in cotton fibres. She's worse in the winter.'

'I can sit with her tomorrow if she wants me to? I'm not on the stall and there's not much for me to do on the farm now the harvest is finished.'

'Thank you. I'll see what she says and get a message to you if she agrees.'

After another long kiss, he let her go and she watched him walk up the lane until he turned the corner onto Potovens Road and out of sight.

~ ~ ~ ~

Stripped to the waist, Noah swung the pick, chipping away at the coalface. The heat cloaked his bare skin. Rivulets of sweat trickled down his back and chest, creating dirty little channels as it ran through the coating of coal dust.

Besides him, his dad knelt hacking away at the coal, and beyond him, his brothers worked in various positions to get as much coal out as possible.

Light flicked from several safety lamps, pushing back the darkness, creating a golden cave around them as they worked. Their twelve-hour shift was not far from finishing, and Noah couldn't wait to get above ground and see how his mam was doing.

Since fetching the doctor yesterday, he and his brothers took turns of sitting with their mam as she lay in bed, struggling to breathe. By early morning as they left to start their shift, she had rallied and looked better. Some colour had returned to her cheeks. She even smiled and received a kiss each from her sons, promising she'd be sitting up when they returned, and no she hadn't wanted Beth to come sit with her. Noah had asked Mrs Neilson from next door to pop in and make her a cup of tea and warm up some soup, and she was only too happy to agree.

Still, Noah wanted to see how for himself how Mam was getting on, and, if all was well, he'd visit the Beaumont Farm and spend an hour with Beth before it became too late.

'Away!' Sid yelled, signalling to James and Alfred to push the full trolley load of coal along the track until they met with the pit pony, who'd then pull it to the bottom of the shaft.

Sweat dripped from beneath Noah's flat cap. He turned to grab a drink from his flask and shuddered when a rat ran out from the shadows. He hated the bloody things. Ginger, the pit's resident cat, needed to get down this tunnel and do his job.

An almighty crack shattered the air.

The sound so loud, he ducked and covered his ears. The boom juddered through his body.

A whoosh of air hit him hard. Knocked off his feet and carried down the tunnel, Noah cried out as he thumped into a thick timber prop. Rocks and dirt fell. Another timber prop, the main supports for holding up the roof and earth above them, splintered like a toothpick. The flickering lamp lights spluttered out. Noah lay in utter blackness.

Something pinned him down. Terror threatened to overcome him. He couldn't see his hands in front of him. The darkness pressed in on him, smothering, clawing. He gasped for air and his mouth filled with dust. He coughed, trying not to panic, but instinct made him want to yell and run.

A moan came from somewhere to his left. He quickly felt around his chest. A large rock trapped him. Using all his strength, he shifted it sideways enough to slither out from under it. The relief in being able to suck in air made him sag. He took many deep breaths, tasting dust.

The moan came again.

'Who's moaning?' Noah called out.

'Me.'

'Who's me for Christ's sake,' Noah growled out, crawling on his hands and knees towards the voice.

'Albie.'

The blackness confused him. He didn't know which way he was going. Was he at the face or further up the tunnel?

Blinded by the darkness, Noah steadied his breathing, slowly feeling his way forward, stubbing his hands and knees on rocks. 'I'm coming, Albie.' He coughed.

'My foot is trapped, Noah.'

The roof creaked and groaned. Noah froze, praying the whole lot wouldn't come down again. 'What can you move?'

'Everything but my right foot,' Albie murmured from somewhere in front of him.

Ahead, Noah heard the shifting of rocks. Was that Albie or the roof caving in again. He reached out a hand into the black abyss. 'Keep talking, Albie.'

'I can feel my toes, Noah.' Relief made Albie's voice high.

'That's good, mate, really good.' Noah kept searching, knowing his brother was close. He pulled off his gloves and searched in front of him. Suddenly he touched material. 'Albie?'

Albie's hand knocked Noah's shoulder. 'It's me!'

Noah grabbed his brother's upper body and held him in a tight embrace, emotion running fever pitch. 'I've got you.'

'Thank God. I don't want to die down here alone.'

'We aren't dying. They'll dig us out.' Noah sounded more confident than he felt. A mine disaster would alarm the village. Rescue teams would be formed, men would risk their lives to dig out fellow miners. He and Albie just had to survive the wait.

Noah took a steadying breath. 'I'll feel down your leg and see if I can move what's on top of your foot.'

'Where are the others?' Albie's voice held a touch of panic.

'Maybe they got out.'

'Pray to God they did,' Albie whispered.

Secretly, Noah wondered if that was the case. All six of them were in the same tunnel. No one else was moaning. He touched around Albie's foot. 'It's a prop. It feels like wood not rock.'

'Can you move it?'

'I'll try. I've nothing else better to do, have I?' he joked. Talking to a faceless voice messed with his mind, but he had to concentrate and not give into fear that they were buried alive.

~ ~ ~ ~

Crossing the lane in front of the farmhouse into the field opposite, Beth carried a tray of cups and the tea-pot, while Ronnie followed carrying a basket filled with beef or ham sandwiches. Mam was behind him with another basket of jam tarts and fruit cake.

Dad, Will and the labourers saw them coming and were happy to stop their work of lifting the heavy clumps of two-year old rhubarb, which would be planted into the forcing sheds. Several fields had been lifted in the last couple of weeks, while other fields had been planted with new rhubarb. In the far fields, one-year old rhubarb was left to grow for another year. The farm seemed to throb with industry, especially as they'd employed extra field hands at this time of the year.

As usual Beth spent Mondays gathering and harvesting the last of the summer vegetables for the stall she'd be opening the next day. Soon all she'd have left to sell was the winter vegetables and the stall wouldn't look as vibrant or as lush as in the summer months. Years ago, Mam had come up with the idea that they'd sell other things to compensate, such as holly wreaths at Christmas and jars of pickled onions and other preserves. Aunty Hilda spent every day by the range cooking and pickling for the Christmas season.

'Ho now, Beth, I'm fair parched,' Reggie said, taking the tray from her.

'Hungry too I should imagine.' Beth began pouring out the tea while Ronnie walked around the men with the food basket. Reggie helped Beth with the familiarity of a long-standing friend. He'd been working for her dad since before she was born.

At first no one was quite sure they'd heard the strange noise. Then suddenly everyone stilled as a siren wailed, splitting the air like a banshee's keen. As one they all turned to gaze across the fields in the direction of the mine which was beyond the village.

Beth stared at her mam's frozen face. 'The pit?'

Of course, it was the pit. Everyone lived in dread of the pit's siren broadcasting that something terribly wrong had happened at the coal mine.

'Noah!' Beth thought her heart would stop. 'He's working his shift.'

'Now, we don't know what's happened.' Mam held up her hand.

'Nowt good, that's for certain,' Reggie mumbled.

'I must go to him.' Lifting her skirts, she ran from the field, ignoring her parents' protest.

Along the lane she kept running until she reached Potovens Lane and joined the swell of people heading for the pit top.

Miners off shift, miners' wives and children all made a hurried course for the pit's gates, where they filed into the filthy yard and stood in silence, waiting for news as the last wail of the siren died.

Activity at the entrance to the shaft building, which held the cage that took the men down into the bowels of the earth, kept the crowd alert as they searched for loved ones. The shaft wheel cranked slowly.

The mine's office door was open and men in suits stepped in and out to talk to workers covered in black coal dust. Heads together, their murmurs didn't reach the crowd.

'They need to tell us what's going on,' a woman grumbled beside Beth.

'They will, soon,' another replied.

Miners not on shift went to offer their assistance. Rescue teams were organised.

Beth stared around the gathered families, knowing many by name and nearly all by face. They were her people, her village community and when a disaster hit, it affected everyone, whether they worked in the pit or not for they would know someone who did.

A baby cried and its mother bundled it up in her shawl, never taking her eyes off the building that housed the shaft cage. Two filthy men came out, coughing and spluttering and were taken into another long building.

Wrapping her coat around her tighter, Beth tried to forget the cold. The mine was on a rise and the breeze was stronger up here than down on the farm.

As she waited for news, she refused to believe anything bad had happened to Noah. They had a whole life together and nothing would shatter that. To think otherwise was defeatist.

An hour went by and no forthcoming information started to wear thin on the nerves of families.

'Come on now!' a man shouted from behind Beth making her jump.

'What's going on?' another yelled.

The mood of the crowd changed from silent waiting to fidgeting frustration. Children played in the dirt at their feet, babies slept in mothers' tired arms.

Finally, an official-looking man came towards them and the murmurings grew louder. Beside him a man carried a wooden crate which he put down for the suited man to stand on.

'I'm Phillip Carruthers, mine owner. Thank you for your patience while we have been gathering information.'

Beth stood, hands clenched, fearing his words.

'We have ascertained that there has been a rock fall in one of the main tunnels. We have twenty-two men underground working this shift. Two men have returned to the surface to give us details on what they know. We need to take careful measures for the safety of the rescue teams going down to find these men and bring them out. The cage is working, and two rescue teams have already gone down to determine the damage and how we can begin to liberate the trapped men.'

'What the hell does ascertain mean?' one old woman mumbled next to Beth.

Mr Carruthers continued, 'Now we understand your anxiety for your loved ones. Let me assure you all that we are doing everything we possibly can to find the trapped men and bring them out, but we must do it safely. It will take time. We ask for any off-duty miners to report to the office to help with the salvage work and clearing of the tunnels. We will provide you with any updates as the afternoon progresses. Thank you.' He stepped down off the crate and he and other man, who Beth recognised as Mr Whitehead, the mine manager, walked back into the office and shut the door.

'Well, now we know,' said a young woman with a child clinging to her skirts.

'We've got a long wait ahead of us,' another woman spoke.

'Let's get ourselves organised then. We've been through this before, haven't we?' A woman about the same age as her mam gave the crowd a nod. 'We need fires lit, tea and food, blankets. Our men will be cold when they come out if night has fallen.'

Beth watched the miners' wives disperse with each of them in their own way helping the other, while she remained rooted to the spot, feeling useless.

'Lass.' Her dad weaved through the crowd to her side. 'No one has come up yet?'

'No, I don't think so. The women are organising fires and tea…' She glanced around at the people who had stayed in the yard. Not all had the means of providing tea and food for everyone. An old man was breaking up crates with the help of some young lads. They lit fires in several old tin barrels across the yard so people could gather around them and keep warm, while they waited for further news.

'I'll go home and fetch some chairs, some food and a flask of tea. One of us will come and sit with you.'

'No, it's fine, Dad. You're all busy with the lifting. I can see to myself.'

'Are you sure?'

'Yes. You go.'

He kissed her forehead and then took off his own woollen scarf and wrapped it around her neck. 'Get by one of those fires. It'll be freezing once the light fades.'

'I will.' She nodded, emotion thick in her throat.

'He'll be all right. Noah is fit and strong. He'll make it out.'

'Yes, he will.' Beth was convinced of it. To think of anything else was unfaithful to the love that burned fiercely in her heart.

As the hours wore on, families and friends converged on the pit, swelling the numbers out of the yard and into the surrounding waste areas. Children ran up and down the slag heaps, getting filthy but at least they left their mothers in peace to wait.

Reverend Simmons came and held a prayer meeting for those who found comfort in his words.

Beth stayed aloof from him, finding his prayers annoying. She didn't want God's love at this time. She wanted Noah. If God loved his people, then why did he cause such misery? She'd been a child who'd

attended Sunday school, and who many times had
been sent out of the building for asking questions and
refusing to believe in the nun's teaching about seas
being parted, five loaves of bread and two fish feeding five thousand people. The nun often spoke to her
mam and she was scolded and in trouble even more
when she got home. Still, the teachings of Sunday
school and every sermon by Reverend Simmons rein-
forced her opinion that religion wasn't the answer to
all. To blindly have faith in some sort of God was not
Beth's way of dealing with life. She trusted in common sense. Things happened because they happened,
and no God could save the lives of the men trapped
below. It would be their fellow miners, who with
knowledge and a bit of luck would bring those men
out alive, or not, to their families.

The weak sun was low on the horizon when finally, there was movement from the shaft building.
Those that were sitting surged to their feet and the
crowd gathered closer. Three men stumbled out of the
shaft building, bleeding and black with coal dust.

Beth stood on tiptoes, trying to see over the shoulder of the man in front of her. Was it Noah coming
out? It was so hard to tell when the men all looked the
same covered in grime.

A cry from a woman in the middle of a group of
women to the right, made Beth's stomach lurch. The
woman, Mrs Thwaite, a customer she'd served on the
stall and who Mam spoke to whenever they passed in
the street, ran forward, and embraced the tallest of the
three men to her. Beth recognised Mr Thwaite now,
and beside him was Terry Jones and his son, Mikey
Jones, who Beth knew from school.

The sight of three men having been rescued brought the crowd to life and the talk grew louder as hope rose. The mine's nurse and Doctor Beatty, the village doctor, hurried the men into a building beside the mine's office.

'My that's good to see, isn't it?' said an old man, regaining his chair by the fire closest to Beth.

Beth looked beyond him to the door of the shaft building, willing Noah to be the next one to walk out.

Dusk fell and then the night crept in, cold and crisp. Stars pinpricked the sky and a crescent moon shone.

Movement and growing whispers brought Beth's head up from gazing down at the pattern she was making in the dirt with the tip of her boot. She craned her neck to see past those in front of her.

Four men walked out of the shaft building carrying a stretcher between them.

Beth's heart somersaulted. Noah? She pushed through the crowd. It looked like Noah. She managed to get a few feet from the men before she realised it was James Jackson.

'James!' she cried out.

Dazed, James frowned and then spotted her. 'Beth.'

She glanced at the stretcher. It wasn't Noah but someone else. 'Have you seen Noah?'

James handed the stretcher handle to another helper and came over to her. 'No. The blast knocked us all flying. I was at the entrance to where Noah, me dad and the others were working. I was blown back twenty yards at least. There's nothing but a wall of rock where I was working.'

She tried to digest the information. 'So…' Suddenly, she couldn't form the words.

'They're buried, Beth.' His voice choked.

She hugged him to her, not caring of the muck coating him. 'They'll get them out. Noah won't leave me.'

James's smile seemed forced. 'No, I don't think he would.'

'Are you hurt?'

'Not badly. Just some bruises and scratches.' He rubbed a dirty hand over his dusty face. 'It's all caved in,' he whispered into her ear so only she heard him.

'They'll dig. It's what miners do, isn't it?' She tried to inject a positive note into her voice.

James stepped back and wiped his eyes, leaving black streaks across his face. 'Is me mam here?'

'Oh. I don't know.' How had she forgot Noah's mam? She felt terrible.

'She's been poorly.' James scanned the crowd.

'Noah told me. I'll go to your house and see her, shall I? I'll tell her what's happened. Sorry, I should have done that earlier.'

'Thank you, Beth.'

Turning away, Beth ran from the yard, eager to do this errand and have something else to think about. Guilt plagued her the entire way. Poor Mrs Jackson, bedridden while her whole family was trapped underground.

Chapter Eleven

Noah opened his eyes. Blackness disorientated him for a moment. Panic raced through his veins.

He'd fallen asleep leaning against Albie's shoulder, listening to him singing some ditty about a Spanish girl that was often sung in the village pub. Now there was no singing, just the drip drip drip of running water.

'Albie!' Noah shook his brother, terrified he'd died while he'd been asleep. 'Albie!'

'What? What?' Albie's gruff mumble eased Noah's dread.

'Stay awake. Sing again.'

'I can't, my voice has gone,' Albie rasped. 'I need a drink.'

'There's water running somewhere I can hear it. I'll have a search around.' On hands and knees, Noah left his brother's side and headed towards where he thought he heard water seeping through the rocks. He bumped his head and swore. The ceiling was low in this part of the tunnel.

Suddenly, his fingers touched something metal. 'I've found something.'

'What?'

Noah groped all around the object. 'It's a lamp!'

'One of the electric ones? Please say it is,' Albie urged.

165

Noah looked back over his shoulder in the direction of Albie's voice though he couldn't see him. 'It feels like the electric one Dad won in the poker game last Christmas. It's damaged. There's a dint in the side.'

'Try it. Turn it on.'

With fumbling fingers, Noah tried to get the device to light up. 'It's broken.'

'Keep it with you. Have you found the water?'

'I think it's just ahead of me.' Noah kept the lamp tucked in one arm and crawled forward, reaching out until his hands hit the wall. He slid one hand along until he felt wetness against his palm. 'Water.'

Above his head the roof creaked and groaned. Fear froze him.

'Can you lick at the water?' Albie asked.

Taking a deep breath, Noah ignored the settling earth above him and shuffled up to the wall and, going by feel only, he leaned against the wall until water trickled over his mouth. Although gritty and tasting of coal, it was refreshing. He sucked at the water until his lips hurt. 'We've nothing to catch the water with, Albie. You'll have to crawl over to me.'

'Bloody hell. My foot is throbbing.'

'I'll tap the wall. Come to the sound.' Between taps, Noah heard Albie scraping along the floor, dragging his damaged foot.

Albie's breath laboured but he finally managed to get to Noah's side and with his hands guiding him, Noah showed Albie where to drink.

'That's fantastic.' Albie sighed when he'd finished.

166

'We should stay here, close to this water source.' Noah shifted a rock to one side.

'How long have we been trapped for do you think?' Albie asked.

'No idea. Hold the lamp while I move more of these rocks.' Noah didn't want to consider the time spent down in their tomb. He concentrated on moving the lumps of earth and rocks to give them some sort of space to sit side by side near the trickling water.

Abruptly, a weak light filtered back the darkness. Noah blinked in surprise.

'I did it.' Albie crowed, holding up the lamp. The weak light showed his grinning face.

'Bloody well done!' Noah glanced around at the cave. In front of them was a solid rock wall but to the left, next to Albie's shoulder, a trickle of water ran down the wall.

'Take it further down there, Noah.' Albie handed him the lamp.

Turning on his heels, Noah held the lamp at arm's length. He could see the broken timber prop which had trapped Albie's foot. 'I'll go down a bit further.'

He climbed over the broken prop and a heap of rocks and dirt. The cave continued for another ten yards or so. Noah could stand upright in one area and he stretched his back, easing the cramp out of it.

Something caught his eye. He swung the lamp over to the right and his breath stopped. Was the light playing tricks on him?

'Dad?' he whispered.

He hurried to the pile of rocks and the jagged wall where at the bottom his dad lay, eyes open in death.

Noah fell to his knees. 'Dad?' He shook him hard, but he knew instinctively his dad was gone. Gently, he closed his eyes.

'What is it, Noah?' Albie called from further up the cave.

'Dad. He… he didn't make it.' Noah picked off all the rocks and dirt that covered his father's body and then crossed his arms over his chest.

Noah stayed with his dad for a moment longer, shutting out Albie's quiet sobbing.

None of it seemed real. He'd never been close to his father, indeed at times he wanted the old man to leave the house and never come back. Yet, confronted with his body, he shuddered with shock. It wasn't so much the sadness of losing his parent but the realisation that he or Albie could be next.

His dad was dead. Would they soon follow him?

~ ~ ~ ~

Slowly, Beth opened the bedroom door. Noah's mother, Peggy Jackson lay in bed, propped up on two pillows. Dressed in a white nightgown, her black hair, liberally streaked with grey, lay about her shoulders. She appeared asleep.

Downstairs, Mrs Neilson had let Beth in and, thankful for the break, told Beth to go sit with Peggy while she slipped back across to her own home to feed her husband and daughter.

Beth hovered in the doorway. The room had faded wallpaper, the pattern hardly distinguishable. Mould patches dotted the ceiling. Hooks on the wall hung a variety of clothes but the room only held a small chest of drawers and nothing else besides the bed.

Beth had noticed the lack of comforts in the sparse kitchen. Coming up the stairs, the treads held no carpet and the walls were painted a dirty yellow colour. She'd been in other people's houses before, mostly Jane's first home and then her grandparents' rundown little cottage, but even that was in better condition that the Jackson house.

Edging closer to the double bed, Beth faltered when Peggy Jackson's eyes opened.

'Who are you?' Mrs Jackson asked, lifting her head.

'Beth Beaumont, Mrs Jackson.'

'Ah, Noah's girl.'

'Yes.' The statement made Beth happy and weepy at the same time.

'I told Noah not to bother with you. You're busy with the stall…' Mrs Jackson coughed, a hacking sound that distressed her.

Beth quickly held the glass of water from the bedside table to her lips and helped her to drink.

Panting, Mrs Jackson laid back. 'Thank you.'

'I've come with some news.' Beth replaced the glass on the table.

'Oh?'

'There's been an accident at the pit.'

Mrs Jackson's eyes sprang wide. 'An accident? My lads? I didn't hear the siren.' Her Welsh accent became stronger.

'Mrs Neilson said you slept through it.'

'I did? It's so loud normally.'

'You must have been exhausted.'

'I was up all night coughing.' Mrs Jackson reached for Beth's hand. 'My boys?'

'I saw James. He is well.'

The other woman's face paled. 'The others?'

'They are still underground.'

Mrs Jackson closed her eyes for a moment then threw back the thin bed covers. 'Help me get dressed.'

'But you're too ill. It's cold out.'

'I need to be there. I'll not sit here worrying.'

Beth didn't argue with her, she had no right to and she knew if she'd been in her place she'd want to be at the pit, too.

While Mrs Jackson visited the lavatory, Beth made her a flask of tea. She grabbed a blanket off the bed, for the night was cold, and with that and the flask tucked under her arm, and her other arm hooked with Mrs Jackson's, they took the slow walk to the pit.

'You are thoughtful.' Mrs Jackson indicated the blanket and flask. She coughed again.

'I'll find a chair for you near one of the fires.' Beth gave a grim smile, noticing Mrs Jackson's frayed woollen gloves and scarf full of holes.

The streets were busy with people walking to and from houses, grabbing coats and blankets, food, and tea.

The atmosphere when they reached the pit seemed tense, expectant. Dogs barked at the commotion and children stared wide-eyed not understanding why adults were whispering and clinging to each other.

'Have more men been brought out?' Beth asked a lad named Paul, a friend of Ronnie's, who found a crate for Mrs Jackson. Beth made her comfortable near one of the fires in the yard.

'No,' the lad said, adding more coal to the fire. 'Nowt's happening.'

'It's a disgrace,' an old man muttered from his crate beside them, the smoke from his pipe billowing up.

'What's taking them so long?' a woman complained on the other side of the fire.

Beth poured the tea for Mrs Jackson. 'I'll go and find James.'

'Thank you.'

Weaving through the crowd, Beth found James in front of the mine manager's office talking to two other rescued men.

'James.'

'Beth. How's Mam?'

'She's sitting over there by that fire on the left.'

'Mam shouldn't be out of bed.' He dashed over to where she pointed.

'She insisted.' Beth followed him. 'I've made her warm.' She stood back as mother and son embraced.

'Now, lad,' Mrs Jackson whispered. 'Where are your brothers?'

'They'll bring them up soon, Mam.' Tears shone in James's eyes.

Mrs Jackson nodded. No more words were needed.

Beth waited with them and had a fleeting thought that Mrs Jackson hadn't once asked about her husband.

In the wee hours of the morning, Beth woke from a nap. She'd been sitting on the freezing ground next to James and they'd both fallen asleep leaning against each other's shoulder.

James slept on but Beth glanced over his head to Mrs Jackson who sat wrapped in the blanket, a shawl over her head and her gaze on the shaft building.

'Sorry I fell asleep.'

Mrs Jackson smiled down at her. 'It's nearly three o'clock in the morning, you're bound to be tired.'

Yawning, Beth wiped her eyes. 'Anything?'

'No, nothing.'

'I can't believe it's taking so long.'

Abruptly, the shaft building's door opened, and a group of men walked out, some were being carried, others assisted.

As one, the crowd rose, wide awake and eager for a glimpse of a loved one. Whispers grew louder, waking those that were napping.

'Who is it, Beth?' Mrs Jackson asked.

Beth stood up, waking James who leapt to his feet.

'Go and find out!' Mrs Jackson barked, then began coughing.

Beth and James raced to the front of the crowd. James being taller spotted Alfred and yelled.

'Is Noah there?' Beth tugged at his coat. She hung onto him as James dodged between people to reach Alfred's side.

Alfred carried Sid on his back.

'It's good to see you both.' James patted Sid's shoulder.

'Give us a hand,' Alfred puffed.

Together he and James carried Sid into the long barn which had been set up as a make-shift hospital.

Sid groaned in agony when they put him on a table. A blanket was wrapped around his thigh and blood soaked it.

Doctor Beatty was quickly beside him. 'Your leg, Sid?'

'Aye, Doc. It's broken.'

Doctor Beatty unwrapped the blanket and cut away Sid's trouser leg. The thigh bone poked against the skin. Swelling and bruising added to the disfigurement. 'He needs to be taken to Clayton Hospital.' He gestured to his attendant and made plans for Sid's removal.

'Is it just us three then?' Alfred asked, as the nurse inspected the cuts on his arm and neck. 'Where's Dad and Noah and Albie?'

'They've not been brought up.' James told them.

Alfred watched the nurse do her work. 'They had to dig us out, which means they're further in the tunnel.'

'Jesus Christ,' Sid swore, wincing as he was moved onto a stretcher.

Beth's heart constricted. What did Alfred mean? Was Noah buried beneath earth and rocks without air? Might he have survived the fall? Was he dead already and they would only find his body?

Sid winced as the nurse covered him with a clean blanket. 'At least the three of them are together.'

'They'll find them.' Beth's words sounded braver than she felt. 'I'll go and tell your mam.'

'We'll join her in a moment, once Alfred has been cleaned up and they've taken Sid,' James said.

Beth fled the building, focusing on Mrs Jackson who waited for her. She couldn't give into her emotions, not yet.

'They're all right?' Mrs Jackson gripped Beth's hands.

'They are. Sid has broken his leg. He'll have to go to hospital so they can set it. Alfred has cuts and bruises. He'll come out and see you shortly.'

'Oh, thank God they are safe. Now, just two more,' Mrs Jackson whispered, turning her gaze back to the shaft building. 'Two more.'

Beth held the other woman's hand, intrigued why she didn't mention her husband.

~ ~ ~ ~

Noah heard the tapping as he woke. When he and Albie decided to sleep for a bit, they'd turned the lamp off to save the battery, but now he felt for it in the dark and turned it on.

Albie stirred. 'What?'

'I can hear tapping. Listen.'

Breath suspended; Noah focused on the noise coming from the bottom end of the tunnel.

'It's someone digging. They've come to get us,' Albie whispered.

Noah stood and reached down to help Albie up. 'Take your weight on your good foot and lean on me.'

Arms around each other, they made the slow walk down to the rock fall blocking the end of the tunnel. The weak lamp light threw shadows and Noah glanced away from the body of their father. He'd spent a few hours before they slept throwing rocks at rats which had been scrambling over the body until he finally killed the horrible vermin.

At the rock fall, Noah lowered Albie down and together they began pulling rocks away from the fall. At times they'd stop and bang a rock against another in the hope that those men on the other side could hear them and know they were still alive.

'Turn the lamp off, Albie. We can work in the dark for a bit,' Noah instructed.

When the tunnel was plunged into darkness, Noah flinched. The tunnel was a black airless tomb and he hated it passionately.

'Sing, Albie,' he muttered, straining to shift a heavy rock. His brother had a good strong voice and it would help pass the time away as they worked.

~ ~ ~ ~

The greyness of dawn lifted the darkness of night. On the horizon a thin line of pink heralded a new day, though the temperature remained low and cold.

Beth shivered in her coat, her eyes gritty with tiredness. People who had gone home last night began arriving again. Miners changed shifts, as did the rescue teams. Large urns of tea started boiling as the inhabitants of the yard awakened and stretched out cramped, stiff limbs, their breath steaming in the frigid air. James and Alfred had gone for more coal to feed the fire.

'Beth.'

Frowning at her name being called, Beth turned as her mam came around a group of men. 'Mam?'

She instantly felt guilty as she should have been getting the cart ready with produce to take to the stall.

Mam eyed the small gathering near Beth, she nodded to a few women before straightening her shoulders and giving Mrs Jackson the briefest of nods of acknowledgment. She thrust a flask into Beth's hands. 'Hot chocolate. I've got you a bacon butty in my bag.'

'Thank you.' Beth would have liked her mam to embrace her but that wasn't her mother's way of showing emotion. 'Mrs Jackson and I have spent the night together. I'll share the hot chocolate with her.'

'Thank you, lass.' Mrs Jackson coughed into a handkerchief.

'What's the latest?' Mam asked, eyeing the other woman.

'Noah, Mr Jackson and Albie are still underground, along with two young lads. They are the last to come out. James, Sid, and Alfred are out and several others. One man has died. Mr Finkley from Silcoates Lane.'

'That's a tragedy. I know his sister.' Mam glanced to Mrs Jackson. 'Do you…' She cleared her throat. 'Do you want me to fetch you anything, Mrs Jackson?'

'No, thanks, Mrs Beaumont. Beth has been most kind to me all night. She's looked after me as good as any daughter would. I'm most pleased she'll be soon joining my family.'

A muscle ticked in Mam's jaw. 'A daughter is heaven sent, indeed. I'm blessed with two.'

Beth watched the edgy exchange between the two women, knowing their history now, she was aware of the tense undercurrent between them.

'You're not to worry about the stall today, Beth.' Mam placed the bag at Beth's feet. 'I'll do a few hours and close it up early.'

'Thank you, Mam.'

'Right. Good.' Mam turned to go. 'Stay warm. Eat.'

Beth smiled. 'I will.'

Once her mam had left, Beth found a crate no one was using and sat down to open the bag. Inside she found, four bacon butties, the family's largest flask of hot chocolate, cups, and slices of fruit cake. At the bottom of the bag was a thick blanket. Beth's heart warmed at kindness of her mam's gesture. Her mam might not be one to give embraces and kisses, but she showed her love in other ways — ways more practical and fitting to the woman who ran a large family and bustling farm in a no-nonsense manner.

'Here, Mrs Jackson. Have a butty, and some hot chocolate.' Beth helped the other woman into a more comfortable position. Her lap being a table for her food. When James and Alfred came back, Beth gave them food and drink, which they ate with gusto.

The sun rose higher and people drifted in and out of the yard as the day wore on.

An update from Mr Whitehead the mine manager told them they were still digging out the collapsed tunnel. They remained hopeful.

Around noon, James and Alfred went back down underground with two other men to help relieve one of the rescue teams. Beth thought them to be terribly brave to return to the place that nearly took their lives.

As the afternoon wore on, Beth found her spirits flagging. She'd tried for twenty-four hours to keep her hopes high and to convince herself that Noah would walk out of the pit. However, when the men carried out the two dead lads late in the afternoon, silent tears flowed down her cheeks.

The cries of the boys' mothers echoed around the yard. Grown men cringed at the sound of the keening. Ripples of talk drifted on a wave of subdued anger as miners spoke of safety regulations and ways to make the mine safer.

After four hours working non-stop, James and Alfred came back to the surface to let another group of men go down. Mrs Jackson insisted James and Alfred have a break and sit with her. She wanted her sons with her.

Exhausted, James and Alfred sat on crates next to their mother as women from the village brought around hot potatoes and cups of tea.

Beth watched the undertaker arrive and disappear into the long building. She wondered vaguely if she'd soon be standing at Noah's grave.

'I'm sorry, Mam.' James leapt to his feet once he'd finished his food. 'I can't sit here, not when me dad and brothers are down there.'

Alfred stood also. 'We have to go back down, Mam.'

'No. You've done your bit. You're too tired to go down again. They need fresh men down there to work fast. Stay here.'

'No. I won't.' James strode off and Alfred, giving his mam an apologetic smile, hurried after him.

Mrs Jackson started to cough, a great hacking sound that bent her over.

Worried, Beth offered her some tea, but Mrs Jackson shook her head and covered her face with her shawl as she continued to cough.

When finally, Mrs Jackson could breath without coughing, she gave Beth a wan smile and Beth took her hand and held it. Together they kept watch on the building.

'Lass.'

Beth smiled as her dad joined her by the fire.

He pulled her into his wide chest and let her rest her head for a moment. 'Do you want to come home for a break?'

She straightened and sighed. 'I can't leave until I know Noah is… out.'

'Well, I'll sit with you for awhile. I've just collected your mam from the stall and taken her home. She had a busy morning.' He smiled at Noah's mam. 'You must be so anxious, Peggy. I'm pleased three of your sons are safe.'

'Thank you, Rob.'

A friend of her dad's came over to talk to him and Beth resumed her watch on the shaft building.

The light was fading, and her dad had gone back to the farm when the door opened, and a cheer went up from the people gathered closest to the front.

Beth jerked up from the crate to see.

'What is it?' Mrs Jackson asked, gripping Beth's arm as she rose.

'I can't see.' Beth wanted to cry with frustration. 'Come on, Mrs Jackson.' Without waiting for the older woman to protest, she pulled her along behind her towards the front.

The crowd were all on their feet, some were clapping, others cheering.

Beth pushed through burly miners and got to the front.

Her heart flipped.

Noah.

She stared at him. Head down, he walked with his brothers alongside a stretcher carrying a covered body.

Beth hung back, but Mrs Jackson continued to the stretcher. The Jackson brothers were crying softly.

Doctor Beatty pulled back the blanket to reveal Leo Jackson. The crowd hushed. In turn each of her sons embraced Mrs Jackson. Instructions were given and the stretcher was carried into the long building.

Noah hesitated and turned to search the crowd.

'Noah!' Beth took a step.

'Beth.' His expression changed from searching doubt to sagging relief.

She ran into his arms not caring who saw. She held him tightly as he held her, his face buried into her neck. He was filthy, black with coal dust and grime, not that she cared. His lips found hers and she clung to him, loving him with such power it overwhelmed her.

The man she loved was alive and well and in her arms and that was all that mattered. Everything would be fine now.

Chapter Twelve

Sitting at the kitchen table, Beth listened to the rain outside while eating her porridge. Across the table, Ronnie and Will sat discussing the latest football match and arguing over whose turn it was to muck out Snowy's stable.

'Be quiet you two!' Beth snapped, pushing her bowl away.

Aunty Hilda came in from the scullery and lightly slapped both boys up the back of the head. 'Get out, go on. You've work to do and sitting around here is wasting time and you're getting on your sister's nerves. She has a funeral to attend this morning and she don't need your nonsense!'

Will and Ronnie scuttled from the table grumbling as they went into the scullery to don boots and coats.

'And Ronnie Beaumont get to school on time,' Aunty Hilda shouted after Ronnie.

Beth smiled at Aunty Hilda. 'Thanks.'

'Idle hands create idle minds, and those two are prime examples of it.' She grinned.

Beth cleared away the table knowing full well that Aunty Hilda loved those boys more than anyone in the house, herself included. Aunty Hilda fiercely loved Will and Ronnie who, in her heart, replaced the two sons she lost in infancy many years ago.

Aunty Hilda added more coal to the range as Mam walked in from outside. 'Your dad has the cart ready. He'll drop me off in town. I'll see you later, Beth.'

'Thanks, Mam. I'll come and take over the stall as soon as the funeral is finished.'

Mam nodded but remained silent, collected her bag, and left the house.

From the range Aunty Hilda watched her go then glanced at Beth. 'She feels guilty.'

Surprised, Beth paused in washing the dishes. 'Why?'

Aunty Hilda pushed away a strand of grey hair out of her eyes. She still wore her curling rags in her hair and didn't take them out until after breakfast and her jobs were done around the kitchen. 'Mary hated Leo Jackson and likely wished him dead many a time. Now he is.'

'That's not her fault.'

'It doesn't matter. The mind is a funny creature. All these years she's been comfortable in her behaviour of blaming Jackson for his wrongdoing towards her. He's gone and her hate for him will fade because he's not around for her to see in the village. It's a kind of loss for her, too.'

'I never realised.'

'No, you wouldn't. Mary hides it well, but I know her better than anyone, even your dad, and I understand what goes on in her head.'

'What can we do?'

'Nothing. It's Mary who will have to mend.' Aunty Hilda put a pot of water on to boil. 'Leave that, lass, and go up and ready yourself for the funeral. I'll see to everything down here.'

Two hours later, Beth left the house in a break of rain showers. She waved to her dad and Reggie who were inspecting the coal fire's flue which provided heat in the forcing shed. Last night in the storm, part of the flue had broken, and Dad and Will had been out for hours fixing it. Most of the rhubarb had been lifted now and long hours were needed in the forcing sheds to replant the rhubarb, but without heat they wouldn't grow. Hence the frantic repair work during the night.

Carrying her umbrella, she walked in the rain up the lane towards St Anne's Church where the funerals of all the victims of the mine disaster were being held. As she passed the ploughed fields, she waved to the three lads that Dad had employed on clearing the drainage ditches. They looked sodden and cold.

She didn't envy them their work and had donned an extra pair of socks before putting her boots on. Soon enough she'd be standing behind the market stall in the freezing weather herself. Thankfully, she wore her best coat with its black fur-lined collar and black felt hat, which although not practical for the stall it was entirely suitable for the funeral.

A large crowd gathered outside of St Anne's. On such a dismal day, to see so many wives and mothers with pinched faces holding onto the hands of silent children brought a lump to Beth's throat. Alongside Leo Jackson, the two lads, and another man were to be buried today as well.

She smiled wanly and nodded to different people as she made her way to find Noah and his family. She hadn't seen Noah since the day after he was rescued. He'd needed sleep and rest and she wanted him to have that. Yet when she had knocked on the Jacksons' door the day after the rescue, all the brothers had been sitting around the kitchen table, drinking tea, and barely talking. From upstairs came the hacking noise of Mrs Jackson's cough. Beth hadn't stayed long as Noah seemed preoccupied with organising the funeral.

That had been four days ago, and she'd been busy on the stall since then and not been able to visit him.

'Beth!' Noah waved to her from near the entrance to the church.

'Such a crowd.' Beth took his hand as she reached him.

'More than expected. There aren't enough pews for everybody. I've waited for you out here and the others have gone in and saved us a seat.'

Few flowers adorned the inside of the church. November wasn't the month for flowers and poor miners didn't waste what little money they had on flowers. The four coffins stood side by side unadorned.

The organist played as Beth squished in beside James and Noah followed her to sit at the end. She reached over and took Mrs Jackson's hand for a moment and gave her a smile for comfort. Noah's mother looked dreadful, blue around the lips and wheezing, but dry-eyed.

Beth smiled in sympathy at Sid, perching at the far end of the pew his leg in a cumbersome brace and stuck out with his crutches leaning against him. He'd been let out of hospital that morning for the funeral.

'I'm glad you came,' Albie murmured to her.

'How's your ankle?'

'Sore. I can't walk on it for long without pain.'

The icy church, although packed with mourners, didn't grow any warmer. While they sang hymns and listened to the reverend speak, Noah held Beth's hand. Finally, the Jackson brothers, except Sid, and other men were asked to carry the coffins from the church.

Outside, the rain fell heavily. Beth groaned, trying to quickly open her umbrella up to cover Mrs Jackson.

'Don't come to the grave, lass,' Mrs Jackson said. 'It's foul out here and we won't linger ourselves or I'll be the next one the boys will be burying.'

'Don't say that. Your sons need you.'

Peggy Jackson glanced to where the five of them stood. 'I won't be around forever.' She gave a shiver and patted Beth's hand. 'Noah said you're off to the stall. Go before you're drenched through.'

Hesitating, Beth's heart melted at the sadness on the brothers' faces. She wanted to speak to Noah, to give him comfort.

'I'll tell Noah that you said goodbye.'

'Thank you.' Beth hugged Mrs Jackson to her. 'Take my umbrella. I'm catching the tram into town to take over the stall from my mam. I won't need it as much as you do. I can survive getting a little wet.'

'Thank you, lass. You're truly kind. My umbrella broke and we've not replaced it...' Mrs Jackson lowered her gaze, and Beth noticed her black coat and hat had seen better days. The Jacksons were poor, Beth understood that, but she didn't understand why when they were all in work.

'Tell Noah I'll see him tomorrow.' Beth gazed at the brothers carrying the coffin on their shoulders while Sid followed them on his crutches.

'I will and thank you. Noah is lucky to have found such a lovely lass as you.'

Beth dashed from the church and down the road. She'd just passed the Methodist Chapel when a carriage pulled to a stop beside her.

'Miss Beaumont,' Louis Melville called from the carriage window.

Groaning, Beth ignored him and walked faster as the rain intensified.

'Please, Miss Beaumont. I offer you nothing but friendship and to be out of this intolerable weather. Do get in.'

If it had been anyone else, she would have done. 'It's not much further to go,' she called back.

Melville ordered the carriage to keep up with her. 'You've a mile at least if you're heading for the tram stop at Newtown. This is silly, Miss Beaumont. I offer you friendship. I thought you were more intelligent than this.'

Rain dripped off her hat, which would now be ruined. Her mam will tut at the saturated state of her good coat, too. She hesitated slightly as the rain fell so hard it bounced off the footpath.

'Get in, Miss Beaumont, please.'

With a frustrated sigh, Beth climbed into the carriage.

Melville made a fuss of her as the horses jerked forward and Beth held onto the seat to stop herself from touching Melville's knees as he sat opposite.

'Here, Miss Beaumont.' He gave her a thick woollen blanket and she placed it over her knees.

Her teeth chattered. 'Thank you. It is… It is kind of you.' She hated saying those words to him after the torment he'd put her through before in the summer.

'I'd like us to be friends. As you are aware, I would like more than friendship.' He put his hands up as she went to speak. 'No, I'll say no more about it. Now is not the time.'

She sat stiffly, swaying with the carriage as they traversed the roads and vehicles into town.

'Is your family well?' he asked, adjusting his cuffs. His top hat and cane were on the seat beside him and he wore a dun-coloured long coat over a caramel coloured suit. He looked every bit of a wealthy man.

'They are. Thank you for asking.' She paused, forcing herself to be polite as she'd been brought up to be. 'Are your family well? Your sister?'

'Indeed, they are. Father suffers from gout from time to time, but he refuses to listen to the doctor. I'm happy he's in Amsterdam and not here so I don't have to listen to his complaints.' Melville shrugged. 'My sister is in London. She much prefers it to Yorkshire. She has many friends there and fills our townhouse in Chelsea every night with parties.'

'Sounds exhausting.'

Melville laughed. 'Yes, it does, doesn't it?'

Beth looked away, noting that they were getting close to Brook Street where the market was situated.

'Perhaps, Mis Beaumont, you would care to visit Melville Manor? We have beautiful gardens, though I confess they aren't at their best at the moment, but the orangery is warm and inviting.'

His offer alarmed her. 'No, thank you.'

'You don't like beautiful gardens?'

'I do. It's not that…' She breathed a sigh of relief as the carriage slowed and the driver called down to them that they were at the market, which Beth thought was stupid as a person only had to look out of the window to see where they were.

Melville climbed down and held out his hand to assist her.

Beth ignored his hand and held onto the carriage door as she stepped down.

'May I walk with you?' he asked, putting on his hat.

'I'm going to work. My mam is minding the stall.'

'I'd like a stroll now the rain has stopped. Stretch my legs and all that.'

She could hardly stop him from walking down the street, but she made a good pace and he smiled at her efforts.

At the stall, Mam was talking to Fred. The terrible weather kept the streets quiet, shoppers having the sense to stay home.

'Mam!' Beth called out before she was even close. Mam's frown made Beth instantly regret it. She turned to Melville. 'Thank you for bringing me into town. Good day.'

He tipped his cane to his hat and gave a small bow. 'Until we meet again, Miss Beaumont.'

Beth clenched her teeth and hoped it would never happen. She slid behind the stall and faced her mam's withering glare and folded arms.

'Firstly, do not shout in the street. You were not dragged up in the gutter. Secondly, what on earth were you doing with Louis Melville?'

'He kindly offered me a seat in his carriage. It was raining so hard.'

'He offered?' she asked incredulously.

'Yes, he did. I didn't take it upon myself to climb in his carriage without invitation I can assure you!' She shook the bottom of her coat which was terribly wet.

'Don't be sassy with me, girl,' Mam snapped.

'Sorry.'

'Why would he take you in his carriage?'

'He likes me.' Beth couldn't face her mam so moved some of the onions about a bit.

'Likes you?'

'Perhaps.'

'You're not making sense, girl.'

'I don't know what else to tell you. Louis Melville has taken an interest in me, but I haven't encouraged him.'

'Then maybe you should.'

Beth whipped around and stared at her. 'Encourage him?'

'Aye. He's the son of one of the wealthiest men in the district. You'd never need for anything ever again.'

'You would be happy for me to marry Louis Melville? Everyone hates the Melvilles.'

'Not everyone don't be foolish and imagine the life you'd lead.'

Beth wondered if she knew her mother at all. 'I love Noah.'

Mam tutted and glanced away. 'That's not love. You don't understand the first meaning of love. And love doesn't provide you with coal and food and a roof over your head. Money does that and the Melville family has it in spades.'

'You would have me marry him for his money even though I don't even like him?'

'You got in his carriage, didn't you?'

'Because it was raining and I didn't want my hat and coat to become more ruined than they already are, as I know how you'd react to that!'

'Don't you raise your voice to me, girl,' Mam whispered harshly, even though no one was near stall. 'Becoming Melville's wife would set you up for life. You'd live in the manor and have servants. Can you imagine never having to lift a finger to do manual work again?'

'Is that what is important?' She didn't understand her mam sometimes.

'Aye, of course it is. The Beaumonts do well. We aren't poor, we have land and a nice house, but you can do even better if Melville wants you. Think about that. Your children would be raised as gentry.'

'I don't want to think about it. I love Noah. I want Noah.'

'And live in a tiny house on the low wages of a teacher?'

'Being a teacher's wife is admirable. You've been a farmer's wife for twenty-five years and you've lived a happy life, haven't you?'

'It's been hard work, girl.' Mam gazed out over the street. 'I just want you to grab any opportunity that comes your way.'

190

'As you did?'

'Pardon?'

'You married up, didn't you? A miner's daughter marrying into the Beaumonts who have a sizeable farm.'

'Aye, I suppose you can say I married up, and if you have the opportunity to do the same then I suggest you do. Make use of having an education and being brought up decently. With a bit of polish, you'd be a fine asset to the Melville family.'

'Similar to a pedigree horse?' Beth laughed. 'A bit of polish!'

'This isn't joke, Beth. This is your future we are discussing. You could become someone important in that family. You would be the mother of the next heir, which is why I encourage you to take this seriously.'

'You didn't encourage Joanna to marry a wealthy man.'

'She didn't have the opportunity you do. Melville didn't take an interest in her, but he has in you. You're a pretty lass. Take advantage of it, you'd be a fool not to.'

'I can't marry him, Mam, not when I love Noah.'

'You'll regret it.'

'Did you regret not marrying Leo Jackson?'

Mam paled. 'I don't know what you're talking about.'

'If he hadn't got Peggy pregnant, you might have married him. A poor miner. You'd be living in a damp two-up and two-down as the Jacksons do. You'd have to work at the mill to make ends meet. You would have endured all that because you loved Leo. Would you have given him up for a better life?'

'I didn't have the choice. You do.' Mam's frown deepened as Joanna came up the street, basket on her arm. 'Why are you out in this weather in your condition?'

Joanna gave a kiss on the cheek to Mam and then Beth. 'I wanted to see how Beth got on at the funeral and I needed a few bits.'

'Couldn't it have waited until it stopped raining?'

'It had stopped at home.' Joanna turned to Beth. 'So how did it go?'

'Sad as all funerals are. The rain didn't help.'

'How's Noah and his family?'

'Coping. Peggy Jackson looked terrible because of her bad chest. Sid has his leg in a brace and is on crutches. Albie was limping. It was a sorry sight to see them carrying their dad in the torrential rain.'

Mam grabbed her bag from under the stall. 'I'm away home. I'll catch the tram and send Will to collect you, Beth. I'll call and see you tomorrow, Joanna.' Without a backwards glance Mam walked up the street.

'What's up with Mam?' Joanna picked an apple and bit into it.

'We didn't see eye to eye on something.'

'What have you done now?'

'I've done nothing wrong.'

'Tell me.' Joanna sat on a stool and waited expectantly.

'Louis Melville wants to court me.'

Joanna's eyes popped and her mouth fell open. 'Never!'

'Lord, don't act too surprised.'

'Louis Melville? I'd never have thought that, not in a million years. He's not in our realm, so to speak, is he? I mean, he's gentry. And he's picked you? I can't believe it. He can have anyone.'

Beth's expression grew incredible. 'Thanks, you are making me sound like a bit of tat in a bottom drawer.'

'Well, let's face it. A Melville? I wouldn't even imagine he knew you existed, never mind asking you to go courting.'

She sagged against the stall. 'It does seem a joke, doesn't it?'

'Are you sure it's not?'

'No, he is earnest, terribly so. He likes my spirit, apparently. Which is odd as whenever we've been near each other we've done nothing but argue.'

'Perhaps some men like the challenge? I would think the women in his society would be rather dull, all afternoon teas and dressing appointments and charity functions.'

'I'm none of that.'

'No, definitely not.'

'Mam says I should accept him and forget Noah.'

Joanna bit into the apple a thoughtful expression on her face. 'I see Mam's side of it. She'd want to you to be taken care of.'

'Noah will do that.'

'He's a miner and look where you've been this morning. Miners don't always make old bones, you know.'

'He's going to be a teacher.'

'Aye, well, that is a better prospect I suppose, but it's nothing on the wealth of the Melvilles, is it?'

'I don't even like Louis Melville. He's been horrible to me in the past.'

Joanna stared at her. 'What do you mean?'

Regretting her slip of the tongue, Beth shrugged. 'We've bumped into each other along the lanes and he's been on his big horse taking up all the road...'

'And you've lost your temper I gather.' Joanna shook her head.

'He's so... arrogant. I couldn't stand being married to such a man.'

Taking another bite, Joanna shrugged. 'Then forget about him. Marry Noah in the spring as you plan to. Besides, Noah is far more handsome than Melville, even if he is poor.'

'Would you marry for love or wealth?'

Joanna grinned. 'Love every time. Who doesn't want to be held by a man who adores you? It's better than sharing a bed with someone you don't like even if the bed sheets are silk.'

Beth laughed. 'I don't need silk bed sheets.'

'Nah. You'd only slip straight out of bed every time you rolled over!'

Despite the chilly rain, and Mam's mood, Beth felt light-hearted. Joanna always gave her something to laugh over. Mam might not be happy for her to marry Noah, but she knew he was the only man for her, rich or poor.

Chapter Thirteen

In the grey light of dawn, Noah sat at the kitchen table, nursing a cup of black tea because no one had thought to buy milk from the milkman. His cup held no sugar either, as no one had thought to visit the grocers and buy staples. They relied so much on their mam doing everything. It wasn't good enough, he'd have to have a word with his brothers, but he had bigger concerns to worry about.

He winced as his mam's coughing drifted down the stairs. He'd heard her during the night when he'd woken from a nightmare of being buried alive in a coffin and no one heard his calls for help. He'd woken drenched in sweat and couldn't get back to sleep afterwards.

The hall door opened, and Sid hobbled in, pain etched on his face.

'I'd have brought you in a cup of tea if you'd hollered.' Noah poured him a cup from the teapot. 'I thought you were still asleep.'

'I can't sleep, not with this thing.' Sid scowled down at the metal and leather leg brace.

'Are you hungry?'

'Starving.'

Noah stood and placed the frying pan on the range's hot plate ready to fry some scraps of bacon. He gave the remaining loaf of bread to Sid to slice.

'Cut it thin,' he said, while he took the pot of fat dripping from the cupboard.

Alfred, James, and Albie stepped into the kitchen, shivering with cold for their bedroom, which, like the others, didn't have a fire and ice formed inside the window and damp ran down the walls.

'I'll cook,' James said, taking over from Noah.

'We need to talk,' Noah said, placing plates around the table.

'Oh aye? What about?' Sid asked, not looking up from his task.

'Money, really, but Mam, too.'

Albie groaned. 'I should be back underground next week, Noah. My ankle should be fine by then. So, I'll be earning again.'

'Aye, but the fact of the matter is we are down four wages now. Yes, Albie you might be back at work next week, but Sid won't be, and neither will Mam. That leaves just James, Alfred and me earning. We'll cover the rent, but we're going to have to do extra shifts for food and coal.'

'We're not paying for coal,' Alfred muttered. 'I'll go out tonight and nick a bag full off the slag heaps from behind the pit.'

'And if you get caught, you've not only lost your job, but you've got a criminal record,' Noah snapped. 'I don't need the police banging on the door on top of everything else.'

'Relax, man.' Alfred waved away his concerns. 'I'll not get caught. No one is about at three in the morning.'

'It's not just coal.' Noah took two sheets of paper from the mantelpiece. 'This is the funeral bill and

Doctor Beatty's bill for seeing to Mam.' From a drawer, he took out several squares of paper. 'All these are gambling debts Dad owed. It's a lot of money.'

His brothers stared at him in shock.

'Gambling debts?' Albie gasped.

'Yes. More than I expected. Dad owed money to half of the village and loads more in town.' The amount of money Noah had added up nearly gave him a heart attack. He had no idea how they were to pay it.

'I didn't realise Dad gambled so much,' James said from the range.

'Mam kept it from us. Hal Broughton asked me after the funeral for the money Dad owed him.'

'What a time to ask. Bastard,' muttered Sid.

'He could have waited,' Alfred grumbled. 'Are not ask at all. Dad's dead. Why should we have to pay up?'

'Will the union help with the funeral bill?' Albie asked.

'I'll go and see them today. They might, but they won't pay it all.' Noah rose from the table. 'And we're paying Dad's debts because I'm not having the whole village whisper that the Jacksons don't pay up.'

'That's the last of the bacon.' James crumpled up the wax paper which the bacon came wrapped in.

The smell of sizzling bacon made Noah's stomach grumble. He'd counted the strips earlier and knew there wasn't enough for everyone. He'd go without.

Donning his coat, he pulled on his boots. Outside flurries of light snow were falling.

'What about your bacon butty?' James asked, flipping the slices.

'There's not enough.' Noah rammed his flat cap on his head. 'We're all going to have to learn how to eat less over the next few weeks. We can't be spending loads of money on food. The rent is due tomorrow.'

'Bloody hell,' Alfred muttered, sipping his tea.

Noah paused by the back door and gave Patch a scratch on the head where he sat in his box by the range.

'Have we got owt to pawn?' Sid winced as he moved his leg.

Noah sighed. 'Mam's pawned everything we had that was decent. It's double shifts for us three until the debts are paid.' Noah gazed at his sombre brothers sitting around the table. 'I'll be back in time for our night shift. Look after Mam.'

Heavy-hearted, Noah plodded along the road into the village. His scarf now lined Patch's bed for Mam had darned and reknitted it so many times that it resembled something only a beggar would wear. He'd rather be cold than look like a tramp.

Snow flurries flew into his eyes, landing on his lashes and cheeks. Hands thrust into his trouser pockets, as he walked he made a plan on what to do to get the family out of the mess they were in. A burning anger filled his chest when he thought of his dad. The selfish man had gambled with no concern to taking care of his family. All those long arduous hours they spent digging for coal had gone into his dad's pockets and out again just as quickly.

The smouldering anger fuelled his footsteps as he headed out of the village and towards the mine. First on his list was to see was the union man.

Three hours later, Noah trod through the slurry of melting snow down Brook Street, passing the market stalls until he came to Beth's. Her welcoming smile and quick embrace gladdened him somewhat after a difficult morning.

'Come and sit on a stool.' She pushed him gently to take a seat. 'I was just about to pour myself a cup of tea. You look frozen.'

'I am. I've been out all morning. I can't feel my feet any longer.'

'Bless.' She poured him a steaming cup of tea from the flask and placed in his other hand a slice of apple and blackberry pie.

The pie tasted incredible and the tea warmed him on the inside. 'Have you been busy?' he asked as she finished serving a customer.

'Extremely busy. As soon as snow starts to fall, people panic that it'll not stop, and they won't be able to get out of their houses. So, they come in droves to buy enough veg to last all week and beyond.'

Noah eyed the stall's display which had gaps in it from where they'd sold out. If only he could take some home.

Beth sat next to him on another stool. 'Tell me about your morning.'

Finishing the last of the pie, Noah took a sip of tea. He didn't know what to say to her. He was ashamed of the way his father had behaved and how poor they had become. What would she think of him and his family? He was asking her to marry into poverty

when she came from a profitable farm with everything comfortable and nice.

'Noah?' she gently prompted.

The love in her eyes made him emotional. He
cleared his throat. 'I'm going to have to work double
shifts for a while.'

'Why?'

'We have some money troubles…'

She took his hand in her gloved one. 'Can I help?'

He reared back. 'No! We'll manage. It's just a
temporary solution while Sid and Albie get back on
their feet, and Mam is still struggling with her chest.'

'But if you're working double shifts how will you
study? Your exam is in a few days.'

He couldn't meet her eyes and stared down at his
boots which needed new soles. 'I'll not be able to sit
my exam.' The admission nearly broke him.

'What? No, that can't happen, Noah.' Beth stood
and paced the small area behind the stall. 'You can't
throw away this chance. You've been studying for so
long. You must sit the exam.'

'I can't, Beth.' He stood and took her hands. 'I
can't concentrate on studying, never mind completing
an exam.'

'You're going to have to, aren't you? I won't let
you miss this opportunity, Noah. Mr Grimshaw won't
want you to either.'

'It's not up to either of you,' he snapped. Her stern
voice annoyed him. She had no idea what his life was
like.

Her eyes narrowed with anger. 'You can't throw
away your future!'

'I don't have a future right at this minute. I've nothing but debts to pay!' He instantly turned away, ashamed of what he'd revealed.

Fred on the stall next to them shook his head before lifting his newspaper higher to block them out.

'I'm sorry, Beth.' Noah's shoulders slumped. 'I'd best go.'

'What are these debts?'

'My wonderful, devoted and loving father has left us a legacy it seems.' His harsh words made her wince, but he couldn't help it. She'd never seen him so sarcastic, but his mind felt ready to explode and his chest was tight with anxiety. Beth had no idea how hard his family had to work to keep a roof over their heads. Another accident or sickness and they might easily be tossed out onto the streets.

Noah thrust his hands in his trouser pockets. 'My dad had a gambling problem. He regularly spent all our wages that we gave to Mam for food and board. She couldn't stop him. His selfishness has created such a mess. We've so many bills to pay. I'm ashamed of him. He never worked hard to see us live decently, to allow Mam to stop working at the mill.'

'Let me help you, please.' Beth's soft words filtered through his humiliation.

'No, Beth. This is my family's problem.'

'And in the spring, I will be a part of the family, won't I?'

Noah shook his head in wonderment. 'I've no idea why you'd pick me. I've nothing to offer you.'

'You offer your love, and that's all I want.' She wrapped her arms around his waist.

He held her, wishing so much could be different. 'You will always have my love, but I fear it isn't enough.'

'Do you want to marry me, Noah?'

'Aye, of course.'

'Then let me help.'

'I don't see how you can.'

'Trust me.' She touched his cheek lovingly, grinning when two old women walking past gasped at the display and muttered about standards dropping.

~ ~ ~ ~

Later that afternoon, Beth packed away the stall with Will's help, but kept a crate of vegetables separate.

'What's that for?' Will asked, loading it onto the cart.

'I want you to drop me off at Noah's house on Potoven's Lane.'

Will set Snowy off at a steady trot through the streets, the wheels squelching through the mushy, dirty snow. 'Are you really going to marry this Noah fellow then?'

'Aye, I am. Why do you ask when you know it's happening?' Beth watched a train chug by as they left town and followed the railway towards the village. She wrapped her scarf up over her face as the icy wind blew.

'I don't like the notion of you not being at home.'

She nudged him with a grin. 'It's not for months yet.'

'The farm won't be the same without you.'

'You'll miss me, will you?'

Will straightened on the seat, not making eye contact. 'Maybe. Ronnie will do more.'

Beth linked her arm through his. 'I'll not be far away.'

'It's not the same though, is it?'

She glanced at him, realising that she'd not thought about leaving her brothers behind when she married. She guessed Joanna hadn't considered her or them either. But remembering how she'd felt when Joanna married, she saw Will with fresh eyes. She and Will had a special bond and were close, always getting into scraps together when they were younger. 'I'll come back to the farm often.'

'That's what Joanna said, and she barely does. We're lucky to see her once a fortnight.'

'I'll be living closer than Joanna does.' She wondered where she might actually be living. With the Jacksons in that tiny damp house?

'In the village then?'

'Yes, likely.'

'I can come and see you all the time then?'

'Of course, you can. Besides, just think with me moving out it means you and Ronnie won't have to share a room any more.'

'I never thought of that!' He brightened as he halted Snowy in front of the Jacksons' house.

'Tell Mam I'll be home in a couple of hours. I want to check on Mrs Jackson and then I'll walk home.'

'It'll be fully dark by then,' Will warned.

'Well, you can come and meet at the top of the lane, can't you?'

'Why should I?'

She thumped his arm. 'Because I'm your sister, that's why!'

Once Will had helped her with the crate and left to go home, Beth knocked on the Jacksons' door and waited. In a few moments it was opened by Albie, still limping but smiling a welcome.

'Beth, this is a surprise.'

'Can I come in?'

'Aye, of course, but Noah isn't here. He's on the night shift.'

'I know.' She struggled into the kitchen carrying the heavy crate.

'Here let me.'

'No not with your foot.' She placed the crate on the stone-flagged floor and gave Patch an ear rub. 'How are you, boy?'

'Is that for us?' Albie gestured towards the crate of vegetables.

'It is. I'm going to make you all a stew.' She took off her coat, gloves, hat, and scarf and rolled up her sleeves. 'And you're going to help me.'

'I can't cook.'

'Then it's time you learnt. With your mam in bed, she needs good hearty meals. Wash your hands and start peeling those potatoes.' Beth unloaded the crate, taking out potatoes, carrots, onions, and turnip. She'd also bought them a five-pound bag of oats for porridge, a pound bag of sugar, tea, a jar of treacle, strawberry jam and from a neighbouring stall managed to get the last two loaves of bread. At the butchers, she bought a ham hock, a beef joint, and a large coil of sausages.

'Bloody hell!' Sid hopped into the room, his leg sticking out and his crutches tapping on the stone floor. 'Where did all that come from?'

'Watch your language!' Albie chastised. 'Beth bought it for us. Isn't she a peach!'

'It's a good job Noah's marrying you, that's all I can say.' Sid sat at the table eyeing the produce.

'Start peeling a couple of onions, Sid,' Beth instructed, searching the cupboards and finding a box of Oxo cubes, she held them up in triumph. They were exactly what she wanted for her stew. Above her head, she heard the rasping cough of Peggy Jackson.

While she cut up the turnip and carrots, Albie found her a large pot which all the vegetables could go in.

Over the next two hours, the brothers told her funny stories of them growing up as she made the stew and put it on to simmer and then made a quick batch of scones.

The hall door opened, and Peggy Jackson ambled in, bent over and wheezing, wearing a thin shawl over her nightgown and her socks had holes. Beth helped her to a chair at the table.

'What smells so nice? I smelled it from my bed.' Mrs Jackson eyed the pot on the range.

'Beef stew,' Albie supplied. 'Beth here has made it for us all. We helped to chop up the vegetables.'

'Isn't that lovely.' Mrs Jackson squeezed Beth's hand. 'What a smart fellow my boy is to choose you. We are lucky to soon have you in our family.'

'I'll put the kettle on, shall I?' Beth bustled away, embarrassed by the sentiment. It pleased her no end to have the support of Mrs Jackson.

'It's far warmer down here than upstairs, even in bed.' Mrs Jackson sighed, a handkerchief over her mouth.

'Alfred is bringing some coal home with him, Mam. We'll make you a fire as soon as he does,' Albie said, getting out cups for them all.

Beth mashed the tea in the teapot and took it to the table. 'I've got oats soaking for porridge in the morning.'

'We can have jam in our porridge in the morning. Beth bought us a jar.' Sid smiled happily like a child.

'You are too good, lass.' Mrs Jackson coughed.

'Well, we'll soon be family. It's the least I can do under the circumstances.'

'How can we repay you for all of this food?'

'You can repay me by encouraging Noah to sit his exam.'

'Why wouldn't he sit it?' Mrs Jackson frowned, and Sid and Albie paused in drinking their tea.

'He says there's too much going on right now. He needs to work double shifts and he hasn't the time or inclination to worry about studying. The thing is, he's put everything into this. We can't let him give it all up now, can we?' She looked at each one of them. 'He can't give up on his dreams of becoming a teacher.'

'I'm not having him sacrifice himself for us lot,' Sid said in annoyance. 'He'll sit that bloody exam even if I have to drag him there on one leg!'

Mrs Jackson patted Beth's hand. 'Don't you worry about it, lass. We'll make sure he sits that exam.'

Relieved, Beth sipped her tea as a knock came at the door. 'That'll be Will, my brother.' She rose and pulled on her coat. 'I'll come around tomorrow after I'm finished at the stall and see how you're getting on, Mrs Jackson.'

'Thank you, lass.'

After saying goodbye, Beth left the house and linked arms with Will as snow fell lightly, whitening the landscape and making it easier to see in the dark.

They laughed and joked, skidding on ice patches, and holding each other up as they slipped and skated down the icy lane towards home.

Beth's smile faded though as she entered the kitchen and saw her mam still up and sitting at the table, darning.

'You'd best get to bed, our Will,' Mam said, not looking up. 'You've an early start in the morning.'

'Aye. Night then.' Will left the room and Beth was about to follow him when her mam lowered her darning and stared at her.

'Why have you been so long?' Mam asked.

'I made the Jacksons a stew and some scones. Mrs Jackson is still poorly.'

'You could have made that here and taken it up tomorrow. It's not right you being there so late and not fair on Will to ask him to go out in the freezing night air to bring you home.'

'Sorry. I'll not ask him again.' Beth's answer was clipped as she tried not to be defensive.

'I've given it a great deal of thought after our talk at the stall today and I think it's best if you don't marry Noah.'

Beth gripped the back of a chair.

Mam folded away her darning into a small basket. 'And instead, I want you to accept Louis Melville.'

'I wish I had never told you about him,' she muttered. 'I'll marry Noah, Mam. We love each other. Surely you want me to be happy?'

'A Jackson won't make you happy and a Jackson doesn't know how to love someone.'

'How can you say that?'

'Because Noah is his father's son.'

'That's not fair, Noah is nothing like Leo. You know nothing about him. He doesn't gamble and works hard. He's the complete opposite.'

'At the moment maybe, but you watch. He'll turn out just like Leo. Untrustworthy and disloyal.'

'You are basing this on your history with his dad, not on Noah personally. What Leo did to you was wrong and… and sad, but—'

'Leo Jackson was a liar and a scoundrel and he's likely to have bred five replicas of himself!' Mam launched herself from the table and stood by the range, breathing heavily.

'I won't give him up.'

'Noah will hurt you.'

'No, he won't. You're being unreasonable.'

'And you're being stupid and blind.' Mam banged her hand on the mantlepiece. 'I'm trying to help you here to save you from a lifetime of misery. Look at Peggy Jackson and the state she is in. That's what happened to a pretty young lass from a good decent family. Her father was educated, a mine manager, and she's ended up fighting for every breath because she's had to work in a mill to help support her family. She could have had anyone, but Leo wormed his way into her affections and her knickers just as he did mine!'

Beth stared at her, trying to make sense of what she'd said.

Realising she'd revealed too much, her mam stumbled to sit back at the table. 'Go to bed.'

Ignoring the command, and pulling out a chair, Beth sat and gazed at her mam. 'What really happened between you and Leo Jackson?'

'Forget it.'

'No, I won't, not now. Did you give yourself to Leo?'

Mam bowed her head. 'I did, yes. I made a mistake and have regretted it ever since.'

'So, Leo was courting both you and Peggy at the same time?'

'Yes. He was making promises to both of us. I loved him dearly. He was everything to me. He made me think he loved me, too. Only, it was all a game to him. He had the two of us eating out of his hands. Peggy won because she became pregnant and told him before I had the chance to tell him…'

'Tell him what?'

'Nothing.'

'To tell him what, Mam?'

Her mam closed her eyes. 'To tell him I also was with child.'

'A child?' Beth's eyes widened in shock. 'You mean… You mean Joanna is Leo's child?'

'No!' Mam jerked in her chair. 'No. Not at all.' With tears in her eyes she stared at the doorway where her husband stood.

Dad walked into the kitchen and put his arm around his wife's shoulders. 'Your mam means the child she was carrying was taken care of... got rid of.'

Beth stared at them both. How was any of this real and she knew nothing?

Dad sat at the table next to Mam and held her hand. 'One day I found Mary, the woman I had loved for years, since we were kids,' he smiled lovingly at his wife, 'anyway, I found her ill by the side of the road. Naturally, I stopped and lifted her into the cart. Mary begged me to take her home, but she was... bleeding heavily. Blood had soaked through her skirts and I knew something serious was happening.'

'Rob, enough.'

'No, Mary. Beth needs to understand. She's the one marrying into that family. The story needs to be told.' He looked at Beth. 'Leo Jackson, back then, wasn't a decent chap. Anyway, I took Mary to Doctor Templeton, my family's doctor in Wakefield at the time.'

Her mam touched his cheek tenderly and Beth sat amazed at the display of affection for her mam wasn't one to show it. 'Your dad was my saviour. I didn't know it then, but he saved my life. Doctor Templeton managed to stop my bleeding...' She looked at Beth. 'You see I'd gone to a woman who lived down a back lane in town. She was known through whispers for what she did for girls in trouble.' Mam twisted her wedding ring on her finger. 'I got her to get rid of the baby.'

'Oh, Mam.' Beth's heart constricted for her.

'I couldn't have it. Leo and Peggy had just announced they were getting married and I heard the rumour that Peggy was with child. So, I knew Leo would pick Peggy over me. Peggy's family had status in the community with her father being a mine manager. Whereas I was only a miner's daughter. All that meant I had to get myself out of a terrible situation. To be unmarried and have a child was out of the question. Everyone would know it was Leo's. My father would have thrown me out of the house.'

'Did Leo ever find out about your condition?'

'No.' Dad squared his shoulders. 'I wanted to tell him. I actually wanted to ram my fist down his throat on many occasions, but it wouldn't have done any good. Leo Jackson wouldn't have cared. He was cock-a-hoop about marrying Peggy. Her father promised them a lovely new house, rent free.'

Beth found it hard to imagine this was her mother's past. 'I'm sorry Leo treated you so badly, Mam.'

Mam grimaced. 'Yes, well, it was a long time ago and he is dead. I had thought the ghosts would die with him but now you bring another Jackson into the family…'

'This is why your mam has been acting like this towards you ever since you started walking out with Noah.'

'But it's not Noah's fault, or mine. Why punish us?'

'We aren't.' Dad took both of Mary's hands in his, his gaze never leaving his wife's. 'No more, Mary. It's done. Over. Leo is dead. You're to give your blessing to our Beth and Noah.'

'But—'

'No, buts. From what I can see Noah is a good fellow. No one has anything bad to say about him. He's not his father.'

'She still could do better,' Mam argued. 'Beth has the chance to move up in the world.'

Beth stood. 'Noah is the man I want, Mam. No one else. Please give me your good wishes on this.'

Mam sighed deeply. 'Very well. Marry him then and on your head be it.'

Disappointed that there weren't any words of comfort, Beth walked to the door. 'Good night.'

She would say no more. She left her parents in the kitchen and climbed the stairs feeling weary and out of sorts. What Leo did to her mam was shameful and nasty, but Noah wasn't anything like his dad, and nor would he ever be.

Should she tell Noah what happened to their parents? Or was it a secret she should keep from him? He didn't have a good opinion of his father as it was, this would only further sully his thoughts about the man. She didn't like to think that she'd have secrets from him, but the alternative was to reveal her mother's past actions, too.

The dilemma made her toss and turn in bed, not able to fall asleep as quickly as she usually did.

She felt so naive. Not once had she thought of her parents as children. Obviously, she'd been aware her dad had grown up in a comfortable well-off family, and her mam had been a coal miner's daughter. How different would Beth's life have been if her mam had married Leo Jackson and not Rob Beaumont? Beth would be in the mill alongside Jane. She wouldn't have this lovely bedroom and a wardrobe of pretty dresses.

Her childhood had been idyllic. True, she and her siblings had worked hard at the jobs around the farm that her parents believed they could manage as they grew older, but the Beaumonts were a successful farming family, which meant they never went without food or warmth, good clothes or an education.

The Beaumont children never had the fear of going to work down the pit or at the mill at the age of twelve or going to bed hungry. Their family had the money to employ workers on the farm in summer and Mam was talking of employing a girl to work in the house to help with the cleaning now that Joanna had left and Aunty Hilda was getting older.

Beth had taken it all for granted. Her world consisted of the farm and the stall and her own amusements all bathed in the luxury of having a loving family and a decent home. Yet tonight she learnt how her mam had suffered in the past and why she never gossiped and kept her own counsel. It was also why she pushed for Beth to consider Louis Melville, so she'd want for nothing. Marriage to a Melville would mean Beth would never have to live in a cramp house and watch every penny.

Beth punched her pillow and turned over. Noah would be a teacher, she was sure of it. He wasn't like his father. He'd never cast her aside.

Chapter Fourteen

Laughing, Beth grabbed Jane's arm as they slipped on the icy puddles. The country lanes between Wrenthorpe and Alverthorpe were thick with snow.

'You'll have me over in a minute,' Jane protested, her basket swinging wildly. 'And if I lose all that lovely veg your mam gave me, I'll not be happy.'

Steadying herself, Beth concentrated on stepping in previous tracks worn down by farmers and animals. 'It's going to snow again any minute.'

'Turn back. I'm serious. I can make my own way home.'

'I said I'll walk halfway with you. Besides, we've not had much chance to talk, not with playing cards all afternoon with our Will and Ronnie.'

'It was nice. I've not had a Sunday dinner like that in a long time. Grandad eats like a bird now, so we cook small meals. I can't remember the last time I had a bit of lamb.'

'Well come again next weekend.'

'I can't. I promised Alfie I'd spend it with him and his family.'

'Are you two getting serious?'

Jane nodded and stopped walking. 'I've wanted to tell you for weeks, but you've been busy with Noah's family.'

'I'm sorry. Mrs Jackson has been so bad with her chest and Noah is working all hours. I barely see him, and I only do if I go to his house.'

'Aye. Aye, I know all that and it's fine, truly. But I wanted to tell you that Alfie and I are getting wed.'

'Oh, Jane!' Beth hugged her friend to her, laughing with happiness. 'When?'

'Saturday, December thirteenth.'

'Wow. That's only weeks away.'

'Alfie didn't want to wait and nor did I.'

'I'm so happy for you. You should have said at the house. Mam would have been pleased to hear it.'

'Aye, well I wanted to speak to you first as I want to ask if you'll be my bridesmaid?'

'Of course!' Beth enveloped her in another embrace. 'You're going to make me cry!'

'I'll leave it up to you what you want to wear, but what you wore to Joanna's wedding is pretty. You'll look better than me.' Jane's face fell. 'I'll have a new blouse but me gran says she'll just add lace over her best tablecloth to make me a skirt and that'll save money on a wedding dress.'

'No, Jane. You can't do that.' Beth took Jane's hands. 'Listen. Let me buy you a wedding dress.'

'No, Beth. Your mam will go mad and your saving up for your own wedding. I don't need anything fancy, really, I don't. Gran will make my skirt look wonderful and I'm splashing out on a new blouse. I'll try and get one with a bit of extra lace on that, too.'

'You'll do no such thing. If you won't let me buy you a dress, then you'll wear the bridesmaid dress I wore for Joanna's wedding. What do you think?'

'Beth…' Jane's eyes filled with tears. 'That dress is beautiful.'

'And now it's yours.' Beth grinned as snowflakes fell on them like powder. 'I'll bring it over next Saturday once I've closed the stall. Now this weather has set in Dad wants the stall closed by eleven on a Saturday, so I'll come straight over.'

'You're the best friend ever.' Jane kissed her cheeks. 'Wish Noah good luck from me for tomorrow. I hope he passes.'

'I'll tell him. Bye.' Head down against the flurries wafting over her face, Beth turned and retraced her footsteps towards the village and home. The fields between the two villages were white, hiding ditches and paths and so she stayed on the main lane coming out of Alverthorpe, not trusting to cut across the fields in case she fell into a beck or a ditch.

Her thoughts, as always, turned to Noah. He'd been working so many hours down the pit that she'd hardly seen him for any length of time, but she called into the Jacksons each afternoon to check on Peggy and Sid. Albie was back underground now, so Beth did odd jobs around the house to ease the burden on them. Peggy, although better, still couldn't work and Noah mentioned daily that he didn't want his mam back at the mill.

Beth sighed, wishing Noah was with her now. She missed him. For when he wasn't working, he was studying. His brothers refused to allow him to not sit the exam and between her and them and his mam, he'd given in to their demands and continued his studying again.

Tomorrow he was to sit the exam at the grammar school, and Joanna had promised to mind the stall for Beth so she could wait for him to come out once he'd finished.

She smiled to herself as she walked, feeling the icy flakes land on her cheeks. Last night, Noah had walked her home from his house, and they'd kissed all the way down the lane. By the time they reached the farm gate, she was breathless, and he was tense with frustration, wanting more than just kisses. Her skin tingled. What would it be like to do more than just kiss with Noah? The thought made her blush.

The jingle of harness and a horse's snort made Beth turn. A carriage came slowly along the lane, its wheels crunching in the snow.

She groaned, recognising it to be the Melville carriage. She hoped it was old Mr Melville inside and not Louis but as the horse slowed, her hopes died. Louis climbed down from the carriage and trudged through the snow to her.

'Miss Beaumont. I am surprised to see you out in this weather. What is it with you walking in all the elements?' He chuckled.

'I was walking back from my friend's house.' She wanted to add that unlike him she didn't have a carriage at her disposal.

'Please, allow me to take you home.' He glanced up as the snow fell harder, quickly reducing visibility. 'Please, I insist. It's treacherous out here.'

He had a point, though she was annoyed the weather had changed so suddenly. 'Thank you, Mr Melville. That is kind of you.'

'We need to go, sir,' the carriage driver called. 'We'll soon not be able to see our way and the horse could stumble and break a leg.'

'Yes, yes. We are coming.' Melville took Beth's elbow and they half ran to the carriage as a strong wind whipped up out of nowhere, swirling the snow into their faces.

Gasping, they entered the carriage.

'Good heavens.' Melville took off his hat and knocked the snow off it.

'It's so wild out there now,' Beth spoke as the carriage lurched into motion.

'Here, put this around your legs.' Melville gave her a thick blanket. 'I didn't expect this weather. It's not snowing in London.'

'You're just returned from there?'

'Yes. Well, I've been to Oxford as well, to see an old professor of mine who has been ill recently.'

'Sir?' The flap opened above their heads. 'Is it Melville Manor or to this lady's home?'

Louis stared out of the window. The storm had blocked the view of the landscape. 'Melville Manor, Bell, if you please. It's closer.'

'Oh, but…'

Melville held up his hand. 'I promise the minute the weather clears, Bell will take you home. But my home is just down the way.'

'I know where you live.' Beth smarted at his decision making.

'I can send a servant to try and get to your farm and inform your parents that you are safe?'

'No, there's no need. They'll think I've stayed with Jane. I'll go home the minute the storm passes.'

'In that case, I'll be honoured to give you a tour of my home while you wait and perhaps, we may indulge ourselves in a nice cup of tea and a piece of Mrs Handry's delicious cake?'

Beth gave him a tight smile. She had no wish to spend time with Melville but a devilish part of her wanted to see inside the manor, a large house she'd only ever seen from the road. She also wanted to eat some of Mrs Handry's cake, who she knew was the manor's cook and who had won many ribbons at the village fair in the cake baking competition.

A butler opened the door and came hurrying out with an umbrella, which the wind nearly blew out of his hands. Melville took Beth's arm and rushed her inside where they shook themselves like a dog with a wet coat.

'Goodness.' Melville smoothed down his oiled hair when they had given over their outdoor clothes. 'How utterly awful that weather is. Come, let us go into the drawing room.'

Beth glimpsed at the large entrance hall with its polished timber flooring and dark green wallpaper. A carpeted staircase curved up to the floor above, but the drawing room took her interest. The room held a blazing fire in the fireplace, sending out welcoming heat.

'Mr Melville, sir,' the butler stood in the doorway, 'on receiving your telegram about your return, I have instructed cook to set a menu for yourself. I did not anticipate you'd be having a guest. Shall I have a room made ready?'

'No, thank you, Staines. Miss Beaumont will be returning home as soon as the blizzard passes. Have a

219

message sent to the stables for them to be prepared. Do send in afternoon tea, will you?'

'Very good, sir.' The butler gave Beth a sharp look, bowed and closed the door behind him.

'Are you warm enough?'

Beth nodded. 'Yes, thank you.'

'What do you think to this room?' Melville asked her. 'And do sit down, please.'

Beth sat on the edge of a blue damask sofa near the fire. The room was light and airy, filled with several occasional tables and the odd gilded chair. Imposing paintings of serious-faced ancestors studded the cream walls. A tall mirror hung above the fireplace.

'It's a nice room.' She couldn't lie. No expense had been spared in the decorating of the room. She imagined the sun streaming through the tall windows, its beams dancing on the porcelain figurines and crystal bowls in the cabinet on the far wall.

'After tea, I'll show you the rest of the house.'

Beth prayed the tea would come soon.

'I tried to see if your farm was visible from the attic windows. I'm certain it is. If you don't mind the climb to the attics you might be able to advise me if I am correct or not?'

She didn't know how to respond to that. He'd gone up into the attic to look for her home. How odd. She gave him a tight smile as the door opened and Staines brought in a tea tray. The silver service gleamed, and the slices of cake looked lush and delightful. The small plate of pale macaroons also seemed rather tempting.

'Leave us, Staines.'

'Yes, sir.' Again, the butler gave Beth a puzzled stare before leaving the room.

Alone with Melville, Beth watched him pour out the tea and pass her a cup. The pretty flowered cup and saucer were so delicate, she was sure she'd break the little handle.

'Tell me about yourself,' Melville inquired, sitting back, and crossing one leg over the other.

'You already know of my family.'

'Yes, I do, but I want to appreciate you better. Do you like to read or draw or paint?'

'I enjoy reading. I'm not particularly good at drawing and haven't painted at all since I was a child.'

'Can you play the piano?'

'No.'

'Do you like riding?'

'I can ride my brother's bicycle. I enjoy that.' She wondered if it was rude to just pick up a slice of cake.

'A bicycle?' Melville's eyes widened. 'How fascinating. I have never done that. I had meant riding a horse.'

'Really? You've never rode a bicycle?'

'No. I do not own a bicycle. Should I buy one?'

'I don't know. Perhaps, but only if you have the time to ride it. My mam doesn't think I should ride one. She says it's not ladylike.' Beth shrugged and not caring about manners, picked up the cake plate and using the little fork began eating the delicious carrot cake.

'I shall purchase one and ask you to teach me to ride.' His eyes watched her every movement.

Beth had difficulty swallowing the delicious cake. 'I wouldn't be allowed.'

Melville sipped his tea and then placed it back on the tray. 'Shall we have that tour?'

Having no reason to say no, Beth gave up her cake. Surely it was bad manners on his part to not let her finish? Still, she smoothed down her skirt and followed him out of the room.

For the next twenty minutes she dutifully nodded and made polite comments on each downstairs room he presented. The house was large and well-cared for, naturally. She spotted the odd maid, but other than that the rooms were quiet, lifeless.

She had a terrible thought he was going to show her every bedroom upstairs, too, but instead he merely showed her one guest room with its view over the fields and then they climbed a narrow flight of wooden stairs up to the attic, which was half fitted out for the female servants and the other half were storage rooms.

In one freezing cold storage room, Melville led her over to the window and from the sill took up a spying glass and handed it to her. 'Look to the right.'

It took her several moments to adjust her sight to make out a small white square in the shallow valley. 'Maybe, yes.' She wasn't sure.

He took it from her, beaming. 'I was correct! I focused on Wrenthorpe Village and then trained my eyes down to the left. I'm certain it's your farm.'

She shrugged uncertainly. 'It's a lovely view.'

Melville watched her closely and stood too near for her liking.

'Look, the blizzard is easing.' She quickly turned for the door not waiting for him.

Once down in the entrance hall, she glanced around for Staines so she could ask for her coat.

'Wait, Miss Beaumont. Come sit down while I have the carriage brought around for you. The snow is still falling.'

'No, I can wait here, thank you. I just need my coat. I can walk. I must get home before the lanes are impassable.'

'Nonsense, you cannot walk out in that. There will be drifts. It's dangerous. I insist on the carriage.'

It would sound childish to refuse. 'Very well. Thank you.'

Hearing voices, Staines appeared and was given his instructions.

'Come by the fire, Miss Beaumont.'

Trying not to sigh, Beth joined him by the fire and watched the flames.

'What do you think of Melville Manor, Miss Beaumont?'

'It's a beautiful house.'

'I agree. However, it is ready for a mistress, children.'

Beth shivered.

'My sister remains in London a great deal of the time and my father enjoys an apartment in Amsterdam. He is rarely here. My wife will have full control over the house and staff.'

She couldn't look at him.

'Miss Beaumont…' Melville stepped closer, forcing her to look at him. 'I would dearly… What I mean is, it would be my greatest wish for you to become my wife. I admire you enormously. As my wife you would want for nothing, I promise you.'

'I'm sorry, Mr Melville, but it isn't possible. I've told you.'

'But why? Please, think about it.' He swept his arms out wide. 'All this would be yours. We have a townhouse in London which we can visit whenever you want to go to the theatre and shopping. By becoming my wife look at the advantages which you could bestow on your family, who you can visit every day if you wish. Your brothers might wish to go to university? I would pay for that. I could aid your father's business. I know he sends his rhubarb to London. I have many contacts there. With my help the demand might easily double or even triple his output.'

'Your offer is very generous, Mr Melville. Any other girl would jump at the chance…'

'Please think about it, yes?'

Staines knocked on the open door. 'The carriage is ready, sir.'

Beth hurried out to the front door and grabbed her coat, scarf and gloves and hat from Staines and pulled them on as fast as she could, noting the warmth of them. They must have been hanging by a fire somewhere.

'Miss Beaumont may I call on you tomorrow?' Melville asked, standing behind her.

'Um…er, no, not tomorrow. I'm not home.' Her mind went blank trying to find an excuse.

Awkwardly, Beth stuck out her hand for Melville to shake. 'Thank you for your hospitality. Goodbye.'

In a flash, she was out the door and into the carriage. She closed her eyes as the horses pulled away. She felt like she'd escaped prison.

As the horses struggled through the drifts of snow covering the lanes to her home, Beth was remorseful for putting them into danger. Yet for the whole journey her mind replayed the visit to the manor. Why wouldn't Melville take no for an answer? How many more times must she tell him? She'd been as blunt as possible. He was like a dog with a bone, never letting go.

The carriage driver stopped the horses outside of the farm's gates and she scrambled down and thanked him. He grunted in response and she didn't blame him.

Will and Ronnie were shovelling snow off the drive down beside the house so the cart was able to get in and out.

'We thought you might stay at Jane's the night,' Will said, pushing the shovel into the snow.

'Whose carriage was that?' Ronnie's eyes widened with interest.

'Beth!' Mam called from the path.

Swallowing a groan, Beth trudged inside. In the scullery she knocked the snow off her boots and took off her coat.

'That was the Melville carriage, wasn't it?' Mam asked.

'Yes.'

'What were you doing in that?'

'Mr Melville offered me a lift as the blizzard hit as I was leaving Jane.'

'And?'

Beth hung up her hat and scarf. 'He allowed me to wait out the blizzard at Melville Manor.'

'The manor? You were in his house?' Mam was incredulous.

'Is there a problem with that?'

'A problem? Do you want to be the talk of the town?'

Beth followed her mam into the kitchen.

Aunty Hilda sat at the table cutting vegetables. 'What's gone on now?'

'She's spent the blizzard at Melville Manor, that's what.'

'What's it like?' Aunty Hilda asked. 'Is it very fancy?'

'It's a lovely house.' Beth watched her mam's face, which looked ready to explode. 'I don't understand your concerns, Mam.'

'No, you wouldn't because you breeze through each day without any thought to the consequences of your actions.'

'I've not done anything wrong.'

'Was his sister there?'

'No. She was in London.'

'Was anyone else there?'

'Some maids and the butler.'

'I know Staines,' Aunty Hilda piped up, cutting carrots. 'His father was a right nice man, too.'

'People will talk.' Mam went to the range and added more coal.

'There is nothing to talk about.'

'A young lass doesn't go to a wealthy man's house alone, Beth. Have some sense. Did he mention anything about his intentions?'

'Intentions?' Aunty Hilda gasped.

Beth longed to be upstairs in her room. 'Yes, he did. He wants me to be mistress of Melville Manor. To be Mrs Louis Melville.'

'No, I never!' Aunty Hilda rocked back in the chair as though slapped.

'Oh aye,' Mam's tone was brimming with sarcasm. 'This one gets an offer to be the next Mrs Melville of Melville Manor and she turns him down to marry a miner. Can you believe it? Because I certainly can't.'

Beth's temper rose. 'That's not fair, Mam. You know I love Noah.'

'But it wasn't Noah you were with this afternoon was it?'

'You are making it sound like I was up to no good with Melville,' Beth snapped.

'Don't you raise your voice at me, madam.' Mam banged a pot. 'You're thinking with your heart not your head. Can you imagine the life you'd have with Melville? Can you? You'll never want for anything. You could help your brothers in some way, get them ahead.'

'Why is that my responsibility?'

'I'm not saying it is. I'm saying you have the opportunity to do some good for your family.'

'We are fine as we are. We don't need Melville money. My brothers will inherit this farm. They don't need me to whore myself to Melville to—' The slap to her cheek from her mam's hand surprised Beth. In shock, she stared at her mam.

'Mary!' Aunty Hilda gasped.

'Hey, what's all this!' Dad stood in the doorway to the scullery. 'What's the shouting all about?'

Mam, her lips tight with anger, stormed out of the kitchen and upstairs.

'Beth?' Dad asked.

Her cheek burning, Beth lifted her chin, anger pulsing through her body. 'Louis Melville wants me to marry him. I've said no. I love Noah. Mam believes I'm making the wrong choice and that I should think how being married to him could help our Will and Ronnie. I said no. Mam slapped me.'

'I'm sorry, lass.' Dad closed his eyes momentarily and sighed deeply.

Beth shrugged, fist clenched.

Dad leaned against the door jamb unable to come in as his boots were caked with snow. 'Melville? That's a turn up for the books, isn't it?'

'I don't want him or his manor,' Beth said, teeth clenched. 'I just want Noah.'

'And turn away from the Melville fortune?'

Beth stared at him. 'You think I should marry him for his money, too?'

'No, lass, not at all. Money isn't everything.' Dad gave her an affectionate smile. 'Marry Noah if you love him.' He walked back outside.

Aunty Hilda added the cut carrots to a pot. 'Noah will give you lovely looking babies. Melville... his eyes are too close together.' She glanced up. 'Put some snow on that cheek.'

'I'll be fine.' Beth rolled her eyes and plodded upstairs to her room and closed the door. She heard her mam in the bedroom opposite, slamming wardrobe doors.

Was she always going to be at odds with her mam? Just once she'd like her mam to hold her hand and say she was happy for her, whatever she decided.

Louis over Noah. Mam made it out to be so simple. It wasn't. Louis repulsed her and her heart nearly lifted out of her chest when she thought of Noah. Money would never replace Noah's love.

At that moment all she wanted was Noah's arms around her.

Chapter Fifteen

Noah left the lamp shed, where the men hung up their lamps after each shift. The murky and cold December afternoon made him shiver after the heat of underground.

Men were collecting wages and having a smoke as the union man chatted to them in groups. Noah was too tired to hang around. After working a shift and a half, he was ready for his bed. For a moment he contemplated even forgoing a bath but no, that would be filthy.

For the last four weeks, he'd done six days in a row of extra shifts and his body ached with an energy-sapping fatigue he'd never experienced before.

'Hold up, Noah,' Harold, the foreman called to him.

Sighing, Noah waited for him to cross the yard. All he wanted was to get home. 'What can I do for you, Harold?'

Harold grimaced. 'You're not to come in tomorrow, lad.'

Noah stiffened. 'What? Have I been sacked?'

'No, now hear me out. You're working too much, it's no good.'

'I need the money.'

'Aye, I know you're going to be short a wage after the accident but working yourself into the ground isn't going to help and we're worried you being so tired will cause another accident.'

Annoyance filled Noah's voice. 'I've never been the cause for anything to go wrong underground.'

'Aye, aye, and that's how we want it to stay. You're to have two days off, lad. Get some sleep. Rest. Come back on Monday refreshed. Yes?'

'I'm fine to work tomorrow and I'll rest on Sunday.'

'No.' Harold shook his head, frowning at him. 'Monday and not before.' He walked away to prevent further discussion.

Noah swore under his breath and walked the road to Wrenthorpe. He'd budgeted on that extra eighteen hours of work tomorrow. He still had so much to pay. James and Alfred were only working eighteen hours when it suited them. Half the time they had some flimsy excuse of things they needed to do after shift and wouldn't work the extra hours. Did they all expect him to pay off the debts by himself? He needed to have a strong word with them.

Walking into the village, his boots squelched through the dirty slush left by the snow as it melted. Recent rain had turned the whiteness of the snow showers they'd had on and off for weeks into a dismal grey bleakness. He hated winter.

'Noah!' Beth ran towards him and behind her stood Mr Grimshaw.

Noah smiled for Beth, but his stomach clenched looking at Mr Grimshaw.

His results. He'd forgotten all about them. Sitting the second exam had been a blur. So much had been playing on his mind that the exam hadn't taken a priority as it should, and he believed he'd failed so he had put it from his mind.

'This is a pleasant surprise,' he said as Beth reached him and kissed him, mucky face, and all.

'I couldn't wait until Sunday to see you.' She tucked her arm into his.

'I'm filthy, Beth.' Her beautiful face radiated with happiness and something else he couldn't name but it made him feel better. His tiredness receded a little as she beamed up at him. He'd missed seeing her. In the last few weeks, he'd only been able to catch the odd hour with her before he had to sleep or work. Damn his bloody father and his debts.

'Noah, it's good to see you.' Mr Grimshaw shook Noah's hand. 'I met your delightful young lady at your home. Miss Beaumont was leaving at the same time as I knocked on the door. She told me you were working, and we decided to walk together to meet you.'

'It's a pleasure to see you, Mr Grimshaw.' Noah was ashamed he'd not made time to see his tutor since the day he sat the exam last month.

'I hear you're working all hours, Noah. That's a grim life.'

'Has to be done, I'm afraid.'

'Well, not for much longer we hope.' Mr Grimshaw took out a buff envelope from his pocket. 'This is for you.'

Noah stared at the envelope. His future lay with what was inside it.

'Open it,' Beth urged.

His hands shook as he ripped the top of the envelope. He paused for a moment before pulling out the sheet of paper inside. He couldn't focus on the words. They all jumbled together, and he was so tired he couldn't make them out. Wordlessly, he handed it back to Mr Grimshaw who quickly read it and suddenly grinned.

'You did it, Noah!' His tutor shook his hand vigorously. 'I knew you would.'

'I did?' The blood drained form his face, with the shock of passing and the tiredness in his legs turned to jelly, and he leaned against a garden wall of someone's house. 'I can't believe it.'

'I'm so proud of you.' Beth rained kissed on his face and he laughed.

'Come and see me when you can, Noah, and we'll discuss your future. Well done. Really, well done!' Mr Grimshaw, grinning, strode away.

Beth gripped his arm as he leaned against the garden wall. 'As if you'd fail. Not you!'

'I wish I'd had your faith in me.' He didn't know what to think or feel. The future he wanted, had planned for, was now his to claim. Yet, he wasn't able to, not yet. He couldn't afford to spend thirty weeks attending college in Leeds. He needed to be earning down the pit working extra shifts.

'I wonder what school you'll teach at after college? Mr Grimshaw's? Or perhaps private tutoring?'

He grasped Beth's hand. 'It'll have to wait. I can't afford to leave the pit just now.'

She pulled back to look at him fully. 'Noah, the pit is dangerous. This is your chance to get out of there.'

'I know but I need the money to pay the debts first.'

'Then let your brothers do their share. I just had a right go at James, sitting around all afternoon when he could have been down there working alongside you.'

'What was his excuse?'

'He had to go to football training!' she fumed. 'I'm sorry but that's not a good enough excuse. They are letting you take on all the extra shifts to pay this money while they're doing nothing to help.'

'I'm going to talk to them.' Noah pushed himself away from the wall. 'Are you coming back home with me?'

'No.' She sighed heavily. 'I've to go home and your brothers are annoyed with me because I spoke my mind earlier.'

He kissed her gently. 'I can fight my own battles, sweetheart. Leave my brothers to me.'

'Will I see you on Sunday?' she asked, holding his hand as they walked past St Anne's Church and to the top of Trough Well Lane, where Beth would leave him to walk down the lane to the farm.

'I'm not back at the pit until Monday,' he told her.

'Monday?' Her eyebrows rose. 'But I thought you were working tomorrow, too.'

'No, not any longer.'

'That's wonderful.'

'So, I'll see you tomorrow afternoon? I'll pick you up from the stall and we'll go have tea somewhere and—' His words were cut off as she kissed him.

'Yes, yes,' she said. 'It feels like forever since we've spent any time together.'

Someone walked by and whistled at them.

Beth stood back, smiling. 'I'll see you tomorrow.'

'I'll plan for somewhere we can go where we won't be disturbed,' Noah said, aching to hold this wonderful girl of his and kiss her properly.

'I'll be counting down the hours.' She reached up to kiss him once more.

'And we'll set a date for our wedding too,' Noah called as she walked down the lane.

She spun back, her smile wide, which lifted his heart just as much as the letter in his hand did.

He watched her for a while until his feet grew numb with cold and she was close to the farm gates. Then he turned for home.

Stepping into the scullery, the aromas of some kind of roasting meat hit him, and his stomach growled. Patch jumped up at him and he stroked his head and made a fuss of him. A bath had been filled and his mam came through and poured a kettle of boiling water into the tin bath.

'Were have you been? I've been trying to keep this hot for you.'

'Sorry.' He stripped off his clothes until he stood in his underpants.

'Were you with Beth?'

'Aye, and Mr Grimshaw.'

'Oh?'

'I'll tell you in a minute, let me get washed.'

His mam stood stirring a pot of something on the stove and she gave him a smile as he came in ten minutes later, clean and wearing the clothes she'd left for him. He dried his hair on a towel as he sat at the table.

'Where are the others?' he asked as his mam passed him a cup of tea.

'Sid is with Meg at her house. He's been there hours. The reverend is visiting apparently to talk about the banns. They need to be quick for Meg is showing. Everyone can see she's with child.' She checked the ham roasting in the oven. 'The other three have gone to the Malt Shovel.'

'They've gone to the pub? How can they afford that?' His brothers had no sense!

'Calm down. They've already had an ear bashing from your Beth.'

'They deserve one.'

'Well, they didn't take it well coming from a scrap of a lass. You two aren't married yet, you know.'

His hackles rose. 'She's been taking care of us all for weeks. Without her none of us would have been eating as well as we have.' He broke off as the back door opened and his brothers walked in, even Sid hopped in behind them on his crutches.

'I thought you were having a pint?' Mam asked.

'We did. Just one,' James grumbled. 'No money for any more.'

'You shouldn't have had that!' Noah snapped. '*I'm* not going to the pub, am I? No. I'm working all hours in that black hole to keep a roof over your heads.'

'Saint bloody Noah,' Alfred sniggered.

Noah shot up from the chair and grabbed his brother's shirt front. 'How about you do my hours then, Alfred, hey? How about that! And I'll swan off to the pub or football training or whatever lazy arse excuse you lot come up with.'

'Get stuffed, Noah. You're not me dad to tell me what to do.' Alfred pushed him away making him bump into James who shoved him back.

Noah turned on James. 'You'll work extra shifts and no more slacking. I can't pay these debts by myself.'

'Stuff the debts,' James shouted. 'I've been working just as hard as you have. Why should I have to work my fingers to the bone to pay off Dad's debts?'

'Why should I?' Noah shouted back.

'Enough! Stop it,' Mam yelled and started coughing.

'We all work hard, Noah. You're not the only one,' Alfred said.

'Really? Then why weren't you finishing at the same time as me this evening then? Answer me that!'

'Because I also have a life outside of that bloody pit!'

'Oh, is that it?' Noah said sarcastically. 'You have a life, do you, and I don't?'

'Oh, right I forgot, sorry, yes you and your stuck-up Beth think you can rule us all.'

'Don't you dare mention her,' Noah growled.

'I will if I want. She thinks she can rule us just because she brings us some poxy crates of food and cooks us a meal every couple of days.'

'You don't mind eating it though, do you? You selfish bastard.' Noah's fists tightened in anger.

Albie put his hands up. 'Enough now.'

'Get stuffed, Noah, you bloody sanctimonious prick,' Alfred muttered.

Noah swung for him, hitting him on the jaw. A pain speared up his wrist and he flinched.

Alfred fell back but recovered quickly. He swore loudly and punched Noah on the cheek bone.

Pain rattled through Noah's head and a red-mist rage filled him. He threw himself at Alfred, knocking over James and Albie.

The fight escalated as tension rose and egos ruled supreme. Their mam's yelling and coughing was ignored as the frustrations of the brothers reached boiling point and they took it out on each other. Chairs were overturned, the table was pushed against the wall, teacups fell to the floor and shattered on the stone flags, making Patch yelp and flee into the scullery as all hell broke loose.

Using one of his crutches, Sid thumped each of his brothers on the head until, dazed, bleeding, they broke apart, panting.

'What bloody good is this?' Sid snapped. 'Fighting amongst ourselves like bloody idiots!' He hobbled over to their mam and rubbed her back as she continued to cough.

She stood, leaning on the table, and stared at each one of them. 'I won't have it, do you hear?' She coughed again, wheezing. 'I've put up with so much over the years from your father, do you think I'll continue to do so with you lot?'

'Sorry, Mam.' Noah filled a glass of water and handed it to her.

She ignored it. 'You are brothers. I don't have much to be thankful for, or much that I pride myself on, but the one thing I can raise my head about is you five. If I've done nothing else with my life, at least I can say I raised five good men. Well, that's what I thought until now.' She coughed again. 'Since the

238

accident you've all, except Noah, acted like selfish little brats. Well, no more. You're better than that. I refuse to allow you to be like your useless father, do you understand me?' She bent over coughing.

They nodded, not able to meet her eyes. Her Welsh accent had deepened in her anguish.

'You are brothers. Blood.' She stared at each one in turn. 'Last month you all assumed you might be dead. James and Alfred helped to dig you out Sid, they continued to help dig out Noah and Albie. In that cave, Noah looked after Albie. You're brothers. Looking out for each other is what you do. Don't you dare do this again. It might have been funny when you were kids but not now. You're grown men and we are a family.' Tears rolled down her face. 'I've suffered enough.'

Noah righted a fallen chair. 'It'll not happen again, Mam.'

'No, it won't.' she replied. 'All of you will help Noah pay off your father's debts. I'm sorry beyond words that he has left us in this mess. I'm returning to the mill next week, too.'

They all protested as one, but Noah stepped forward and took her hands. 'No, Mam. You're not strong enough. We can manage.'

Albie stepped beside him. 'He's right, Mam. You can't go to the mill with your chest. I'll go back down the pit and work more days than just the two a week I've been doing. My ankle is much better, and I can start doing extra shifts. It'll be another full wage.'

'I'll work more shifts, too, Mam,' James said, coming to put his arm around her. 'I'm sorry I've been selfish. I'm ashamed of myself. I'll give up football.'

'How much money have we left to pay, Noah?' Sid asked, righting another chair, and sitting on it, wincing in pain at his stiff damaged leg.

'I've paid off the funeral costs with the help of the union. It's just the gambling debts, rent arrears and the daily living expenses.' Noah glanced at his mam. 'John Kilmarsh cornered me the other day in the lamp room. Dad owed him eight shillings. He said he'd take half, but he's got six kids to feed so he needs some of it. I told him he'd get the full amount. I've added it to the list.'

She bowed her head in shame. 'I'll never forgive your father.'

Quietly the brothers made the kitchen back to what it was, and Patch slinked in to jump up on Noah's lap, his little body shaking. Their mam bathed cut lips and put cold wet cloths on bruised eyes and cheeks.

'We'll all work double shifts,' Albie said, subdued, holding a wet flannel to his eye.

'Aye.' James nodded, dabbing his split bottom lip.

Alfred put his hand on Noah's shoulder. 'I'm sorry what I said about Beth, Noah. I didn't mean it. It's just she had a go at me and James today and it riled us.'

Noah rubbed his sore cheek. 'She's got a temper on her has my Beth.'

'Good luck being married to that one,' James scoffed with a grin.

'How did it go with the reverend, Sid?' Mam asked, accepting a cup of tea from Albie.

'We're getting married on Saturday the twentieth. The reverend is putting up the bans on Sunday.'

'Five days before Christmas.' Mam beamed.

Sid scratched his chin. 'I'm going to move in with Meg and her parents after the wedding. It'll give you one less person to feed.'

Noah frowned. 'You don't have to. I told you I'll bunk in with the others and you and Meg can have the front room to yourselves.'

James mashed the teapot while Mam basted the roast ham. 'Can't you get a pit house?' he asked Sid.

'There's not one available yet. I've got my name down on the list,' Sid replied. He turned to Noah. 'Have you got your name down for one for you and Beth?'

Noah remembered the life-changing news he'd received, and which hadn't really sunk in. He went into the scullery and from his jacket pocket pulled out the letter Mr Grimshaw had given him.

He gave it to Sid. 'I'll not be needing a pit house when I marry Beth in the spring. I'm hoping by then we'll be in a better state and I can be a teacher.'

'You've passed?' Mam looked up from the roasting tin.

Noah grinned. 'I did.'

Whereas ten minutes ago his brothers were trying to knock seven bells out of him, now they were thumping him on the back and wishing well and offering congratulations. That was the Jacksons. They'd never be any different.

'I'm proud of you, Noah.' Mam left the range to embrace him, tears filling her eyes once more.

241

'Will you get a schoolhouse being a teacher?' Jamie asked.

'No, schoolhouses are for principals, head teachers. I need to talk to Mr Grimshaw next week some time about my future. But I can't leave the pit yet. We need the overtime I can do. Then, once the debts are paid, I'll need to save for the wedding and a home for Beth and me.'

'When will you get married then?' Albie asked.

'I'm going to talk to Beth about it tomorrow. Perhaps March or April.' He rubbed a hand over his tired eyes. 'I need some sleep.'

'What about our dinner?' Mam asked as he rose from the table.

'I'll have some when I wake.'

He crawled into a freezing bed and wrapped the thin blankets around him. His cheek hurt from Alfred's fist and it'll likely be bruised by morning, not the look he wanted to present to Beth as they talked about marriage. He smiled as he grew sleepy. Soon he'd have Beth to cuddle up to in bed. He gave in to a minute's dream of what it'd feel like to touch her body, to move inside her, then he purposely put the thought from his mind. He was randy enough for the want of having her, he couldn't think about it too much or he'd go mad. Spring seemed a long way off.

He sighed and drew his knees up to try and keep warm. He was a certified teacher. Soon he'd never have to wash off coal dust again. He smiled to himself. Suddenly life had become a whole lot rosier.

Chapter Sixteen

Glancing around the restaurant, Beth felt mature and modern as she and Noah celebrated his exam results with a meal at a small restaurant on Upper Kirkgate in Wakefield. Their table was by the window and she watched as a tram rolled by, the bell ringing.

Beth sat back and smiled. Full of a lovely meal of steamed fish in a creamy sauce, she sipped at the white wine Noah had ordered. She wished every meal could be as enjoyable as this one. Drinking wine was only done in her family on special occasions, and Beth felt it go to her head, making her slightly fuzzy.

After being on the stall since early morning, standing in the chilly weather, she'd been eager to pack up. Noah had arrived in town as planned, just as she was closing the lock-up.

They first visited the library, for Noah to return some books, and then they strolled through the indoor market for Beth wanted to find something for Jane and Alfie's wedding present. She bought them a small carriage clock, joking with Noah that soon they would need to start shopping for their own house.

'Do you want a pudding?' Noah asked, refilling her glass.

'I'm rather full but well, why not?' She couldn't wipe the smile from her face. 'I saw on the menu there was vanilla ice cream or mint sorbet, jam roly-poly, rice pudding, trifle and orange posset with shortbread fingers.'

'Which do you prefer?' Noah relaxed in his chair.

Beth couldn't take her eyes off him. He wore a dark grey suit, his best, and he looked so handsome, she wanted to kiss him and never stop.

Bringing her wayward thoughts under control, she sat straighter. 'The orange posset sounds nice.'

'I'm going to have the trifle.' Noah spoke to a waitress nearby and ordered. 'When I'm a teacher, I hope we can have meals like this at least once a month,' he said, sipping his wine.

'Wouldn't that be lovely?' She wondered if such a thing was possible. Certainly, her parents never did, and it wasn't as if they were strapped for money, because the farm was profitable. Perhaps it was more a case of being set in their ways. Mam liked to cook their meals and have the family around the table. She came from a mining family where such a thing as dining out wouldn't have been possible. The best they got was fish and chips on a Friday night.

This was how the other half lived, and Beth was clever enough to realise that she could live this life without marrying Melville. Granted, she wouldn't be draped in furs and pearls married to Noah, but the odd meal out like this was more than enough for her. No matter what Mam said, Melville's money wasn't enough for her to give up Noah.

'What shall we do next?' Noah asked as they ate their dessert.

'I want to give you a present.' Beth pushed away the posset as her corset protested at how much she'd eaten. She reached down beside the table where she'd hid her shopping.

'A present?' Noah grinned, which banished some of the tired lines around his eyes.

Earlier that morning Beth asked Fred to mind her stall while she visited a men's hat shop in Westgate and spent some of her hard-saved money.

She passed over the oval box.

Noah opened it and brought out the black bowler hat. 'Goodness.'

'It's fitting for a teacher. Do you like it?' For a moment she had doubts.

'Oh, Beth.' Noah's expression softened, his love shone from his eyes and she swelled with emotion. She'd made the right choice, even if it had cost her a small fortune.

Noah admired the hat. 'I'll wear this with pride.' He gripped her hand across the table. 'Thank you. I don't have the words to say how much this means to me.'

'I'm pleased you liked it. Shall we go for a walk?'

'After all this food it's probably a clever idea.' Noah paid the bill and escorted her outside, where the wind had dropped, and a weak sun appeared between dirty grey clouds.

'My hat fits perfectly.' Noah turned his head this way and that to show her. His flat cap was pushed into his coat pocket. He tucked her arm through his as they walked along Upper Westgate.

She looked up at the hat that suited him perfectly. Suddenly, he seemed lifted, important, a man of distinction. She couldn't have been prouder to be on his arm. 'Your brothers will call you a right dandy in that.'

'Aye, I'll have no end of grief about it.'

'You couldn't wear a flat cap to school.'

'No. I agree.' He glanced down at his best suit. 'I'll have to save up for another good suit, too.' Noah sighed, the happiness seeping out of him. 'I can't be a teacher yet, Beth. I don't have the money to kit myself out with new clothes and books and pencils and all the stuff I'll need to teach a class. Every penny is needed at home.'

'I understand, but once those debts are paid, you'll get a position at a school. Mr Grimshaw will have this extra time to find you a suitable place.'

'What if it is away from Wakefield?'

She squeezed his arm. 'When we are married, I'll be your wife and will follow you wherever you go.'

He stopped and gazed at her. 'I'm the luckiest man alive.'

'Miss Beaumont?'

Beth's head snapped around at Louis Melville's voice. She'd been so intent on Noah she'd not seen him cross the street to stand before them.

'Mr Melville.'

Melville stood with two male friends, men dressed in black suits, silk ties and top hats, but it was Melville's annoyed tight expression which made Beth shrink inside herself.

'How fortuitous that we meet. I was expecting you to return to Melville Manor to see me and tell me your answer.'

She stared at him as though he'd lost his mind. 'Your answer?'

'To the question I asked you before you left last week.' He turned to his friends. 'Miss Beaumont was caught in the blizzard and I rescued her. We had a lovely afternoon at home. We discussed our future.'

Beth felt Noah stiffen beside her. How dare Melville spoil this day! Did he never give up? 'Excuse us, we must go.' Her eyes sent a silent message to Melville to not say anything else.

'You are Noah Jackson?' Melville stuck out his hand to Noah.

Noah ignored it. 'I am.'

'A local miner, is that correct?'

'At present but soon to be a teacher.' Noah spoke through clenched teeth, his anger visible in his narrowed eyes.

'A teacher? Without a university degree?' Melville mocked. 'Do they still allow that to happen?'

'Indeed, they do, Mr Melville,' Noah grounded out, his temper rising.

'Do they allow teachers to have black eyes?' One of Melville's friends laughed.

Melville guffawed. 'Hardly. But I'm sure whatever little village school Mr Jackson ends up in will not care about the state of him, after all he'll only be teaching poor parish bastards and imbeciles.'

'How dare you!' Beth snapped, fury making her heart race.

'Forgive me, my dear. I should not insult your friend. It is remiss of me. I must make allowances for your... connections. Once we are married, I'll try harder.'

'Married?' Noah jerked around to stare at Beth.

Melville bowed to Beth. 'I invite you and your parents to Melville Manor for afternoon tea on Sunday, Miss Beaumont. We have much to discuss. Do let me know if you can make it. Good day.' He sauntered away with his pals, chatting about the joys of future heirs.

Beth released a pent-up breath.

'Care to tell me what that was all about?' Noah ground out.

'It was nothing. Melville making trouble as always.'

'You spent an afternoon with him at his house?'

'A brief time while the blizzard raged, that was all, and then I left. I didn't want to be there.'

'What was his question? He mentioned marriage. It's not true, is it?'

'Noah, please, forget about him.'

'What was his question, Beth?' Noah was very still.

She closed her eyes momentarily. 'Yes, he did ask me to marry him.'

'He wants you to be his *wife?* Not a joke?'

'For real, yes.'

'Why?' His eyes widened.

'Why?' She frowned. 'Because he likes me.'

'Oh yes, he likes you all right,' he scoffed.

'What does that mean?'

'He can have any woman he wants, Beth. Men like him see working-class women as objects to amuse them, that's all. They don't marry them. He's a wealthy man why would he want to marry you?'

She glared at him. 'Why wouldn't he want me? What is wrong with me? I come from a decent family.'

'Men like him marry women from wealthy families, Beth, not a rhubarb farmer's daughter! He's playing you for a fool. I bet all this is one huge joke to him. He won't mean a word of any of it.'

Instant rage built from his words. 'So, I'm not worthy of the attentions of a wealthy man, am I?'

'He wants you in his bed, not as his wife. Don't you see? He'll make you promises and then when he's got you and used you, he'll fling you to the side and marry a woman of his own class.'

'How dare you!' Her heart thumped in anger.

'And how dare you keep something like this from me!' he shouted back.

'Because it means nothing. It's not worth talking about!'

'Oh, I think it's definitely worth talking about. When another man wants to marry the girl I'm walking out with, then, yes, it certainly needs talking about. What else happened while you were at his manor? Did he show you how the other half live? Did he promise you a carriage of your own, perhaps?' His sarcastic tone irritated her further.

Heat flushed her cheeks.

Noah pounced. 'So, he did! I bet he gave you a tour, didn't he? He wanted to show you all you could have. Did you tell him about me? Did you talk to him about the miner you'd already promised to marry?'

Now the blood drained from her face.

Noah saw that too and took a step back, the light dying from his blue eyes. 'You didn't mention me at all, did you?'

'I... I... It wasn't like that.'

Noah took the bowler hat off his head. 'I don't want to marry someone who hides me in conversation.' He gave her the hat and walked away.

'Noah!'

He jumped on the tram just departing around the corner and was gone.

Astounded, Beth stood holding her shopping and Noah's hat.

~ ~ ~ ~

'You've only got yourself to blame.'

Beth looked up from her cooling soup to her mam, her harsh words painful to hear. 'I do realise that.'

She and her mam hadn't been talking much since her mam slapped her. Beth wanted the silence to continue rather than speak of Noah and Melville.

'I didn't want you to marry Noah, but I wouldn't want to see him treated like that. It's not fair on him.' Mam put a large earthenware bowl into a cupboard. 'You know what he'll be thinking, don't you? That you've been hedging your bets between him and Melville.'

'But I haven't,' Beth protested. 'I've never wanted Melville.'

'More fool you.' Mam placed some cups in the sink full of hot soapy water. 'Marriage to Louis Melville will set you up for life.'

'I don't want him. Can you please stop talking about Melville!'

'You're a strange one, that's for sure. Any girl would want to marry money, except you.' Mam sighed. 'Wash up these things before you go to Jane's. I'm off to visit Reggie's mam, who's not been feeling well. Aunty Hilda is sorting through the cupboard under the stairs, trying to find more wool. She's in a knitting frenzy for Joanna's new baby. See if she needs any help before you go. Your dad and the boys are out in the sheds.'

Beth nodded and took her bowl to the sink. She'd lost her appetite since yesterday's argument with Noah. She'd gone between crying and rage at the injustice of it all. How had she been able to be so happy one minute and then fall to the depths of despair the next?

She'd deliberately missed church this morning to avoid seeing Noah or any of the Jacksons. Instead she'd pleaded a headache, which her mam had not believed, and stayed inside as light snow fell.

However, she had promised to take the dress over to Jane's in readiness for the wedding next Saturday. A glance out of the kitchen window as she washed up showed it was still snowing but only lightly; the flakes drifting down slowly.

'Aren't you off to Jane's?' Aunty Hilda said as she came into the kitchen with a basket full of coloured wool.

'I am.'

'You'd best get a move on before the snow sets in.'

Beth washed the last plate and quickly dried and stacked them in the cupboard. 'Do you need help finding any more wool?'

'No, lass. I've searched everywhere for a bag of white wool I'm sure I had. I must have used it at some point.'

'I can buy some for you tomorrow.'

Aunty Hilda sat at the kitchen table, sorting out the wool by colours. 'That'll be lovely, pet. Thank you. I need some yellow ribbon for the little jacket I've made. Can you buy me half a yard of that, too, please? Joanna is coming over on Wednesday to have tea with us. I want to give her what I've made then.'

'I didn't know she was coming.' Beth hung the tea towel over the rail above the range.

'Well, your mam mentioned it on the way to church this morning, but you weren't with us. Has your headache gone?'

'Yes.'

'And it's been replaced with heartache?'

Beth fought the urge to cry.

Aunty Hilda shook her head. 'You remind me too much of your mam. She had all this nonsense with young men and love.'

'Mam is pleased Noah and I have fallen out.'

'Your mam wants the best for you, that's all.'

'And that's Melville?'

'Who knows? Your mam went from being a poor miner's daughter to a grand farmer's wife. Not a bad step up in my opinion. Who's to say you can't do the same thing? From a farmer's daughter to a member of the gentry.'

'I can't accept Melville. I loathe him.'

252

'Then you need to go and see Noah and explain.'

Beth slipped off her house slippers and fetched her boots from the scullery. 'He won't listen. He made that clear yesterday.'

'Aye, but he's had the night to think about it and cool down.' Aunty Hilda tucked a wayward strand of grey hair out of her eyes.

'He should trust me.'

'Agreed, but he's done nowt wrong and so he's likely feeling he's in the right to be angry, but he'll also know that you are too good to lose. Pride will play a part, of course. Men are fools, and he'll not want to lose out to Melville. Go and see him. Smooth his ruffled feathers.'

'I've promised to take this to Jane.'

'Do it after then.'

Beth took a deep breath, weighing it up. Part of her was so angry at Noah for not trusting and believing her when she said she only wanted him. The other part of her wanted to have this sorted out. She'd lain awake all night wondering if he no longer wanted to be with her and, if so, then she needed to hear him say it even if it meant facing the pain of it.

After donning her outdoor clothes, Beth collected the dress which was wrapped in brown paper and placed in a leather bag to keep the weather from it.

'I'll be home later,' she called to Aunty Hilda as she left the house.

Despite the snowflakes drifting delicately, the day wasn't too cold. Beth waved to Ronnie who was stacking wood in one of the outhouses.

The lane wasn't completely covered in snow as the flakes were melting as they hit the ground, for the moment at least.

Hood up, Beth slung the bag over her shoulder and head down trod along up the lane towards the village. Some children were out, running about, screeching, but mostly the village was deserted and quiet.

From the village she strolled up Sunny Hill and along Potovens Road, which at the end of it was Alverthorpe Road. Walking gave her more time to think about Noah and his reaction. Yes, she felt guilty for not telling him about Melville, but what good would it have done? It wasn't as if she ever considered Melville. Noah was the man for her, or was he? His behaviour on Saturday made her doubt her choice. Not that she would choose Melville over Noah, but was Noah the one for her when he was so quick to doubt her? Perhaps listening to her heart wasn't the best option? It was all such a muddle.

She couldn't believe her wretched luck when on the Alverthorpe Road she saw a carriage coming towards her. She let out a sigh when it passed without stopping. It wasn't Melville. She hurried her footsteps towards Jane's village and away from the direction of Melville Manor.

When she reached the cottage where Jane lived, her grandmother, always called Granny Jean by Beth, opened the door.

'Oh, lass, it's so good to see you, but Jane is at Alfie's house.'

'That's no problem. I told her I'd bring the dress over.'

'Come in, come in.' Granny Jean ushered her into the small living area of the cottage and to where Jane's grandfather sat by the fire dozing.

'Would you like some tea? We were just about to have a cup ourselves.' Granny Jean was already pouring the kettle's boiling water into a teapot.

'I won't, no, thank you.' Beth put the bag on the floor by the door. 'I'll go along to Alfie's place and see if I can have a quick word with Jane. I need to know what time she wants me here next Saturday.'

'She told me she'd like you to come spend the night with her on Friday. Then you're both here to get ready and walk to the church.'

Beth brightened at the thought. She'd not slept over in years. 'I'd like that.'

'You two can have a last night together before our Jane becomes a married woman.'

'It's hard to believe, isn't it?' Beth grinned. 'We're not kids any longer.'

'Aye, but he's a good lad is Alfie and he adores our Jane and that's all we want, isn't it?'

'It is. And if he doesn't treat her properly, he'll have me to deal with.'

'God help him then.' Granny Jean laughed.

'Alfie lives on Flanshaw Lane, doesn't he?'

'Aye, lass. Opposite the school.'

'Lovely. I'll go and see her now. See you on Friday evening.'

Beth closed the door behind her and headed up the road. She soon found Alfie's house and knocked on the door.

Alfie answered it and welcomed her into a chaotic house of fighting children and a bird squawking in a cage by the window. Washing hung drying from the line strung across the front room and in the kitchen more washing hung, nearly touching the heads of the adults sitting at the table. In the middle of it all Jane sat holding a child of about five.

'I don't want to intrude,' Beth said, smiling at Alfie's family. The little house seemed filled with people. Jane had told her that Alfie was the eldest of eight children, most of them squabbling over something as she stood in the doorway to the kitchen.

'Would you care for a cup of tea?' Alfie's mam asked, getting up from the kitchen table and giving the oldest girl next to her a tap on the head. 'Leave it, Doris. I'll have no more of your fighting. You, Betsy, take Susie upstairs she needs a nap.' Mrs Taylor took the smallest child from the lap of a lad about fifteen. 'Richard give your chair to Jane's friend, quick now.'

'No, thank you, Mrs Taylor. I'll not stop long. I just need a quick word with Jane about the wedding.'

'Oh, of course. It'll be a grand day on Saturday. My first born getting married.' Mrs Taylor smiled proudly at Alfie.

Jane led Beth into the front room, and they stood by the door as the black bird squawked in his cage at them. In the kitchen one of the children started yelling and another cried.

'It's madness, isn't it?' Jane laughed.

Beth grinned. 'Not what I was expecting.'

'So different from our quiet cottage with just me, Gran and Grandad.'

'The complete opposite.'

'I think that is why I like it so much. I get to have brothers and sisters that I've never had before.'

'You get that at my home, don't you?' Beth asked, a little offended that Jane was more at home here than at the farm where she'd spent her childhood growing up with Beth.

'Aye, but it's not the same. At the farm, well… you know what your mam is like. She's house-proud and everything is clean and tidy and, well, I feel like I always have to be on my best behaviour. But here, Mrs Taylor is laidback and it's just… easy. You know?'

Beth didn't know, but it didn't matter. 'I've dropped the dress off at the cottage. That's how I found out you were here.'

'Thanks for that. Will you come and sleep Friday night with me? I thought we could get ready together.'

'Yes, I'd like that. I'll come to you straight after I close the stall. I'll take my dress with me.'

'Great. We can spend the night gossiping like we used to as girls.'

'I look forward to it.'

'How is it with Noah? I got your note from your Ronnie. I was sad to read it.'

Shrugging, Beth gazed at the bird hopping on its perch. 'Your guess is as good as mine. We've not spoken. I hoped he might have come to the farm and want to talk to me but he's clearly stubborn.'

'Why don't you go there, then?'

Beth crossed her arms in annoyance. 'Go crawling to him? No. He walked away without me having the chance to explain.'

'Look who is stubborn now.' Jane chuckled. 'Do you want me and Alfie to walk a little way with you?'

'No, it's cold outside. Stay here in the warmth. I'll head back.' Beth kissed Jane's cheek. 'See you Friday, bride-to-be!'

At the corner of the Alverthorpe Road and Flanshaw Lane, two boys were throwing stones at a ginger cat.

'That's not nice, is it?' Beth chastised them. 'What has that cat ever done to you?'

Both boys looked scruffy and dirty and only about six or seven years old and neither of them wore a coat.

'Get inside out of this weather,' Beth told them.

The boys ran off, as did the cat, scooting over a nearby fence.

Beth ignored the carriage coming under the railway bridge, her thoughts on Jane and how her best friend would soon be a married woman and her priorities would be Alfie's family. She had only met Alfie twice before and really, as Jane's best friend, she should get to know him better. Yet, her concern was for her friendship with Jane. Would it change once she was married? Would they still have the picnics in summer by the beck? Or go on long walks or feed the ducks at the park? Or would Alfie want Jane all to himself?

'Miss Beaumont?'

Beth groaned as the carriage stopped and Melville climbed down. Did the man stalk her like a deer?

'What are you doing in these parts?' he asked jovially, clasping his hands together.

'Visiting a friend.' Right now, she wished Jane lived anywhere else rather than on the Alverthorpe Road.

'I was just doing the same. I have friends at Alverthorpe Hall.'

Beth knew of the hall. It was not much further down the road. 'That's nice. Good day, I must be going.'

'First, I want to talk to you.'

'I haven't the time, sorry.' The light snow pitted and patted against her face and she was becoming cold.

'Miss Beaumont, please. Just a few minutes. Come into the carriage out of this weather and after we've talked you can go on your way.'

Beth sighed and followed him into the carriage.

With the door shut, Melville sat opposite her and smiled. 'This is becoming familiar, you in my carriage. It feels right, don't you agree?'

She looked at him, suddenly tired. The worry over the fight with Noah, the lack of sleep the night before and the walk had worn her out. 'Mr Melville—'

'Let me say something first, please.'

She nodded grudgingly.

'Yes, you have told me that you don't wish to marry me. But after some considerable time pondering on your decision, I have come to the realisation that I hurried you to give me an answer. I was being unfair on you and I apologise.'

Beth waited for him to say more.

'You must understand, Miss Beaumont, that I find you extremely appealing. I am used to getting what I want, until I met you, that is. I will not pressure you, however, may I ask if my offer was even slightly considered by you?'

She wondered if she should lie but then decided why bother. 'Yes, I have given it some thought. How could I not when it was so unexpected?'

'And have you spoken to anyone about it?'

'My parents.'

'And their opinion was?'

'My mother believes it to be something which I should agree to.'

He leant forward, joy flooding his expression which surprised Beth. 'Excellent. Your mother is a woman of sense. I know my asking you to be my wife must have come as a shock. I understand that it wasn't something you'd ever expect. Nevertheless, I mean it, Miss Beaumont. I mean it wholeheartedly. I wish to marry you. Nothing would give me greater pleasure than being your husband. I would love you devotedly and care for you and your family.'

'But I don't love you, Mr Melville.' There was no plainer way to tell him.

He sat back. 'Do you wish for more time? I will wait, of course. Didn't I just mention I wouldn't pressure you? Love can grow if nurtured. We can proceed slowly, I promise you.'

'No, you aren't listening to me,' she snapped. 'I don't need more time. I'm sorry. I love someone else. He is the one I want. He will only ever be the one I want.' She ignored the inner voice which said Noah may not want her.

'That man you were with in the street, who you always seem to be with?' His mouth became a thin line. 'He is a miner, yes?'

'Yes. I will marry him.'

'He cannot give you what I can.'

Beth sighed. 'No, he can't, that's true. He can't give me a manor and a carriage, but I don't care. It is his love I crave more than anything.'

'Love will soon die when you are living in a hovel and have numerous children bawling at you night and day and no food to put on the table.' His tone became edgy, clipped. His fingers tapped on his thigh. 'I beg you to reconsider.'

'No. Thank you for your offer, but I'm sorry, I won't marry you. Please don't ask me again.'

'You haven't had enough time to—'

'I have!' Frustration made her tone harsh.

He reached out and took her gloved hands. 'Please, Miss Beaumont, Beth. I will give you anything you want. I can make you happy. Look at what I can provide for your family.'

'My family can take care of themselves, Mr Melville.' She tried to pull her hands free, but his hold tightened.

'You're making a mistake. We can talk some more. I can visit your parents, perhaps? You must listen to your mother's wise words,' he pleaded, sounding desperate.

'It'll do no good. Please, let me go.'

'I won't! I've told my friends about you.'

She frowned. 'Why?'

'To show them the beautiful woman who would bear my children.'

'Mr Melville I'm sure there are any number of women in your own class who would be happy to marry you.'

'I don't want those insipid women. I want you. Someone with spirit and fire. You're like a wild creature when angry and that is so refreshing to me. You would delight my friends, make dinner parties interesting. I'd be the envy of them all to have a woman who would break the boundaries that restrain my society so tightly. No one would have a wife like mine.'

'I'd be a laughing stock.'

'No.' He kissed the back of her hand. 'You'd never be laughed at. You'd be revered and have men eating out of your hands and women eager to be more like you.'

'It would never work.' She wished he wouldn't touch her.

'Trust me, please. I would spend every moment of my life making you happy. We could travel. I'll take you wherever you wish to go.'

'I'm sorry, Mr Melville. It is impossible. Good day.'

He lurched forward and kissed her hard on the mouth, pushing her lips against her teeth.

Beth squirmed, mumbling through her closed mouth. She tried to push him away.

Melville pulled her down on to the seat, laying his body over her, one hand over her mouth. Using his cane, he tapped the ceiling of the carriage and the driver clicked the horses on.

In the rocking of the carriage, Beth stared at Melville's red, angry face above her, his body pinning her down like a lead weight.

Scared, she fought hard, hindered by her skirts and his strength. Only, it did no good as Melville kept one hand over her mouth while he opened her coat and ran his other hand over her body.

'You're mine, Beth. Don't ever think you will be anyone else's but mine. I've told people that I am to marry. They are expecting it. I'll not let you go. You'll love me in time. I'll be a good husband to you,' he whined.

She shook her head from side to side, trying to be free of his hand over her mouth.

Melville kissed her face, small little kisses rained over her skin. He nibbled her ears, whispering sweet words of his love for her.

When the carriage stopped, Melville straightened, but kept his hold on Beth's arm. His face was impassive. He'd become someone else again.

'Let me go.' Fear clenched her stomach, but she was willing to fight him.

'We are going to go inside, my dear. You are going to behave naturally. I just want us to talk.'

'Let me go or I'll scream the place down! You can't kidnap me like this and force me to do as you want.' Hatred made her rage against him.

'If you don't,' his voice dropped to a whisper, 'if you don't behave, I'll kill your poor miner.' His gaze bored into hers.

She blinked in confusion. Kill Noah. Was he mad? 'You're insane.'

His top lip twitched. 'And don't imagine I'm making an idle threat, because I have the means and the contacts to make sure it happens.'

Once out of the carriage, Staines opened the front door. 'Mr Melville, sir, you have guests. They arrived half an hour ago.'

'What?' Melville snapped in surprise.

Beth took advantage of the moment and jerked her arm free of his hold and ran around the other side of the carriage. She lifted her skirts and ran as fast as she could down the short drive and onto the road.

Her back tingled with the thought of Melville chasing her or sending the carriage after her, but a quick look over her shoulder showed no one followed. She pushed through a hedge and into a field, knowing a carriage couldn't follow across a ploughed field.

Mud sucked at her boots, slowing her down, but she continued on as fast as she was able until she reached the top of the hill and Potovens Road. Slowing down, she half ran and walked, a stitch in her side making her pant.

Tears of anger and fear filled her eyes. Once again Melville had shown his true colours. He was like several different people rolled into one. He scared her. Sometimes he charmed and other times he threatened. She'd never met anyone like him before. It was impossible to deal with such a man. He was someone to avoid, and a man she had made an enemy of. Would he leave her alone now, or would he carry out his threats to harm her family and Noah?

She'd given him no encouragement to develop this obsession with her. Melville was so used to getting his own way that he didn't understand refusals. How was she going to avoid him when the man seemed to be wherever she went? Like a shadow he was always there. She'd wounded his pride, but instead of taking the refusal as a gentleman, he'd turned into a monster. She shivered, slipping in the mud.

How had she got into this mess and would he really harm Noah?

Chapter Seventeen

'Will you get that bloody light shining over here so I can see properly?' Noah yelled at James.

'All right, keep your hat on!' James adjusted the lamp to shine better where Noah dug at the coal seam. 'You won't be able to speak to your students like that, you know.'

'Shut up and get to work.' Noah, stripped to the waist, lay on his side to pick away at the coal. He's been underground for ten hours and for ten hours he'd done nothing but think of Beth as he toiled in the black hole.

Had he done the right thing walking away from her like that? She had lied to him, or more correctly kept something important from him. He had cause to be angry with her. No man wants to think his girl was being tempted by another man, especially when that man had wealth and pedigree.

However, since her revelation about Melville on Saturday he'd spent the next four days alternating between anger and despair at having made a reckless decision. Did he want to end it with her? Could he honestly walk away from her?

No. She was his beautiful Beth, the gutsy girl who he adored. Her kisses sent him to a place where he lost control. She brought out the best in him and now, obviously, the worst of his jealousy.

He wanted her smiles to be only for him, no other man. He liked to make her laugh and see the love in her eyes when she looked at him.

God, he'd been a fool. A stupid thick-headed fool. His mam and brothers had said the same when he told them what had happened. He hadn't listened to them. He'd been so fired up with fury and envy of Melville, who had everything Noah did not. He'd gone to the pub and drunk away precious money which he'd been saving to pay off the next debt. Such a stupid irresponsible thing to do, but at the time he'd needed to drown out his sorrows. How could he ever compete against Louis Melville?

He'd been in a rage at the pub, wanting to fight anyone who looked at him wrongly. Why hadn't Beth told Melville to go hang? Why did the pompous arse think he had a right to ask such a thing of Beth? Had she encouraged him?

He had to talk to her. They needed to sort it out. He had to know all the details.

But why hadn't she come to the house demanding to explain it to him? Was she pleased he'd called it off? Had she changed her mind about him? Was she as fickle as Lillian, the girl who he'd been courting a few years ago and who suddenly decided she wanted someone else? Was he destined to never settle with someone who genuinely loved him?

He'd given his heart to Beth. He thought it would be enough. Yet Melville had come sniffing around and she'd not sent him packing. Did the lure of his fortune make her think she could do better than a miner?

Self-doubt and recriminations filled his mind as he shimmied out of the narrow tunnel and started shovelling the coal he'd broken from the wall.

His brothers, except Sid, were working with him. They were working as many extra shifts as they could physically cope with. Each week he was able to pay a bit more off the debts their father had racked up. His plan was that by the end of January, he'd be able to ask Mr Grimshaw to find him a position in a school. Sometimes, he tried not to think that far in advance. To dream of a life without coal dust under his fingernails seemed a fairy tale. His lofty ideas of teaching, of marrying Beth, appeared to be something forever in the distance.

He wiped the sweat from his eyes. He had to talk to her. He simply had to. He was going out of his mind. If she wanted Melville, then he'd walk away and wish her good luck. If she still wanted to marry him and not Melville, then he needed to make it up to her somehow. Though why any girl would want to marry a miner when they could have a manor and diamonds and furs, he didn't know.

A terrible thought clenched his gut. Had he pushed Beth away with his rash behaviour on Saturday? Had Beth gone to Melville and accepted his proposal? She'd have the support of her family, especially her mam who didn't want her to marry him anyway. A Jackson or a Melville. It was hardly worth considering, was it?

Noah groaned and shovelled faster, the sweat running down his back. He needed to see Beth. He had to speak to her, ask forgiveness and he hoped to God that she still wanted him.

'Hey, watch out?' James shouted as Noah threw a shovelful of coal and missed the trolley and hit James instead.

'Sorry!'

'Get your head on the job, man.' James gave him a rude gesture.

Noah sighed, dropped the shovel, and took a drink from his flask. James was right, he needed to concentrate while down here for lives depended on it. He wished he were on nights so he could forgo sleep and go and speak to Beth, but working day shifts and extra hours meant she was in bed when he was heading home. Saturday would have to be the day. It couldn't come quick enough.

~ ~ ~ ~

A thundery heavy shower sent shoppers home on Friday afternoon. Beth was happy to pack away the stall. She'd been freezing all day and drunk her flask of tea before midday and had to go for a refill at one of the tea rooms from the indoor market. She'd hoped to be kept busy with customers to stop her thinking of Noah and Melville, but the freezing weather slowed trade and she spent too much time looking up the street hoping Noah would come and see her.

'So, you're not open tomorrow then, lass?' Fred asked, placing tools into crates.

Beth added a crate of beetroot to the handcart. 'No, it's Jane's wedding.'

'Your Joanna's not coming to mind the stall? How's she getting on?'

'She's doing well. Getting bigger every time we see her, which is why Mam doesn't want Joanna standing out in this weather all day, and Mam is too busy. So, we'll have the stall closed just this once. The trade isn't great when it's so cold anyway.'

'No, it's not,' Fred agreed. 'I've had about ten customers all day. Now with this rain, we'll have ice everywhere in the morning. It'll keep people home, if they have any sense that is.'

'Hopefully, we'll get the Christmas rush starting next week.'

Fred rubbed his face. 'I doubt that'll help me.'

'Why?'

'I'm just about done, lass. I'm getting too old to be standing out in all weathers.' With a despondent look on his face, he continued packing away.

'But what will you do if you don't have your stall?' Beth added bunches of onions to a crate.

'I honestly don't know, lass. It gives me sleepless nights, I can tell you.' Fred added the last crate to his cart. 'I'll see you next week, lass,' he said unhappily. 'Enjoy the wedding tomorrow. Give young Jane my regards.'

'Bye, Fred.' Beth hurried to finish packing up.

She waved to a few stallholders as they closed their lock-ups. She had to make two trips to the lock-up to store the crates of vegetables as she hadn't sold much today.

After the final trip with the handcart, the rain fell heavier. Traders went home, grumbling about the weather.

In the lock up, Beth sorted through the vegetables and any that were becoming too old for sale were placed in a barrel, which her dad then sold to a pig farmer in the village of Outwood.

Thunder cracked overhead, making her shiver. Her mind was on what she'd buy to take to Jane's house, for she couldn't turn up empty-handed. Perhaps she should stop at a baker's and buy a couple of loaves of bread and maybe a pie, if there was any left. She fancied cake and, at the thought of it, her stomach rumbled nearly as loud as the thunder above her head.

When the lock-up door slammed, banishing most of the grey afternoon light, Beth swore softly. She turned to go open it again but froze on seeing Melville standing there.

Annoyance and alarm made her tone sharp. 'What do you want?'

'Now that isn't very pleasant, is it?' he smirked.

Beth took a deep breath. Did the obliging Melville stand before her or was it the evil, unpredictable one? 'I don't have time to talk to you, Mr Melville. I need to be somewhere and I'm going to be late.'

'Do I look as though I care?' He sauntered further into the lock-up which was a large room sporting a high ceiling. With the wide door closed the only light came from a small window at the top of the back wall.

So, it was the evil, insufferable one then.

Beth adjusted her scarf around her neck, trying not to show how nervous she was being alone with him. She'd have to brazen it out. 'Have you come to apologise for your behaviour in the carriage?'

He snorted. 'I never apologise for anything unless I consider it worthwhile.'

'That doesn't surprise me.' She continued sorting through the vegetables, putting on a brave face despite the fact that his presence made her quiver with dread.

Melville came to stand close beside her. 'I have decided to forgive you.'

'Forgive me?'

'For running away like that. It made it very awkward for me to explain to Staines and my carriage driver why you did so. I told them you were upset after receiving some unwelcome news.'

Beth snorted in derision. 'Yes, because telling them the truth would have shown them how you really are.'

Melville flicked away a spot of rain from his long coat. 'Nevertheless, I feel we need to clear the air.'

'Don't bother yourself.'

'For your benefit and to get us back to being friendly, I will apologise for my behaviour. Unfortunately, you seem to bring out the best and worst in me.'

'Lucky me.' She gave him a sarcastic smile.

'You must realise that my… infatuation with you comes as a surprise to me as well as to you. However, I feel we can have an excellent life together. We are both passionate people. That can only be a good thing, don't you agree?'

'Not in the slightest.' He never gave up. How was she to reason with such a dangerous fool?

Melville sighed deeply, as though she was an unruly child needing his patience. 'Despite all that has happened in the past, I am willing to overlook your behaviour and my proposal still stands.'

She frowned at him. 'Do you seriously believe I would marry you after how you treated me last week? Plus, all those other times? I haven't forgotten you whipping me with your riding crop during the summer or charging Noah, Jane, and me when we had our picnic. I've not forgotten any of that. So how could you possibly think I would marry a beast like you?'

He struck her hard across the cheek in a move so fast Beth didn't see it coming.

She stumbled back against the barrel, holding her throbbing cheek. Why had she goaded him? Yet, anger rose like steam from a boiling kettle. She wanted to hit him back, but held herself in check, hoping he'd quickly leave.

Melville's thin lips curled in distaste. 'I can be a gentleman who will treat you well, or a beast. The choice is yours.'

'I've made my choice!' Beth yelled at him, hating him from her very core. 'It's not you!'

'Are you sure? This is your last chance.'

'I would pick anyone over you,' Beth sneered between clenched teeth. Her cheek was on fire and a rage burned within her. 'You are mad to think I would even look your way. You're a monster.'

Something flickered in his eyes, as though her words had wounded him. 'I can be nice, Beth. If you'd only let me show you. I don't like being angry with you.'

She laughed mockingly. 'I don't want your niceties. I don't want anything from you at all. Just leave me alone! Get out!'

'Out of all the eligible women in the district I have picked you to be the mother of my children. You don't seem to understand the great honour I'm bestowing on you.'

'An honour? Are you mad? I'd rather die than be with you. You're insane.'

Red-faced, eyes narrowed, he grabbed her by the front of her coat, his face inches from hers. 'You will regret this moment. You will regret ever spurning me. Do you understand? I won't be made a fool of.'

Something caught his attention and he grinned evilly. Holding her by one hand, he reached over and picked up the shears from the table where Beth cut the stems of the flowers they sold in the summer.

Melville brandished the shears before her face. 'Let us see how much your miner thinks of you when I've finished with you, shall we?'

'What are you going to do?' Her knees threatened to give way. Her breath caught in her throat.

'Why I'm going to make you look even more beautiful. Allow me to enhance your pretty face.' He pulled away her scarf and then yanked off her hat. The pins which secured it clattered onto the cobbled floor.

He spun her around, so she was leaning over the barrel, her back to him. Beth squirmed, trying to get free but he pushed his weight against her, pining her over the barrel's edge her face nearly squashed into the vegetables. The plait she wore unwound as he pulled away the combs.

'What are you doing?' Frantic, she struggled. 'Let me go or I'll scream!'

'Hold still, or I'll stab you!' he panted, kicking her legs apart, pressing his body hard against her.

Beth groaned as she heard the snipping of the shears. Was he cutting her clothes? In horror, she stared as Melville reached around in front of her and dangled the long plait of hair he'd cut off.

'No!' Her long hair gone! Beth bucked and fought to be free.

His laugh was moronic as he continued snipping.

'Stop! Stop!'

Thunder cracked overhead, drowning out her cries.

Suddenly the shears clattered to the ground. Melville's hand stroked her bare neck. She shivered with revulsion.

'Not so spirited now, are we?' His hand went up inside her skirts, feeling his way over her woollen stockings and the garter she wore to hold them up.

The blood froze in her veins. Was he going to take everything from her? Spoil her for Noah? His other hand squeezed the back of her neck. She wanted to die.

He touched between her legs.

A red mist of rage blurred her vision. She elbowed him hard. Her strength from years of hauling heavy crates took Melville by surprise.

He grunted and moved back a little, but it was enough for her to swing around and land her fist on the side of his head.

Melville swore, stepped back and then his punch to her stomach felled her to her knees.

Doubled over, she gasped for breath. Pain spiralling through her body.

Melville squatted down in front of her, grinning. 'You're a firecracker, aren't you? You'd be great in bed. However, you'd never make a proper lady and so

I withdraw my offer of marriage. You're not good enough to be a Melville.' His hand roughed up her short hair. 'I don't know what I ever saw in you. You'd never be a lady worthy of the Melville name. You'd have made me look a buffoon.'

She glanced up at him, winded and in pain. 'I'd… rather be dead than be a Melville.'

Melville stood, tidied his coat, and straightened his hat. 'You need teaching a lesson, market girl.' He hauled her up and punched her in the stomach again.

Beth gasped at the pain. She couldn't breathe. Her lungs felt like they were trapped in a vice.

He dropped her to the floor where she knelt wheezing for air. 'I'm going to enjoy ruining you, your family and your lover.'

'No…'

'Oh yes, sweet Beth. I'm going to make you pay for rejecting me. And if you go to the police about this, I'll make sure something nasty befalls someone you love, do you understand? And believe me, I can do it so easily no one will even suspect me. Accidents happen, my dear.' He chuckled. 'They happen everywhere…'

'No, please!'

'Too late for begging. You had your chance.' Melville strode to the door. 'A night in here will sharpen you up or kill you. Either way, I don't care. And don't bother shouting. Brook Street is deserted. Everyone has gone home.' He opened the door and looked out. 'Not a soul to be seen.'

Thunder reverberated outside. Rain pounded on the roof.

'Enjoy your night, Beth Beaumont. It is only the start of the pain I'm going to cause you.'

'Please, Melville…'

'Oh, and I might come back in the night and visit you. Wouldn't that be lovely? Maybe it's time I sampled what you're willing to give to that miner. I think I shall have you first.' He smiled, stepped outside, and closed the door. The lock rammed into place.

The weak grey light from the high window didn't filter the whole lock-up, leaving the corners dim and gloomy.

Shocked, Beth didn't run to the door. There was no point. He'd locked it securely; she'd heard that locking sound nearly every day of her adult life. To scream would be pointless. The rain pummelling the roof drowned out all other sounds. She had a fleeting wish that it would stop for Jane's wedding tomorrow.

Coldness whispered over her bare neck. Tentatively, she touched the exposed skin and the uneven tufts of short hair. Her long hair all gone. A sob escaped her.

She slid to the floor and picked up the plait. Tears rolled off her lashes. Dazed, she glanced around and seeing her scarf she quickly wrapped it around her neck. Her basket still sat on the handcart, her flask of tea poking out of the top.

'At least I have drink and food,' she murmured, feeling out of control as the tears fell faster, harder and she sobbed as though her heart would break.

Chapter Eighteen

Noah watched Patch as he jumped over puddles capped with ice. The little dog was excited. The walk to Alverthorpe was different than their usual one around the home lanes of Wrenthorpe and Patch was determined to explore and pee on every tree and bush.

A farmer trundled by on his cart, taking a load of grunting pigs to market. The smell as they passed made Noah's nose wrinkle. He trod carefully to miss the mud from last night's storm. The temperature had dropped below freezing and the countryside and village roofs were sprinkled with ice, shining like millions of stars had landed on earth. No snow had fallen, and last night's rain had washed away the remaining snow from recent falls leaving the landscape ugly and drab in the depths of winter.

Once in Alverthorpe, Noah stopped at a cottage and asked a woman feeding her geese if she knew which house was Jane Ogden's home. He was thankful he had a good memory and remembered Jane's last name.

'Further down. Briar Rose Cottage it's called. Lord knows why as a rose hasn't grown in that garden in many a year.'

'Thank you.' He waved to the old woman and called to Patch to join him as he carried on down the road.

Briar Rose Cottage had a small front garden leading to a black door. Smoke came from the chimney. He knocked on the door and waited.

Eventually, it opened, and Jane stood in her dressing gown, her red hair in rags to curl it. 'Noah?' She looked surprised. 'Sorry, I expected you to be Beth.'

He frowned. 'I thought she might be here to help you get ready for the wedding. I've come too early, forgive the interruption.'

'Well, Beth was meant to be here. We'd arranged for her to come last night after she closed the stall, but she never turned up. She might have finished late, maybe, and decided to come here this morning.' Jane glanced down the road. 'I hope she comes soon. I need help with my hair.'

'I'll go for a walk and see if I can see her.'

'Have you two made up yet?'

He gave a wry smile. 'That's why I'm here. I've been an idiot.'

'Men usually are.' Jane laughed. 'Go and talk to her but be quick about it. I'm getting married in three hours and it'll take that long to sort me out to be halfway decent.'

Noah shook his head. 'You'll be a very pretty bride, Jane.'

She blushed. 'Come to the wedding later. We're having a drink in the pub on Flanshaw Lane. I'm sure Beth will enjoy having you there.'

'I will, thank you.'

'And tell her to hurry up when you find her.'

Noah walked along Alverthorpe Road until he reached Potovens Road turn off and there he and

Patch got a lift on the back of a farmer's cart back into Wrenthorpe Village.

His nervousness grew as he walked down Trough Well Lane to the Beaumonts' farm. Would Beth see him or close the door in his face? He couldn't blame her if she did the latter.

At the farm gates, Ronnie was harnessing their horse to the cart. 'Morning, Noah.'

'Morning, Ronnie. Is your sister about?'

Ronnie steered the horse backwards between the shafts. 'She's with Jane.'

'Are you sure? I've just come from there.'

'Hey there, Noah.' Rob Beaumont came out of one of the rhubarb forcing sheds.

'Morning, Mr Beaumont. I'm looking for Beth.'

'I'm pleased. She's been sorely upset this past week. You two need to sort it out.'

'Agreed. I want to talk to her about that.'

'Good man, but you'll find her in Alverthorpe at Jane Ogden's place. She's getting married today, Jane, I mean.'

A shiver jolted through Noah. 'I've just come from Jane's. She's not there.'

'She has to be. She went there yesterday straight from the stall. She's not come home.'

'No, she didn't. Jane's not seen her…' Noah felt the blood drain from his face.

Rob Beaumont started running for the house. 'Mary!'

His wife came out of the scullery, buttoning up her coat. 'What is it? I can't be held up, I'm late. Ronnie are you finished?' She stopped on seeing Noah.

Rob gripped his wife's arm. 'Our Beth, are you sure she went to Jane's?'

'Of course, she did. She was spending the night there. Jane's getting married today.'

'Noah has just come from there. Jane said she's not there.'

Mary Beaumont scowled, giving Noah a filthy look. 'Have you said something to her?'

'No, nothing at all,' Noah defended. 'I didn't even get to see Beth. Jane said she didn't turn up last night as expected.'

'You've upset Beth. Jane's probably lied and said she's not there because Beth doesn't want to talk to you.' Mrs Beaumont adjusted her hat and headed for the cart. 'Leave my daughter alone.'

Noah followed her to the cart. 'Honestly, Mrs Beaumont, I've not seen Beth since last week. When I knocked on the door Jane thought it was Beth. She looked up the road for her as though expecting her to arrive. She said Beth was meant to spend the night with her but didn't turn up. She assumed she had worked late on the stall or something.'

Slowly, Mrs Beaumont turned to look at him. 'Beth is not here.' She turned to her husband. 'I've not seen her since she left for town to open the stall yesterday morning.'

'God in heaven. Where the hell is she then?' Mr Beaumont jumped into action, helping Ronnie quickly fasten the last of the harness straps and buckles. 'Will!' he shouted.

Will came running out of the house, his coat unbuttoned and a bacon sandwich in one hand. 'What's up?'

'Have you seen our Beth?'

'No, she went to Jane's, didn't she?'

Mrs Beaumont climbed up into the cart. 'Drop me off at the tram stop. I'll go into town and ask Fred what time Beth packed up last night. You and Will go to Alverthorpe and speak to Jane.'

'We'd do better splitting up,' Noah said worriedly.

'Aye.' Mr Beaumont nodded. 'Will, you go into the village and look for your sister. Knock on doors if you have to. Ask everyone you see. I'll take Ronnie and we'll go to Alverthorpe.'

Noah whistled Patch to his side. 'I'll search the rest of this lane and make my way along Jerry Clay Lane and down to Brandy Carr.'

'We'll start at Alverthorpe and head that way into town.' Mr Beaumont took his place on the seat of the cart, his sons scrambling into the back to be dropped off in the village.

'I'll go to Joanna's after the market,' Mrs Beaumont said and then turned to look down at Noah. 'Check every ditch and hedge and the... the becks as well.'

He nodded, fear clutching his innards. The cart drove out of the gates and Noah ran down the lane with Patch panting at his heels.

~ ~ ~ ~

Beth woke to a bang. She huddled further into the corner of the lock-up, the shears clutched in her gloved hand. A weak light from the window helped her to work out that it was morning.

282

She'd stayed awake all night, listening for any sounds that Melville was returning. Empty crates in front of her screened her hiding place in the corner. It was the only thing she could think of doing in the dark hours, hoping that if Melville returned, he'd not find her in the darkest corner of the lock-up and perhaps even suspect she'd escaped somehow.

All night, freezing and shivering, she'd held the shears to her, ready to defend herself. Rats had scuttled in the dark making her skin crawl. The rain on the roof dulled her senses one minute and then the next she thought she heard footsteps. Every creak and moan of the building had her on alert. The storm didn't abate until the first grey light of dawn appeared and it was only then she allowed her eyes to close.

The bang came again.

Shaking from fear and cold, she kept watch on the door. Outside she heard voices. Had Melville brought someone with him? Was he coming to take her away? Was he here to attack her as he said he'd do? She'd fight him with every ounce of her strength. Kill him if necessary.

She wanted to scream but was too frightened. Hiding behind the crates kept her safe for the moment.

Suddenly the heavy door was wrenched open, flooding the room with more grey light. Beth jumped, holding the shears in front of her.

'I'm sorry. I know nothing more,' a male voice spoke.

Beth whimpered. He was back. Her hands shook. Her heart raced faster. The voices came again. Loud traffic rumbling outside of the lock-up mumbled the voices. Beth strained to hear. Could she make a run for it? Would Melville catch her? He wasn't alone.

'I don't know where she could be.'

'I'll go ask around the other stalls.'

The door started to close.

Craning her neck a little, Beth peeked around the crates. Mam? She blinked. Was she seeing things? She moaned, so scared she couldn't think straight.

'What was that?' Mam said.

It *was* Mam! Beth tried to stand but her cold legs cramped when she moved. Pain shot through her legs and back.

'Beth!' Mam shouted.

'Mam…' she cried from the agony in her frozen legs. Pins and needles throbbed in her feet.

The crates were thrown aside, and Mam was kneeling beside her. 'Beth. Good God what has happened to you?'

'Mam.' She couldn't speak for emotion clogging her throat.

Behind her mam Fred stared in horror at her.

'Help me get her up, Fred.' Mam reached for her, but Beth shrank back as Fred stepped closer.

'No!' She thrust out the shears. 'Stay away.'

'She's been attacked,' Fred said. 'I'll get the police.'

'No!' Beth screamed. She gripped her mam's arms. 'Take me home. Just you. Tell no one.' She sobbed, pulling her scarf over her cropped head. She had to get away before Melville found her gone.

'Come on, my love.' Mam hauled her stiffly to her feet.

Beth winced and gritted her teeth to stop crying out as her frozen body moved for the first time in many hours. Beth couldn't stop shaking.

'I'll get her home, Fred. Thank you for your help. I'll hire a hansom cab. We'll be fine. No, we don't need the police.' Mam steered her out of the lock-up and down Brook Street.

Beth stumbled, unable to use her feet. Was she even walking? Her limbs felt as though they were made of jelly. She kept her head down, hidden by her scarf. No one could know it was her, the humiliation would be too much.

The journey home became a blur to Beth. Her body tingled as circulation began in her limbs. She was so cold her teeth chattered, yet her head was hot. The rocking motion of the hansom cab made her ill.

She was vaguely aware of Aunty Hilda crying as Mam half carried her into the house. Aunty Hilda patted her hand as her mam stripped her of her clothes.

'I'll get a fire lit in here, Aunt. She needs warming up. Hot water bottles.'

'I'll heat up some soup, too.' Aunty Hilda disappeared as Mam pulled a flannel nightgown over Beth's head and helped her into bed.

Beth couldn't stop shaking. The blankets icy on her skin. Tiredness gave her a headache, yet closing her eyes scared her, too.

'Are you in pain?' Mam asked.

Wearily, Beth tried to focus on her face which wavered before her eyes.

She closed her eyes; it was all too much effort.

When she woke, she kicked off the blankets. Sweat saturated her nightgown as though she'd had a bath in it. Her airless bedroom baked from a roaring fire and the curtains were closed, but she glimpsed the night sky through a gap. A lamp lit beside her bed gave her enough light to see the clock. Twenty past eleven.

She closed her eyes, too tired to stay awake.

The rooster crowing woke her at dawn. Her mam sat on a chair beside the bed, asleep. The fire had died down and a chill in the air made Beth shiver. She pulled the blankets up to her chin. Her throat felt on fire as she swallowed, and her head pounded.

Mam sprang awake and laid her hand on Beth. 'Lass, you're awake,' she whispered. 'How do you feel?'

'Awful,' Beth croaked.

'Aye, you've caught a fever. You've been burning up all night.' Mam adjusted the pillows and straightened the blankets. 'Do you want some water?'

Beth nodded and sipped at the glass of water held to her lips. The effort exhausted her.

Sitting back down, her mam tucked in the blankets. 'Can you remember any of what happened to you?'

Melville. The nightmare of being trapped in the lock-up all night, holding the shears until her hands cramped, the freezing floor she sat on behind the crates, the rats… Her hair…

It all came flooding back.

She put a hand to her hair, feeling the short tufts at her neck.

'Who attacked you?'

Humiliation and despair filled Beth. 'It doesn't matter.'

'Of course, it matters,' Mam whispered harshly so as not to wake the rest of the household.

Melville's taunting face and his evil threats whirled in her mind, frightening her.

'Tell me, Beth. I demand to know.'

'You can't know.'

'Why?'

'Because he'll harm us all.'

'Who will?' Mam gripped Beth's hand. 'Who did this to you?'

'It doesn't matter now. It's over.' Beth wondered if that were true or would Melville forever be in the shadows watching her, ready to pounce again. The thought made her shiver. Tears burned hot behind her eyes.

'You'll tell me everything, Beth. Now.'

'I can't,' she croaked. 'Please don't ask me to.'

'Did he, did he touch you? I mean did he force himself on you? The truth now.'

'No. He didn't go that far.' Beth gazed at the fire's flames licking the coal in the grate, remembering the feel of Melville's hand between her legs.

'Did you know him?'

'I can't tell you.'

'Why?'

'He threatened to ruin the people I love.'

Mam leaned back in shock. 'Ruin the people you love? He knows you then? And you know him?'

'Don't ask me, Mam.'

'I will ask you,' Mam's whisper was fierce. 'This man attacks you, threatens you, locks you up over-night in freezing conditions and you expect me not to ask you who did this? You could have died!'

'I can't tell you.' Beth's head throbbed as though ready to split open. Her body was on fire and she had no strength to argue with her mam.

'I'll bring the police here to talk to you. Maybe you'll tell them.'

'No.' Beth jerked her hand out to stop her mam from leaving. 'No, you can't get the police.'

'Beth this is serious. Who is threatening you?'

She closed her eyes, wishing all this was simply a bad dream. 'You have to promise you can't tell anyone, not Dad, not the police, no one.'

'Why I can't I tell them?'

'Because he threatens to ruin us. I can't live with myself if Dad found out and did something crazy in revenge. You know what he's like, he's so protective over his family. The minute Dad knows who did this, he'll be straight there and confront him and then get himself into trouble. Or Will might think he needs to take action.'

Mam leaned back in the chair. 'Why would anyone want to ruin us? We have no enemies.'

'We do now.' Beth stared up at the ceiling, wishing all this was simply a dream. 'I rejected Louis Melville.'

Silence stretched between them for a moment.

'Are you saying Louis Melville from Melville Manor attacked you?'

Beth nodded, a tear escaping over her lashes.

'Because you wouldn't marry him?'

'Yes.'

Mam gasped and rubbed her hands over her face. 'I don't understand. He's a gentleman. A man of wealth and status in the community. I can't believe it.'

'He's been persistent in asking me. Watching me. Ever since the summer he seems to have taken an interest in me. Wherever I turned he seemed to be there, waiting.'

'That sounds overdramatic.'

'It's the truth. He'd watch me when I was working the stall, he'd slow his carriage down if he saw me in the street. He even made his sister speak to me as though he wanted his sister's approval that was I good enough for him.'

'His sister spoke to you?'

Beth played with the edge of the blanket. 'When I said no to him at the lock-up, he went mad. He lost all reason. It's like a switch is turned off and on in his head. He's done it before.'

'Done what before?'

'He offered me a lift in his carriage, but he wouldn't take me home, he wanted me at the manor. He threw himself on me in the carriage, kissing me, pawing at me, pinning me down so I couldn't get away. He said I had to go into the house, or he'd kill Noah.'

'Kill Noah?' Mam gasped; eyes wide in her pale face.

'I managed to escape…'

'You should have told us!' Mam's anger showed in her clenched fists.

'I didn't want Dad to confront him.'

'God above. Why did you have to bring this upon us?'

'I didn't want any of this to happen. I didn't ask Melville to like me. He whipped me with his riding crop one time in the summer, and he charged at me on his horse while we were picnicking by the beck. Do you think I wanted any of that?'

'Why did you not tell me any of this months ago? And I thought it was just his dog at the picnic. Why did you lie to me?'

'Because I didn't want Dad to confront him or cause trouble. Dad hates the Melvilles as it is. If he found out about Louis doing this to me, he'd have it out with him, wouldn't he? And then he'd be the one in a police cell.'

Mam jerked up from the chair and paced the bedroom. 'What did Melville do to you at the lock-up?' Mam's tone was wooden, her face emotionless.

'At first, he was telling me he'd treat me well if we married, but he is incapable of being nice. I refused him. I told him I wouldn't marry him as I love Noah. He got so angry. He-he cut my hair. I thought he was going to stab me…'

Mam moaned behind her hand.

'A couple of punches winded me but it could have been worse. I expected at one point he was going to… to…'

'Force himself on you?'

Beth nodded.

'Thank God he didn't.'

'You can't tell Dad.'

'No, I can't for he'd murder the monster for touching you and he'd go to jail for it. I'm not losing my husband because of Melville.'

'No.' Beth burned with fever and mortification. 'No one must ever find out.'

Mam stood at the end of the bed and smoothed down her black skirt. 'I'll tell the family you didn't know your attackers. It was a couple of young men… they were drunk… thought it to be a huge joke cutting your hair.'

'Tell Dad I didn't see their faces… their hats were pulled low and scarves over their faces.'

Mam straightened the already straight blankets. 'Yes. That is the story. The truth is our secret.' Mam couldn't meet her eyes. 'I'm sorry, Beth, for my part in this. I encouraged you to consider Melville. It was wrong of me.' She walked out of the room and closed the door.

Beth turned over and stared at the other empty bed where Joanna used to sleep. Hot tears ran down her hot face. She wished her mam had held her. She felt very alone.

Chapter Nineteen

'You still in bed?' Joanna declared as she came into the bedroom the next day.

Beth looked up from staring at the fire and burst into tears as Joanna hugged her tight despite her pregnant belly getting in the way. 'I'm so glad you came.'

'Dad picked me up yesterday, but you were sleeping when I came up, so I left you in peace. I couldn't take in what he told me. How are you feeling?'

'Terrible.'

Joanna gently touched Beth's cropped hair. 'Bloody buggers! I'm fuming that this happened to you.'

Beth moved away a little. She hated anyone noticing her hair.

'Do you want me to fix it for you?'

'How can you? There's nothing left.'

'I can tidy it up. Get rid of those tufts so it grows evenly.'

'If you like.' She shrugged, not caring either way. She had no wish to step outside of her bedroom ever again.

A few minutes later, Joanna retuned with the sewing scissors and sitting behind Beth on the bed, began to comb and clip the straggly hair.

'Noah has called, both today and yesterday.'

Beth stiffened at the mention of him.

'He seems very worried about you.'

'He'll forget me soon enough.'

Joanna tutted. 'What do you mean by that? Do you not care for him any more?'

Melville's threats filled her head. 'I can't be with him.'

'Why?'

'I don't want to be with anyone.'

Joanna snipped and the sound reminded Beth of Melville cutting her plait off with the shears, she cringed at the sound. Her heart raced as the image of Melville dangling her plait filled her mind.

'You just need time to heal. Noah cares for you. He's so worried.'

'Tell him to stop coming, Joanna. I can't deal with him.'

'I'll tell him to give you some time.'

'No, tell him I don't want to marry him.'

'Um… no, I'm not saying that. If you don't want to marry him then the least you can do is tell him face to face.'

'I can't see him.' Panic overwhelmed her at seeing Noah. What would he think when he saw her?

'Calm down. There's no hurry.' Joanna combed her hair, which with the clumps gone it felt even shorter.

Bits of hair fell over Beth's shoulder and down onto her clasped hands. She stared at it in revulsion. She'd look hideous now and would resemble a boy. Tears blurred her vision.

'There, that's much better.' Joanna smiled. 'Do you want to see it in the mirror?'

'No.' Beth crawled back under the blankets.

'Why don't you come downstairs? Poor Ronnie has been a bit upset since this all happened, and it would help him to see you up and about.'

'No, I'm too tired.' In truth she was exhausted. Her temperature fell and rose by the hour and all she wanted to do was sleep.

'Mam said Jane is calling later. She wants to see you and she has some wedding cake for you.'

'I don't want to see anyone.' Beth glanced away. Guilt gnawed at her, making her feel even more awful. She'd missed her best friend's wedding. How could Jane ever forgive her?

'Beth.'

'I'm tired, Joanna.' She squirmed down into the blankets and closed her eyes. Joanna sighed and left the room.

Tears hung on her lashes as she thought of Noah. There was no way she wanted him to see her like this with a shorn head. Besides, she needed to keep her distance from him so Melville wouldn't hurt him in any way. Breaking it off with him would keep him safe from Melville. But how was she going to keep the rest of her family safe? Could Melville really destroy their livelihood?

Later that evening, Mam came in with a tray of beef stew and slices of buttered bread and a cup of tea.

Beth wasn't hungry but dared not say that to her mam.

Mam placed the tray on Beth's lap. 'Jane's left some wedding cake for you.'

'That's nice.'

'The wedding went off well. Though she was extremely worried about you. She said she'll come over and see you on Sunday afternoon.' Mam walked to the door but hesitated on opening it. 'It would be nice if you came downstairs in the morning. Things need to get back to normal.'

'Normal?' Beth stared at her as though she was mad. 'How is anything going to be normal again? Melville could do anything at any time.'

'Maybe so, but hiding in your bedroom isn't the answer. With luck, he'll forget all about you. He probably already has. You're out of his system now, no doubt. He's had his fun, taught you a lesson and that'll be the end of it. I'd find it surprising if he spends all his time dreaming of ways to hurt you. He must be a busy man and have other concerns.'

Beth stared at her. Why was she so quick to put all this behind them? 'He's evil. He can't be trusted. He meant what he said about seeking revenge.'

'Perhaps, but I doubt he'll do anything further. He was a man spurned. His pride was wounded, that's all. He'll forget all about you now. You need to get on with your life, Beth, and forget him.' Mam walked out and closed the door.

'I don't know how...' Beth murmured. How could she tell her mam about the nightmares that plagued her, of Melville's demented face that haunted her whenever she closed her eyes?

~ ~ ~ ~

'Cheer up! This is a wedding not a funeral.' Albie patted Noah on the back as he sat down beside him.

The pub's back room heaved with people celebrating Sid and Meg's wedding. Noah wished he could join in the party, but he felt low about Beth. Every day for a week he'd gone to the farm only to be told she wouldn't see him. He didn't know where he stood with her anymore. Did she still want him, or had she finished with him for good?

Could he blame her? He'd behaved like a spoilt child by not giving her the chance to explain about Melville. Then on top of that she was attacked by two drunken idiots, locked in a freezing place over night, missed her best friend's wedding and now she was ill with a fever. Of course, she wouldn't want to see him.

Albie supped his beer. 'You're not in the best of moods, are you?'

'No, sorry.'

'At least you put on a happy face for Sid today.'

'I tried my best.'

'It's been a great wedding.'

'I'm happy for Sid.' Noah drank the last of his ale.

'Beth will get better,' Albie said softly, understanding Noah better than any of the brothers.

'Aye.'

'Give her time. She's been through it.'

'I just want to show her that I care. That I'm here for her.'

'Aye, and she will know that.'

'Will she?'

'Have another drink, you're empty.'

'No, I'll call it a night. It's getting late.' Noah stood, knowing he'd not be missed. He'd given his speech and the food was all gone, leaving nothing but crumbs on plates, but the beer was flowing all too well. There'd be sore heads in the morning.

'Take Mam back with you. She looks tired.' Albie nodded to where their mam sat by the fire, talking to a neighbour, but the greyness of her face showed her exhaustion.

'Mam.' Noah stepped in front of her. 'I'm off home. Want to come with me?'

'I will, yes.' She said her goodbyes to friends and kissed Sid and Meg, who would be now living with Meg's family in the village.

Outside the wintry night air made them shiver in their coats after the heat of the crowded taproom. They said goodnight to two men on their way to visit the lav, and others out smoking or needing some fresh air. One man was leaning drunkenly against the pub wall singing, while another vomited into a bush.

'Get home, Tom Newton,' Mam said, with a chuckle.

Noah nodded to the daughter of the landlord as she collected glasses and tankards left outside.

'What a grand day,' Mam said, linking her arm though Noah's so as not to slip on the icy pavements.

'I'm glad it went well.'

'And you'll be next.'

Noah listened to the haunting cry of a fox somewhere in the distance. 'Will I?'

'Beth worships you, lad.'

'As I do her.'

'Well then, that's all that matters. You two need to make up before Christmas next week. It'd be nice to have her come and see us.'

Two men stepped out of the shadows and blocked their way. They stood flexing their fists.

Noah tensed. 'Excuse us, fellas.' He gripped his mam's arm tighter and went to walk around them.

The man on the right shot out his fist connecting with Noah's jaw.

Noah stumbled, letting go of his mam.

The other man lunged forward and punched him in the stomach, sending Noah to his knees, gasping for air.

Again, the first man punched Noah in the face. Pain rocked his brain. Noah reeled, hearing his mam screaming and fight the attackers with her puny strength. 'No, Mam!'

A boot kicked him in the thigh sending an agonising jolt up through his hip. Another punch to the head flung him backwards against a garden wall. Stars burst before his eyes.

Dazed, he tried to get up as another boot kicked him in the stomach taking the breath from his lungs. Open-mouthed, he panicked as no air filled his lungs. He wheezed, bent double.

Shouts and yells came from the pub as his mam's screams for help alerted the men who were outside.

Noah covered his head as the two men gave a last kick and a punch.

'That's a taster from Mr Melville, you scum,' one of the men said, before they both ran off.

Friends helped Noah to his feet. His body recoiled from every step. He stopped and vomited into the bushes of someone's garden. Pain pulsed through his face and stomach. The men wrapped their arms around him, and half carried him home.

In the kitchen Mam thanked the men and sent them on their way, before stirring up the embers in the fire and adding more coal. In silence she heated up some water and found cut up bandages in a bottom drawer.

Noah sat at the table, holding his face, eyes closed. His jaw throbbed and he could taste the blood from his nose running into his mouth and his bleeding split lip added to it.

'Turn to the light.' Mam placed a lamp on the table and soaked one square of bandage in the water. She worked away cleaning the blood from his face. 'Will there ever come a time when I'm not cleaning up the faces of one of you lads?'

'I doubt it.' Noah winced as she pressed on his lip.

The kettle whistled as it boiled, and she stood to make two cups of cocoa.

Sitting back down, she continued her task of stemming the blood running from his nose. 'So, who is Melville and why did he send men to come and beat the life out of you?'

Noah closed his eyes. 'He wants to marry Beth.'

'And he has men to send you a warning to stay away?'

'He's wealthy, Mam. Melville Manor in Kirkhamgate. You must have heard of it?'

'That Melville?' Her eyes sprang wide. 'Good God. And he wants Beth?'

'He does.'

'And she's rejected him over you?'

'Aye.'

'Oh, lad. What are you going to do?'

'I have no idea.'

'It's time Mr Grimshaw found you a school. Marry Beth and move away. Start again somewhere else.'

'You know that's not possible. I can't afford to leave the pit and go to college and run two households. With me and Sid gone, you'll have to rely on Albie, Alfred and James.'

'I'll go back to work as well.'

'You're not well enough and James and Alfred spend more money at the pub than they do on the bills. I'm sick of talking to them about it.'

'We'll manage.'

'Until all the debts are paid, I can't afford to marry Beth.'

'We'll work something out, lad. I'm not having you getting beaten up by that Melville man. You've got to get away.'

'This might be a one-off.'

'And what if it's not?'

Noah sighed and closed his eyes, the painful throbbing robbed him of thought.

His mam kissed the top of his head. 'Drink your cocoa.'

~ ~ ~ ~

Beth sat at the kitchen table, a headscarf wrapped around her head as she cut the pastry circles with the top of a glass. Trays of mince pies covered the table, filling the kitchen with the fruity smell of Christmas.

Aunty Hilda sliced cheese to go on the ham sandwiches she was making for the men harvesting the rhubarb in the forcing sheds.

Will came through the door like a whirlwind as always, bringing with him a blast of frigid air. Tall for his age and with a flop of overlong black hair, he was fast becoming a good-looking lad who turned the girls' heads. Today he turned seventeen, no longer a boy but not yet quite a man.

Will folded his lanky frame onto a chair and grabbed a warm mince pie from the cooling tray. 'It's good to see you downstairs, our Beth.' He munched away.

Beth gave him a nervous smile. She'd come down today for the first time since the attack. With her fever gone and growing bored after a week and a half in her room, she felt the need to go downstairs, though she'd gone no further than the kitchen. 'Well, it's your birthday, isn't it? A special day.'

'You'll stay down all day? Later, Mam said I can open my presents.'

'I'll do my best, I promise.'

'Are the men nearly ready for a break?' Aunty Hilda asked, loading sandwiches into a basket.

'Aye. I've come for the food. The table is set up in the barn.' Will stuffed another mince pie into his mouth.

Aunty Hilda added cups and flasks of tea to the basket, as well as slices of lemon cake she'd made the day before.

Will grabbed the large basket. 'Have you heard how Noah is?'

Beth's heart somersaulted at the mention of Noah. 'I've not left the house, Will. I've spoken to no one,' she said dully.

Aunty Hilda placed several apples into the basket. 'What do you mean how he is?'

Beth looked up, finally realising what Will had said. 'What are you talking about?'

'Noah got beat up on Saturday at his brother's wedding.'

Beth dropped the pastry she held. 'Attacked?'

'Aye by two men as he was walking his mam home. Folk reckon the men were strangers. No one from these parts would attack Noah. He's too well thought of, isn't he?'

'Were they after money?' Aunty Hilda asked.

Will shrugged. 'That's all I heard. They gave him a good pasting apparently.'

Beth stared at Will. 'You need to find out more.'

'How am I meant to do that? We're in the middle of harvesting the rhubarb and it's my birthday.' He left the kitchen carrying the basket.

'You should go to his house and find out what happened,' Aunty Hilda said.

'I can't see him like this.' Beth put a floury hand up to her scarf. It was more than the state of her hair though, it was the thought of bumping into Melville that kept her indoors.

A knock on the front door made them stare at each other. Few people knocked on the front door, all friends and family came around the back to the kitchen.

'I'll get it. Likely it's a peddler.' Aunty Hilda walked down the hallway to answer it.

Beth placed the round circles of pastry into the tart tray, her mind full of Noah. Attacked? How badly was he hurt? Her chest swelled with anguish at the thought of not being able to see him. She craved to hold him and kiss away his pain. Was this how the rest of her life was to be? Always on alert for any mention of Noah? Of spending her days trying not to think of him, hoping she wouldn't see him in the village? How could she cope?

'Would you like a cup of tea?' Aunty Hilda was saying as she came back into the kitchen followed by Peggy Jackson.

Beth stood in surprise. 'Mrs Jackson.'

Wheezing, Mrs Jackson smiled and grasped Beth's hands not caring they were covered in flour. 'It's good to see you, lass.'

'And you. How are you?'

Mrs Jackson glanced away. 'I have good and bad days. Today is a good day so I thought I'd go for a walk with Patch and come and see you. He's out there sniffing in your mother's garden.'

'Sit down, please.'

'I will, if that's all right. I've worn myself out and I dread to think how I'm going to get back up the hill.'

Aunty Hilda mashed the tea. 'We'll take you back home on the cart, Mrs Jackson. The cart is leaving shortly to take the first harvested crop of rhubarb to the train station.'

'Thank you. That's kind.'

After Aunty Hilda had gone outside to tell the men they had a passenger, Beth poured a cup of tea for Mrs Jackson. 'You shouldn't have come so far with your bad chest, not in winter.'

'It had to be done. I had to see you, lass.'

'Oh?'

'It's our Noah. He's in a right state.'

'I only just heard from my brother that Noah was beaten up?'

'Aye.'

'How is he?'

'Sore, bruised. But he's back at work. He rested on Sunday and went back underground on Monday. Nothing would stop him.' Mrs Jackson sipped her tea. 'Looks like you've been under the weather yourself. You're as thin as a rake and so pale.'

Beth adjusted the scarf around her head. She looked a fright with dark shadows under her eyes. She'd lost weight for eating didn't interest her at all. She pecked at her food like a bird and only did that to please her mam.

Mrs Jackson covered Beth's hand with her own. 'Beth, will you not make it up with my Noah? Forgive him, for whatever he's done. He's lost without you.'

'I can't, Mrs Jackson.'

'Was it so very bad what he did?'

Beth bit her lip. 'It's not about the argument we had in Wakefield. I wish it were only that.'

'I see. So, it's something more serious? Has it got something to do with this Melville fellow? Do you prefer him over our Noah?'

'What? No!' Beth jerked back in her chair. 'I hate Melville.'

'It was his men who attacked Noah. They said the beating was from Melville.'

Beth hung her head in shame. Melville had been good with his threats then. Poor Noah. She had done this to him. 'I'm so sorry.'

'You need to tell me everything that's going on, don't you think?'

Their tea went cold as Beth haltingly told Mrs Jackson everything that happened with Melville since the summer.

'So, it's revenge he wants?'

Beth nodded sadly. 'I fear for what Melville will do next.'

'You need to go to the police. Report him for his attack on you. We can go as well and tell the police what those men said. The police will have to take some kind of action.'

'How can they touch a wealthy man like Melville? He'll deny it all. It's our word against his. We have no proof. And I fear his revenge might become even more nasty. I have to protect my family.'

Aunty Hilda came silently into the kitchen, nodding wisely. 'I *knew* there was more to your attack than just drunken men.' She stared at Beth. 'Your mam never was an exceptionally good liar.'

'You mustn't tell Dad,' Beth pleaded. 'He'll lose his mind over it and confront Melville. There will be bloodshed.'

'Maybe that's just what is needed?' Aunty Hilda raised an eyebrow.

'We can't have Dad getting into trouble.'

Coughing, Mrs Jackson stood. 'I'll not have my lad kicked and punched just because Melville's been denied something he wants. I'm going to the police.'

Aunty Hilda smiled. 'I'll come with you, Mrs Jackson. Sergeant Holmes at the station is an old beau of mine. I'll have a word in his ear.'

'No, you can't.' Beth felt breathless with worry. 'Melville will—'

'He'll do nothing, not if he knows what is good for him. The Melville family have always had weak males. Their womenfolk are much stronger but always side-lined, as is the way of wealthy families. Louis Melville has been a nasty one, a coward since a boy. That family isn't very well liked around here, never has been. It's why Sir Melville is away all the time. I can tell you now he'll not be pleased to hear his son is causing havoc. The Melvilles have ghosts in their closets, believe me. There's still the mystery why Sir Melville suddenly found Amsterdam the place he needed to be. It was all very suspicious, and which is why Sir Melville will want Louis to behave.'

Beth was shocked how her old great aunty knew so much. 'I've not heard of any of this.'

'Dear, when you've lived as long as I have you learn a thing or two. Remember I told you the Melville butler, Staines, and I are good friends?'

'Yes.'

'Well, I've had a visit from him.'

Alarmed, Beth had to sit back down. 'Staines came here?'

'Aye, when you were sick with fever.'

'Why didn't you say?'

'Because I was waiting to see if anything else came about. Your mam was in a state when she brought you home. We were all upset, and I didn't imagine Melville had anything to do with you being locked away and your hair being cut off, but since then I've had time to think it over.'

'Your hair has been cut off?' Peggy Jackson gasped.

Beth nodded and unwound her scarf to show Mrs Jackson her boy's short haircut.

'Oh, lass.' Peggy came around the table and squeezed Beth's shoulder. 'What a monster to do that to you.'

'Noah can't see me like this.'

'Lass, he wouldn't care about your hair. It's you he cares about.'

'It'll grow back.' Aunty Hilda was forthright and with a look in her eyes that she meant business. 'Staines told me that he saw you run off from the manor a couple of weeks ago and he felt something wasn't quite right. He's not an admirer of his employer, you know. Staines saw how uncomfortable you were the day of the blizzard when Melville brought you to the manor.'

Beth wrapped the scarf around her head again. 'None of us has the power to stop Melville. He threatened he'd destroy us all. I won't have Dad or Will seeking revenge for what Melville has done. We have to keep it a secret.'

'We don't have any power, but his father does.' Aunty Hilda went into the scullery and grabbed her coat, hat, and boots. 'I'll make a visit to Staines and get him to write to Sir Melville. I'll also have Sergeant Holmes do the same. The last thing Melville wants is his father coming back and curtailing his expenses and activities and Sir Melville won't want the police meddling in his affairs.'

Will came into the kitchen. 'We're ready to go into town now. We need to load the eleven thirty train to London.'

'Good. We're coming. Help Mrs Jackson up onto the cart, we'll drop her off in the village and then I want you to take me somewhere after we've unloaded the rhubarb onto the train.' Aunty Hilda patted Beth's shoulder. 'All will be well.'

'Are you sure you should be doing this?' Beth stood close to her beloved aunty who she adored so much.

Aunty Hilda tapped her hand gently against Beth's cheek. 'I may be old but I'm not dead yet, lass.'

Chapter Twenty

On Christmas Eve, Noah sat with Mr Grimshaw in a tea room on Northgate at his tutor's request.

'It's good to see you, Noah.' Mr Grimshaw had ordered tea and cake, and he was forking a piece of sponge cake into his mouth. 'Are you ready for Christmas?'

'I suppose.' Noah glanced out of the window. Christmas Day was tomorrow and usually he enjoyed the occasion. He and his brothers would cook breakfast as a treat for his mam and then they'd go to the pub for a midday pint and come back to have a meal of whatever their mam could afford to put on the table, but no matter how poor they'd been in the past their mam always provided a little bit of something special for Christmas Day whether that be a fruit cake or a nice bit of roast beef. Sometimes they had small presents to unwrap, a new pair of socks, a handkerchief, or she'd knitted them all new scarves or gloves.

This year, however, money was tighter than ever before. His mam was sick in bed again after her walk to the Beaumonts' farm and his dad was dead, and Sid was spending the day with his wife's family. He didn't even have Beth's smiles to comfort him. This Christmas would be a disaster and he couldn't wait for it to be over.

'Do you want to tell me about the cut lip and bruised eye?' Mr Grimshaw continued eating his cake.

'Not really.'

Mr Grimshaw put down his fork and leaned back in his chair. 'I've not seen you for some weeks and the change in you is very apparent. You're thinner and, aside from your lip, you have a look about you of a man in despair. I'm sorry to see it.'

'It has been a little tough recently.'

'I've heard you say those words before.'

'It seems to be my life's mantra,' Noah scoffed.

'Well, maybe this bit of news will cheer you up. Call it a Christmas present from me to you.'

Noah grimaced. There was nothing that would cheer him up. He'd lost Beth.

'I've found you a position after college.'

'I told you, Mr Grimshaw, I'm not able to leave the pit yet. I can earn more working extra shifts down the pit than I can earn on a teacher's wage.'

'Maybe so, if you were working at a small village school. However, I've been able to speak with fellow colleagues and I even spoke to the governors' board. I am happy to report that I have secured you a position at the junior boys' school of Queen Elizabeth Grammar, depending if certain circumstances are met.'

'The boys' junior school?' Noah stared at him, then looked out the window and down the street towards where the impressive grammar school stood. Could it be real? Was it even possible he might achieve such a dream?

Mr Grimshaw smiled. 'The junior school only opened three years ago. It is a commendable addition to the QEG. Of course, in time you could apply to teach within the senior department, but for now, as your first post, I'd like to think you'd be satisfied enough with the junior school?'

'Yes, of course.' Noah's mind whirled.

'There are even rental rooms to go with the position and situated not far from the school. Nothing grand, mind you, they are only but two rooms converted from a large house, but the flats are neat and damp free and, best of all, at a reduced rent. There is a vacant one for you should you want it.'

'I don't know what to say. I honestly don't have the words... I dreamed of teaching there, but never thought I actually would. A village school would have been enough for me.'

'I've praised you to the board, and, really, to anyone who'd listen. It wasn't an easy sell. You haven't been to university as all the other teachers there have done. But the headmaster is a good man, decent and modern-minded. He's willing to bring in fresh blood, so to speak, someone who comes from a different background to every other teacher there. He believes you would add character and a new way of approaching teaching.'

'I don't know how to thank you.'

Mr Grimshaw held up his hand. 'Now, the board of governors want to see you. They ultimately have the final word on you getting the position. They would like to meet you in the New Year. It will be for them to look you over, ask you questions. Understand? You'll be inspected and interviewed, and you'll have to do well in college, naturally. The position might only be for one term, to see whether they like you and you are the right person for the job.'

'I understand.'

'They expect a high standard, Noah, and turning up with a split lip isn't an ideal way to show them you are a responsible and dedicated person to be teaching in their school. This is your chance to change your life. Are you up to it, Noah?'

He nodded eagerly, touching his sore lip. As depressed as he felt, he would do his best because letting down Mr Grimshaw after all he'd done for him wasn't to be considered. 'I'll make you proud.'

Mr Grimshaw grinned, his shoulders relaxing. 'Of course, you will. I have always had faith in you doing your best. This is a start of a new chapter of your life, Noah. Only you can make it happen.'

'I will. I promise.' And he would. Chances needed to be taken and he had to take this one.

Mr Grimshaw passed over the table a large brown paper wrapped parcel. 'Happy Christmas.'

Noah flushed with embarrassment. 'I haven't got you anything.'

'I don't need anything, but I thought this might be beneficial to you.'

Carefully Noah unwrapped the paper and blinked in surprise at the shiny caramel-coloured leather satchel. The smell of new leather filled his nose. 'Again, you've left me speechless, Mr Grimshaw.'

'I'm pleased you like it. You'll have books and all sorts of paraphernalia to carry with you once you're teaching classes. A satchel will aid you in carrying all that.'

Noah stroked the leather, touched the gleaming brass buckle. He was overwhelmed by the man's kindness. 'It's a thoughtful gift. Thank you.'

'Of all the students I've taught, you have shown such promise and drive to change your life. That must be encouraged, and I hope one day in the future you will be in my position to also help someone to change their life.'

'I'll do my absolute best to fulfil such a legacy.'

Later, having wished Mr Grimshaw a merry Christmas and leaving the tea room, Noah sauntered down Northgate, his satchel slung over his shoulder, to stand in front of the grammar school.

He gazed at the impressive stone buildings, hardly believing that he could be soon working within their hallowed walls. He, Noah Jackson, a coal miner from a little village, was one step away from changing his life forever.

He didn't want to do it without Beth.

She should be standing beside him right now, excited by this news. Not at the farm, scared to leave the house. He couldn't believe his mam when she told him Melville had been the one to lock Beth away, that he'd harassed and tormented her and cut her hair. His first reaction was to find the bastard and knock his teeth down his throat, but his mam held him back, making sense with her words that revenge must be done smartly. It took all his willpower to listen to her.

Mr Grimshaw believed him to be smart, clever. He would prove he was, just not yet. He needed to get something out of his system first.

He stared down at the ground and then back to the school. Melville had ruined this moment for him, he'd ruined Beth's chance to be at her best friend's wedding, more than that, his abuse had left her changed. She was no longer her normal happy self. His mam said Beth looked like a walking ghost. His beautiful girl was suffering. Fury ripped through him that Melville had done all this and got away with it.

Soon, Noah would be a respectable teacher, but today, at this moment, he was a man who needed to teach someone a different kind of lesson.

Less than an hour later, angry and full of revenge, Noah rang the bell pull beside the wide front doors of Melville Manor. He would have it out with Melville. Wealth and privilege didn't cower Noah. A man was a man whether he wore a tailored suit or coarse trousers held up with twine. Louis Melville needed a good hiding and no one else should do it but Noah. For Beth he'd give Melville the thrashing of his life.

Laughter swung him around. Two young maids walking down a side path from the drive were giggling and staring at him before they disappeared around the side of the house.

Noah frowned. He stepped back and surveyed the gravel drive, the dormant garden beds, the ornamental trees. A fountain, not working, stood in the middle of the lawn to the right. A male peacock balanced on the stone edge of the fountain's small wall. Abruptly the peacock dropped down to the grass and opened his glorious tail and shimmied, the aqua and emerald colours more dazzling on such a damp day.

The notion that Melville even had a bloody peacock on top of everything else should have fired him up more, but it had the opposite effect.

A sobering sense of awareness widened his eyes and mind. He stepped back at gazed up at the house, properly seeing the splendour of it for the first time.

Beth had rejected all of this for him. The thought rooted him to the spot. His anger, which had continued to build on the journey here, ebbed away, leaving him dispirited, deflated.

The large wooden door opened. 'May I help you?'

Noah recognised the older man. He was sure he'd seen him play cricket in the past. 'Good day. I'm Noah Jackson. I'd like to speak with Mr Melville, please.' However, as he said the words, the rage which has simmered inside since his mam told him about Melville's attack on Beth no longer had the strength it once did.

The butler stepped out and closed the door behind him. 'That's not a clever idea, Mr Jackson.'

Noah tensed. 'I don't see how you can be the judge of that.'

'I'm Staines, the Melville's butler, but more than that I'm a friend of the Beaumonts and I know your name from Hilda.'

Swallowing back a cutting remark about the man working for a tyrant, Noah strived for a cool head. 'I need to speak with Melville.'

'To what purpose? Mr Melville's actions are being dealt with.'

'Dealt with?' Noah frowned. 'What do you know?'

'Everything.' Staines glanced back at the door. 'Walk with me.' He hurried down the steps leaving Noah no choice but to follow.

They slipped down beside the house. Staines looked about and satisfied they wouldn't be over-heard, relaxed a little.

'Sir Melville has been made aware of his son's be-haviour. He's been summoned to Amsterdam where Sir Melville now lives. Mr Melville leaves the day af-ter tomorrow.'

'He's leaving?' Noah stuck his hands in his pock-ets, the cold intensifying as the afternoon wore on and the sun slipped lower in a grey sky.

'What did you think you were going to do?' Staines asked, blowing on his bare hands.

'Talk to the man. Unlike him, I don't send men around to do my dirty business for me.'

'I heard about that. It's a cowardly thing to do, but that's Melville.' Staines peered at Noah's battered face. 'You're lucky a beating is all you got.'

'His men won't touch me again. Not after I've spoken to him.'

'It'd do no good. Mr Melville is only frightened of one man and that is his father. Let the old man sort him out, if such a thing is possible.'

Noah didn't want to give up. Pride demanded he face Melville. 'Well, it wouldn't hurt to warn him to never look Beth's way again. She doesn't want him and if he ever lays a finger on her again, he'll go missing and never be found.'

Staines raised his eyebrows. 'Really?'

Noah dropped his voice to a murmur. 'Under-ground there are a lot of disused tunnels and unfortu-nately many cave ins. I also have four strong brothers and a good many friends, who for the price of a barrel of ale, will do just about anything you ask of them.'

Staines chuckled. 'I kind of want you to carry that out, to be honest. It's not easy working for such a bastard as him.'

Sensing he was talking to a decent fellow, Noah eased his stance. 'I don't know how you can stand being at the beck and call of that man.'

Staines shrugged his shoulders. 'It'll not be forever and, let's be truthful, there are worse jobs, like shovelling coal in a black hole.'

Noah couldn't argue with him there.

'The days Melville is away from the house makes it worthwhile though. I'm only staying here until I've saved enough money to open a little pub of my own.'

'Sounds like you're itching for a change of scenery?'

'Too right. A life in service has lost its appeal for me. I want to be my own man.' Staines looked up as a gardener wheeled a barrow along a path at the edge of the garden. 'I'd best go in.'

They walked back to the front of the house.

'You want justice,' Staines said, 'but truthfully, you'd only end up in jail. Melville's an evil bugger for sure. He's not worth ruining your life over.'

'My mam said something similar.'

'Then listen to her. The only person who has any influence on him is his father. Do your best to forget about him. Concentrate on that pretty lass of yours. That's the best revenge of all.'

Knowing that to be true, Noah smiled, wincing as his lip protested at the movement. He liked Staines. 'Will you be playing cricket in the summer?'

'No. I'm past that now. I gave it up two years ago. Besides, it was too hard getting time away from here.

Melville thinks I've no life at all and doesn't understand the need for time off.'

'Typical.'

'Well, now Melville has made a nuisance of himself with young Beth and his father has sent for him, I'm hoping he'll be gone for months. I might be able to come and watch you play. You're rather decent with the willow.'

'I do enjoy cricket. You should play this summer.'

'Maybe.' Staines glanced at the closed door. 'I'll send word if I hear any of his plans regarding Miss Beaumont, but he'll not have time. Right now, he's busy sorting out his affairs in his study and the maids are packing his trunks. We're hoping we won't see him for a year or more.'

Noah shook Staines's hand. 'Thank you. I hope so, too.'

Feeling lighter of heart, Noah left the estate and trod across the fields towards the Beaumont Farm. As much as he'd like to have spoken with Melville, and threatened him, he had to be careful. He couldn't risk anything damaging his reputation if he wanted the position at the grammar school. Melville deserved a good beating but giving him one, would only inflame the situation more. As Staines mentioned he had to concentrate on Beth, and he had to show her she'd made the right choice.

~ ~ ~ ~

Beth stood in the scullery and hung up her coat. She been out in the forcing sheds helping with the harvesting of the rhubarb. Since Melville's attack she'd not been on the stall. Her mam had run the stall, leaving Beth to stay home and work around the house and sometimes in the sheds. Little by little she was feeling more herself. Yet the thought of leaving the farm and running into Melville horrified her. So, she stayed within the farm's boundaries.

Taking off her hat and unwinding her scarf, Beth heard voices in the kitchen. She smiled, hearing Joanna's voice as she pulled off her boots.

'It'll take her some time, Mam. You can't expect her to be on the stall after what happened to her,' Joanna said.

'I understand that but the longer she mopes around here the longer it'll take for her to get better,' Mam answered back.

'She needs our support and if she's not ready to face the world outside of these farm gates, then that's fine.'

'No. I'll not have it, Joanna,' Mam snapped. 'Beth has to start returning to normal before she's scared of her own shadow. She's always been the noisy, bossy one. Out of the four of you it was her with the quick temper, the loud laugh, the sunny nature, always running when she ought to walk. I want that girl back.'

Beth stood still; emotion caught in her throat.

'What about Noah?' Joanna asked. 'Does she still like him?'

'Oh, who knows?' Mam scoffed. 'One minute she was all over him like a rash and planning a spring wedding and now she refuses to speak his name and that was before the attack. They had words over Melville before Jane's wedding. Beth didn't tell him about Melville's attention, but then she didn't tell any of us, did she?'

'But since the attack?'

Mam sighed. 'Noah, to give him his due, came every day for a week but she refused to see him. I never thought I would feel sorry for a Jackson, but I do for him.'

'Has Aunty Hilda heard anything more from Staines?'

'Nothing yet. Did your dad tell you our prices were low for the rhubarb we sent to London?' Mam asked.

'No. Does Dad know why?'

'He doesn't, but I worry Melville has spoken to his contacts in London and deliberately found ways to sabotage our deliveries. Our buyers in Covent Garden gave us less than we normally get, and some didn't turn up at all. In the end we had to sell cheaply.'

'And you think Melville has that power? That he could know all of our business?' Joanna sounded incredulous.

'It's not hard to find out, is it? We are known in the district for sending our rhubarb to Covent Garden. All Melville has to do is press enough money into the right hands and our produce is ignored.'

'I can't believe that would happen. Surely Melville hasn't sunk so low as to do that?'

'Your dad is travelling with this afternoon's delivery to London. He's going to look into it.'

'Does he know what Melville did to Beth?'

'No, not yet. I'm trying to keep it from him but if our sales continue to drop and Melville is behind it then I'll have to tell him everything.'

'What a mess.'

'Indeed.' Mam sighed again, something she did a lot of now, Beth realised.

'Jimmy and me will come for Christmas tomorrow,' Joanna said brightly.

'I thought you were going to his family for the day?'

'No, not now. I want to be here at home. Beth needs us all around her.'

'I'd like that, lass.'

Upset, Beth donned her coat, scarf and gloves. From the peg she took her felt hat and pulled it down low over her ears. Like a little mouse she quietly opened the door and slipped outside.

She walked through the kitchen garden and around to the drive. The weight of guilt rested heavy on her chest. She was a burden to her family. She'd caused this trouble. What if Melville was taking revenge on her by making their produce not sell well in London? How could she stop that from happening? Would he listen to her? First, he beat up Noah and now he was affecting her dad's business? He said he would ruin them, and it looked like it wasn't a bluff.

What would be next? She dreaded to think.

At the gates she paused and looked back at the sheds and the house. No one was about. No one was wondering what she was doing. Could she leave the farm? Anxiety made her palms sweaty inside her gloves. This was her mess and she had to fix it. She couldn't have her family worrying over her for another minute nor could she allow Melville to ruin her family's farm. Only she was able stop that. She'd have to reason with Melville. The thought of facing him made her stomach clench.

Taking a deep breath, she forced herself to take the steps, to leave the sanctuary that was her home. Twelve days and she'd not left the farm. Was that really her? Normally she was never home. If she wasn't at the stall, she was in town shopping, or walking the lanes with Jane, visiting people she knew in the village, running errands for Aunty Hilda or her mam. She knew everyone and everyone knew her. These lanes and the village were part of her, a part of her home. She'd always felt safe here.

She had to trust they still were.

Swallowing back her nervousness, head down she turned out of the farm gates and along the lane. Maybe she could persuade Melville to leave them alone somehow? But how? She'd been relying on Aunty Hilda's plan to alert Sir Melville to his son's wrongdoings, but what if that didn't work? They'd heard nothing so far from either Staines or the police sergeant.

'Beth?'

She nearly jumped out of her skin. Her head jerked up. 'Noah.'

'Beth, lass.' He ran the few yards to her.

Beth stepped back. Her hands pulling down her hat further. 'Go away.'

'I didn't expect to see you out and about.'

She spun on her heel and headed back to the farm. No one must see them together in case it got back to Melville and she had to hide her ugliness from him.

'Beth!'

'I don't want to see you.'

'Why?' He marched alongside of her. 'Beth, please. I know about your hair. It doesn't matter in the slightest to me. You're still beautiful.'

She groaned in despair, as if that was all she cared about? 'Go away, Noah.'

'I want to talk to you.'

'No. There's nothing to be said. We're finished.'

He grabbed her arm and pulled her around to face him. 'I refuse to believe it!'

Beth pushed him away. 'Leave me, Noah. We can't be together.'

'For Christ sake why!' He stared at her.

'I'm sorry,' she mumbled, running from him.

'No, I'm not letting you go until you talk to me.'

'There's nothing to say.'

'Well, I have something to say so just bloody stop for a minute, will you?'

At the gates she felt safer, puffing slightly, she turned to him. 'Go away, Noah.'

'Beth?' Her dad walked quickly down the drive from the sheds, Will hot on his heels. 'What's wrong?'

Noah reached out to her. 'Beth, please. Can't we talk?'

She blinked away the tears that gathered behind her eyes. 'No.'

'Is everything all right, Noah?' Dad asked.

'Aye, Mr Beaumont. I just want your stubborn daughter to hear me out.'

Dad grinned slightly and put his arm around Beth's shoulders. 'Listen to him, lass. Make things right between you.' Dad walked back to the house taking Will with him.

Beth gripped her hands together and looked at Noah properly. He seemed thinner, tired. She noticed the cut on his lip and the bruised eye and guilt washed over her.

He gave her a small smile. 'I've missed you.'

Her heart twisted but she remained silent.

'It was wrong of me to walk away that day in town when Melville spoke to you.' Noah glanced down at his boots. 'I should have stayed and listened to you when you wanted to explain. I'm afraid my temper got the better of me. I was a stubborn fool. All that week I should have come to see you, but I didn't and then when I realised I needed to sort it out with you, it was too late. You were attacked and missing.'

She stayed quiet, watching him.

He sighed. 'I nearly went out of my mind when you couldn't be found. The relief when your mam brought you home was… well, there aren't any words. I was so happy you were safe.'

'I'm sorry Melville's men attacked you,' she said softly.

He touched his lip. 'It's nothing compared to what he did to you.'

Beth took a deep breath. 'I was just on my way to speak to him.'

'You were?' Shocked, Noah's eyebrows rose. 'Why?'

'Our rhubarb prices have been affected in London. I wanted to see if Melville was the cause of it.'

'What good would have come from you facing him?'

'I needed to find out if it was him. I can't let him ruin our farm.'

'That's not your responsibility, Beth.'

'It is. It's my fault he is acting this way.'

'So, what would you have done? Told him you'd marry him after all to save the price of rhubarb?'

She stiffened, anger rising fast. 'Don't be a fool. I hate the man.'

'Then what were you going to do? He won't listen to reason, will he?'

She sagged. 'I have to do something. This is all my fault.'

Noah took a step closer. 'No, it's not. All this is on Melville, not you.' He took another step. 'Anyway, I've just come from Melville Manor.'

It was her turn to be shocked. 'Why?'

'I, too, wanted to speak to him. Actually, at first I wanted to punch him into next week.' He grinned.

'You haven't?'

'No.' Noah glanced down at the muddy lane. 'When I was there it suddenly hit me all that you had given up in saying no to marrying him and yes to marrying me.'

'I didn't give anything up. It was never mine in the first place, and I never wanted it.' She searched his face for clues to how he felt. Was he as distraught as her? Had he missed her as much as she missed him?

'But I did speak to Staines instead. Sir Melville has ordered his son to Amsterdam.'

'Louis is leaving?' Dare she believe it?

'Yes. The day after tomorrow.'

'Then Aunty Hilda's plan worked?' Beth sagged with relief.

'My mam told me about it, and, yes, it seems so.'

'Oh, thank heavens.' She bit her bottom lip, her chin quivering with suppressed tears. 'I hope he never returns.'

'Even if he does, he'll never touch you again. I promise you.'

She nodded but dared not consider it. She would always be wary of Louis Melville and always looking over her shoulder.

'I want to protect you, Beth. You'll never have to be scared again.' Noah's gaze locked onto hers. 'Can you forgive me?' he asked gently.

She took a deep breath and let the tears trickle down her cheeks.

'I love you, Beth Beaumont. Can you love me again?'

'I do,' she whispered. 'I never stopped.'

He took the last step towards her. Love shone in his eyes. 'Are we still getting married then?'

'I'd like to think so, yes.'

His cheeky smile appeared, and he held out his hands. 'Then you'd better kiss me.'

Her eyes widened at his words. Yet, just being near him made her feel more of her old self. She placed her hands in his and then stopped, her confidence falling away once more.

Her mind whirled with what ifs… Would they be strong enough to face Melville if he ever returned? Would Noah accept that he was always the one she wanted? Could she trust Noah to not turn his back on her when things got tough?

'I'll never give you reason to doubt me again, you have my word,' he said as though reading her mind.

Slowly, she took off her hat. The chilly air whispered around her ears and neck. As much as she wanted to hide her cropped hair with her hands, she kept them by her side and raised her chin, daring him to reject her.

Noah gently touched her short dark wispy hair with his fingers. He gazed into her eyes. 'You're still my beautiful Beth and I can't wait to marry you.'

A sobbed escaped her and he crushed her into his arms.

❖ Beth and Noah's story continues in the sequel, *The Woman from Beaumont Farm,* which is planned to be released in 2021.

Author Notes

Writing this book was a nod to my parents, grand-parents and ancestors that lived and worked in the Wakefield area for generations. The idea for this book came in 2019 when driving in the car with my uncle, Peter Brear, and he was showing me places where my mum and dad worked and lived before they emigrated to Australia in the 1960s.

Over the years my parents, Ken and Betty Brear have told me stories of their childhood, but they have both passed away now and their stories only live on in the minds of those left behind. I am terribly worried that soon those stories will be gone, too, when my siblings and I are no longer here. I'm a huge fan of genealogy and spend many hours finding ancestors on ancestry.com and when I do find these generations who ultimately created me, I am always intrigued by their stories, and wished someone had written down what they were like, where they worked, not just a note on a census.

The Market Stall Girl isn't my family's story. However, the fictional families could easily have been mine. I wanted to set a story in the area where my parents and ancestors lived. My characters walked the same streets, worked the same jobs and lived in a place rapidly changing. For me this was a chance to recreate a time that would be familiar to my grandparents.

Trough Well Lane still exists and is where my own family had a farm when my great grandfather Jesse

Brear was alive. I have one photo of Jesse and his wife Lillian in Trough Well Lane.

My ancestors were coal miners or agricultural labourers. I've managed to research as far back as Nathaniel Brear born 1720 in Flockton, Yorkshire but then moved to Wragby, near Nostell Priory and worked as agricultural labourers. Nathaniel's grandsons went down the pit and that avenue for work continued right up until my dad, who preferred working the land and with animals than being down a black hole. On my mum's side of the family tree, the inspiration for Noah and his four brothers comes from my great great Ellis uncles who went to war in 1914, but I'll leave that thread for the sequel...

From Wakefield Council I was able to obtain a map of Wakefield and surrounding villages for the years 1907-1919, which helped me enormously, as it showed the original names for roads and lanes. In the last one hundred years many places have ceased to exist or have changed and been renamed.

Potovens Road is now called Wrenthorpe Lane.

There was a Potovens Lane, which Noah lived on and a Potovens Road which went over Sunny Hill and towards Alverthorpe. It confused me at the start I can tell you!

Alverthorpe Road is now called Batley Road.

Where Alverthorpe Mills used to be is now a housing estate, but Flanshaw Lane still exists. My mother worked at Haley's Mills in Flanshaw in the 1950s.

Brook Street outdoor market is no longer. The area of Brook Street has been redeveloped into a shopping mall. I do remember walking around both the indoor and outdoor markets in the early 1980s with my mum.

In the 1950s, my parents went courting in the lanes around the fields of Wrenthorpe as both families lived on Sunny Hill. My parents married in St Anne's Church in Wrenthorpe as Joanna and Jimmy did.

My father left the pit and worked as a farmer, including helping out at Asquith's Rhubarb Farm in Brandy Carr. The current owner, Ben Asquith, remembers my dad. Sadly, Ben is the last in his family to own the family farm which has been going since 1870s. http://www.brandycarrnurseries.co.uk/history/

Wrenthorpe Mine is no longer in use and the land is now the Wakefield Metropolitan District Council offices. My father, grandfather and great + grandfathers all worked at a local mine in Newton between Wrenthorpe and Outwood.

I would like to thank Mark Carlyle from the National Coal Mining Museum for England https://www.ncm.org.uk/ for his help in answering my many questions! He was very generous with his time and any factual errors are mine alone and are down to fictional licence.

In 1913 the land between the villages of Wrenthorpe, Alverthorpe, Kirkhamgate, etc was all farming. There were also more railway lines, all of which have been demolished in that area. The railway line that left the Wrenthorpe Junction and crossed the village of Alverthorpe is no longer there.

Alverthorpe Hall (Melville's friend) was actually demolished in 1946.

Rhubarb farming links: Wakefield is in the Rhubarb Triangle. https://en.wikipedia.org/wiki/Rhubarb_Triangle

Miners' Brass bands: A long tradition where collieries have their miners form a brass band and play in competitions. The movie Brassed Off with Ewan McGregor is good to watch and depicts the closing of the British mining industry, yet the bands played on. It brings a tear to your eyes!

Thank you for reading The Market Stall Girl. I want to thank all the readers who support me and review my stories, it means a great deal to me. I love your messages!

A special shout out to Deborah Smith and her facebook group for their support, not just for me but for all authors they read. I'm truly thankful they enjoy my books!

My books are found on all Amazon sites:
https://www.amazon.co.uk/-/e/B00705A120
Say hello on Facebook!
http://www.facebook.com/annemariebrear

Best wishes,
AnneMarie Brear
http://www.annemariebrear.com
2020